FEROCITY

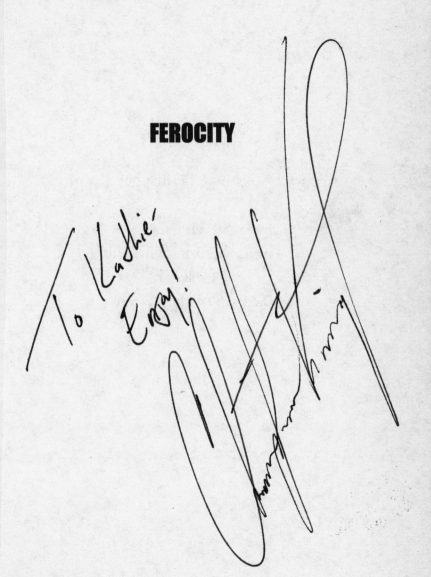

To Kathie
Enjoy!

other books by Christopher Knight

St. Helena
The Laurentian Channel
Bestseller
Season of the Witch

FEROCITY

by
CHRISTOPHER KNIGHT

AudioCraft Publishing, Inc.
Topinabee Island, MI

This book contains the complete
unabridged text of the original work.

FEROCITY

An AudioCraft Publishing, Inc. book
published by arrangement with the author

ISBN: 1-893699-03-X

AudioCraft Books are published by
AudioCraft Publishing, Inc., PO Box 281, Topinabee Island, MI 49791

PUBLISHER'S NOTE
This is a work of fiction. Names, characters, places and
incidents of the author's imagination or
are used fictitiously. Any resemblance to any person
living or dead is purely coincidental.

Second Printing - June 2003

Printed in the United States of America

A note:

It would be a gross injustice if I did not thank
some of those who selflessly offered their time and expertise:

Jim Hammond, for getting the ball rolling;

Ed & Paula Dombroski, for the 'fish on loan';

Sheri Kelley for editing assistance;
(and lots of it)

Tori Adams, for typographical assistance;

and-

Chuck Beard & Straits Area Printing, for continued hard
work...patience...and *more* hard work.

-The Author

for Boots

PROLOGUE

Craig Sheldon left the bar after his shift was over, cursing the heat as he started up his car and backed out of the gravel parking lot. It was just after two a.m., and the boiling heat from the kitchen had kept him perspiring for hours. A swim—a quick dip in the lake—was definitely in order. He rolled down the window of the car and sped up, cursing the heat for the umpteenth time that day.

He took a long, final drag on his cigarette, pulled the Marlboro from his lips, and was about to flick the half-smoked cigarette out the window when he thought twice about it and snubbed the butt out in the ashtray. The forest was drier than Wabash County, Tennessee, a county that had been receiving a lot of rain this year, but if you lived in Wabash County, Tennessee and wanted a nice Chardonnay or a Miller Lite, then brother, you knew what *dry* really was.

No sense in burning down the entire goddamn town this early in the summer, Craig thought. *We'll leave that to the tourists.* He nudged the radio volume up a bit with his thumb and forefinger and hummed along to an old Aerosmith tune, tapping the steering wheel in perfect timing with his right palm as Old US-27 sped beneath him, glowing like a black snake in the headlights. The wind rushing through the open car windows was a welcome, cooling relief, and he pushed away the thoughts of sweat and grease and smoke and fryers.

Life was good despite the heat. And despite the fact that the air conditioner at the bar had broken. *Again.* Oh, it wasn't so bad if you were on the floor waiting tables, but if you were in the kitchen grilling up the burritos and the nachos and the burgers like Craig had been for ten hours . . . well, you better look out. The heat from the fryers and stoves kept the kitchen a balmy, tropical hundred and twenty degrees and it was more than just miserable.

Perhaps the only thing that kept Craig going on this particular night was the fact that Cheryl Townsend was going to be waiting for him at her house, clad only in her birthday suit or maybe some itty-bitty fledgling piece of skimpy clothing she'd ordered from *Victoria's Secret,* or any of the other seven or eight mail order catalogs that Brad found laying around her house. His personal favorites were *Frederick's of Hollywood* catalogs, featuring dozens of beautiful, succulent women in clothing so tiny the models probably had to dress themselves with a pair of tweezers. Craig had ordered something from *Frederick's* once and presented it to Cheryl as a Valentine's gift, racking up innumerable carnal favors . . . making the forty-nine ninety-five plus four dollars shipping and handling a very worthwhile purchase indeed. And, although Cheryl left a bit to be desired in the intellectual department, no one would deny that she had breasts that could stop a charging bull elephant . . . which, in Craig's mind, more than made up for the fact that Cheryl Townsend couldn't tell you where the state capitol was. (Somewhere near Flint, she thought, but she couldn't be sure.) Craig and Cheryl had a very simple, respectful understanding: sex was more of a matter of convenience than a matter of commitment, and that was just fine with both. Neither of the two was interested in any type of long-term relationship with each other, which was a good thing—being that Craig had already screwed Cheryl for his last time.

He just didn't know it yet.

✳ ✳ ✳ ✳

Craig turned off the highway and into the lakeside picnic area, a bit surprised to find that there was no one else around. Usually by this time of the morning (right after the bars closed) there were two or three cars parked in the small circle drive that wound dangerously close to the water. Most were just teenagers nervously swigging that glorious *Under Age* brand beer. Which was just like any other brand of beer, but it tasted oh so much better in its youthful prime. *Under Age* brand beer was specially brewed somewhere between the hazy, small towns of Youth and Stupidity and was pretty easy to come by if you knew where to look or who to talk to. When you reached the legal drinking age of twenty-one, it took the taste and fun away from *Under Age* brand beer, and most enthusiasts graduated to drinking Coors

Light or Budweiser or Miller Genuine Draft or some other *Legal Age* brand beer. And if you were a *Legal Age* brand beer drinker, you probably headed to Mullett Lake at this hour with the same idea as Craig Sheldon: a quick, refreshing swim after a long day at work. A day that was made so much longer by that damned broken air conditioner.

Craig reached into the back seat and grabbed a beach towel that, when spread out, looked suspiciously like an enormous *7–Up* can. It seemed like just about every clothing article bought these days had some kind of American corporate logo on it, and beach towels were not immune. The tactic probably wasn't working as well as thought; upon further inspection the article was usually found to be made in Korea or China or Mexico. Or, in the case of Craig's terrycloth *7-Up* can, *Malaysia* of all places. Most people couldn't *pronounce* Malaysia, let alone find it on a map. No doubt Cheryl Townsend would probably say it as Mal-lay-SIGH-yuh.

He stepped out of the car and slammed the door closed, kicking off his Nike's and strolling across the wet grass that grew almost to the shoreline. A heavy rainstorm had raked through earlier in the evening, bringing brief high winds and a torrential downpour. The storm did nothing to drop the temperatures as everyone had hoped. The rain was warm and had moved on as quickly as it had arrived, leaving a gray, hazy mist to rise from the pavement and rooftops like the sleepy steam from a vegetable fryer. The rain had drifted off to the northeast, and for a few brief moments before dusk the sun had peeked through purple and orange thunder heads that hung passively over the horizon.

An old wood pier jutted out from a small beach area and Craig walked slowly along the dock, listening to the sounds of the night as his bare feet padded the weathered planks. The bright chorus of crickets faded as he made his way farther over the water, anticipating a well-deserved swim after a day of slinging burgers and fish baskets and whatever the hell else was written on the endless wave of tickets that the wait staff pushed through the window. He pulled his T-shirt over his head, rolled it into a ball and carried it loosely as he walked, unbuttoning his jeans and unzipping the fly as he reached the end of the dock.

He stopped, gazing out over the dark waters, slowly turning his head to survey the tiny beads of light on the opposite side of the lake some two miles away. The serene stillness of Mullett Lake whispered to him, licking at his ears with the soothing melodies of a sultry summer night.

To the north, about a half mile from where he had parked his car, the jovial laughter of a late night party drifted across the lake. The flickering orange glow of a campfire reflected on the water and in the faces of those who stood around the roaring blaze, and the revelers were laughing and talking, their voices interspersed with broken fragments of reggae music. A car moved steadily north along Old US-27, the low drone of tires on pavement growing stronger, then fading as it passed. Craig turned to watch the car as its headlights continued by, finally disappearing through the trees.

Beneath him the water lapped at the moorings of the dock, gently slurping at the old wooden pilings. Here at the end of the dock the water was deep: ten feet or so at least with a perfect sandy bottom, which made this particular dock and its beach a rather popular swim site. But tonight the water was *black*. Not just a dark, murky black, but a thick, full black . . . a black that seemed to swallow up the night.

Craig dropped his clothes and the *7–Up* towel on the dock, stretched, took a long, deep breath, and plunged headfirst into the cool, dark water.

The water was refreshing and invigorating despite the fact that it, too, was quite a bit warmer than normal. It filled his pores and washed away the smells of grease and french fries and buffalo wings and shrimp ka-bobs that had become trapped in the oil of his skin.

He continued to swim slowly beneath the surface, bringing his arms above his head and pushing himself along as he swept his cupped hands back to his sides, enjoying every glorious, cleansing second. He felt renewed, refreshed and re-energized, and the prospect of burying his face right between Cheryl Townsend's delicious silver-dollar sized nipples grew more tantalizing by the moment. Amazing what a good shower or a dip in the lake can do for your libido.

He suddenly surfaced and shivered. It wasn't a shiver because he was cold or chilled, but he had suddenly sensed something very *odd*. Not at all a premonition, not a vision, just . . . *a feeling*. Craig wasn't afraid of the water; not even at night when demons and ghoulies and ogres came out, if, of course, there actually *were* such things as demons and ghoulies and ogres. If so, they had been slain long ago when Craig was a teenager, when the thoughts of scary monsters lying in wait beneath his mattress and box springs dwindled and were replaced by real fears: getting caught skipping school or having your dad find your pack of *Zig Zags* in the family station wagon.

And yet, oddly enough, that was what *this* feeling was like.

A slight uneasiness began at the base of his neck and trickled down the sliver of his spine. His head bobbed above the surface and he glanced quickly around, watching the waves fade away and distort the moon in the glossy reflection on the surface before him. Tiny lights dotted the shoreline on the other side of the lake more than a half-mile away, and far to the southeast a vertical row of red lights from a radio tower blinked every few seconds.

Craig cocked his chin downward and stared into the black water before him. He could see nothing except the occasional glitter of a reflecting star dancing on the wavering film.

A splash was heard in the distance and the giggle of a woman was cut short as she plunged below the surface, only to re-emerge laughing and sputtering, hollering something unintelligible to the partygoers that had thrown her in. The night was a carbon copy of last night, the night before that one, and the night before that one. Summertime on Mullett Lake, Michigan, and the living was oh, so easy. Spring came early and the warm weather had brought many vacationers to the lake in advance of the season to get a head start on summer, and the lights from their cabins and homes glowed brightly from the shoreline. Everything was beautiful and perfect, just like it should be on a lake in the scenic north. All the travel brochures guaranteed it; tonight was no exception.

And so in the blink of an eye Craig brushed aside his nervousness and began to swim easily, steadily crawling arm over arm through the refreshing water.

His foot kicked something hard, and he stopped swimming immediately and tread water. Once again the odd sensation of apprehension came over him and he turned to look at the dark shadow of the dock some thirty feet away, half expecting to see his father standing there, holding a pack of *Zig Zags* in his hand with a *what in the hell do you call this, boy?* expression of boiling rage on his face. Quite obviously he wasn't there, as the elder Sheldon had died of cancer three years ago. A pack and a half a day for thirty years had proven the Surgeon General correct, after all.

Craig snapped his head back around quickly, searching the

shadowy, inky waters for . . . for *anything*. His leg had hit something . . . perhaps a sunken log. But then again, he was certain that it was too deep for him to be able to reach bottom. And in the pitch-black water it was impossible to see beneath the surface. He couldn't even make out the vague form of his hand only a few inches away, let alone the object that he had kicked. His head darted nervously around and he decided to return to the dock. After all, he reminded himself, he just needed to get the stench of the bar off of his skin so when the horizontal bop was in full swing later on, Cheryl wouldn't be getting stale whiffs of everything he'd cooked that day. It was just polite.

He turned and began to swim, forcing the demons and ghoulies and ogres back to his pre-teenage years where they belonged.

With the impact of lightning his body suddenly shot below the surface, and a searing pain screamed from his thigh. In a flash Craig bolted back to the surface, gripping his leg with one arm, flailing frantically with the other, gasping for air. He reached down and his fingers met squishy flesh, and Craig shuddered in horror as he felt his bone through torn muscle and tendons. His leg had been completely severed just above the kneecap, torn away as easily as one of those *take-a-number* roll-tabs at the Secretary of State's office. His mind was a whirling blur of confusion and intense, fiery pain. He tried to scream but another jolt snapped him quickly under water. Now he was moving. Beneath the surface something seized his whole body and was moving fast. A hundred razors tore through his flesh and powerful, vice-like jaws bound tightly around his torso. In the blackness he could see nothing, but the pressure building in his ears and the movement of water against his face told him that indeed he was being carried deeper and deeper into the lake.

Craig hadn't had time to get a good breath, and his lungs began to throb. Terror and disbelief spun through his head. He was being violently shaken under water, shaken the way a dog plays with its favorite toy. Back and forth and sideways and back again, each motion causing excruciating agony. Sharp incisors crimped his body and forced the remaining of the air from his chest. He gurgled and screamed as he exhaled, but the sound was muffled by the rush of bubbles that escaped and began rising to the surface.

He managed to pull one arm free and he flailed it about in the water, trying to struggle away from whatever it was that had attacked him, tearing his flesh away with every powerful, twisting snap. Craig was a good swimmer, but he'd always thought that drowning would be one of the worst ways one could possibly die.

No!! his mind screamed. *Not this way!! NOT THIS WAY! I don't want to drown! I DON'T—*

He could no longer bear the burning pain in his chest. His air had completely run out. He opened his mouth and water poured in, rushing down his throat, pushing down his esophagus and deep into his lungs. His stomach tried to expel the onslaught of water by regurgitation, but the results were only compounded by more water surging back down.

One arm was still trapped by his side, but his free arm began to grow limp and he felt himself losing consciousness. The pain began to fade and the dark black around him was giving way to a hazy, calming blue. He began to relax, his body growing slack, his muscles relaxing, his eyes wide and bulging.

Suddenly Craig realized that his fears of drowning were unfounded. There was something much more terrible, much more evil to be afraid of than merely drowning. Something that had been lurking in the depths, waiting for its opportunity to attack and devour its next prey. The demons and ghoulies and ogres of his childhood *had* been real, after all. They had missed their opportunity in his golden youth, and they had come back for him.

And man, were they *pissed.*

Hey Craig-geeee, they whispered from the dark depths. *We gotcha now, Craig-geeee . . . .*

No, Craig thought, as consciousness dwindled away. *I'm not going to die drowning. I'm going to die by being eaten. I'm being eaten alive! I'm—*

One more violent, powerful snap shook his body, whipping his head forward and slamming his chin to his chest. He was being carried within some massive mouth, moving swiftly through the water. Craig's world slipped further away and the darkness was no longer. The hazy blue took over, becoming brighter and warmer as the black faded away. Suddenly, even the blue was gone. It was replaced by—

Nothing. There was no color, no sounds. In his mind he saw his father standing at his bedroom door, holding a pack of *Zig Zags.*

You're in one heapa trouble now, boy, he was saying. *One heapa trouble indeed.*

Indeed.

Then, as simply and gently as if someone had clicked off a light switch, Craig Sheldon quietly gave in and succumbed to the overwhelming rush of calming nausea. Horror and terror were replaced by quiet serenity and calm. Craig's light blinked out like the last flicker of a candle that had struggled to burn to the very bottom of the wick, only to run out of wax and diminish into nothing more than a tiny orange spark that grew dimmer and dimmer, finally extinguishing altogether.

Unseen from the surface or the shore, the enormous creature slipped silently back to the murky depths of Mullett Lake.

✳ ✳ ✳ ✳

The phone buzzed a dozen times in Cheryl Townsend's ear before she put the receiver back on its cradle. Three candles burned, illuminating the room with a soft, yellow glow. Two open bottles of Busch Light beer sweated on the same table in the same place that they had been for the past two hours.

Finally, she returned them to the fridge (no sense in wasting two perfectly good beers) and went from candle to candle, reluctantly blowing each one out. At the last candle she stopped, gazing out the window into the darkness, hoping to see Craig's car pulling into the driveway.

No such luck.

She leaned over and blew the last candle out, locked the front door, fumbled her way in the darkness to her bedroom, let her black lace teddy slip to the floor, and crept into bed.

Damn him, she thought as she pulled the thin sheet up to her waist. *That's IT. Hope he enjoyed it last week cause it's the last he's ever gettin' from me again.*

Funny how things just worked out like that sometimes.

ONE

It had been the kind of summer that made sweat bead on your forehead the moment you stepped out the door to walk to the mailbox. *Hotter than hell's furnace,* the old folks around the lake liked to say, which, of course, no one really knew for sure if hell even *had* a furnace, but if it did, the Big D himself probably paid his gas bill right there smack-dab in the middle of Courville, a small town on the shores of Mullett Lake in northern Michigan where the daytime highs had turned most parking lots into flaming waffle irons. Not that there *were* many parking lots in Courville in the first place; there were only a dozen or so small shops and most of their parking amenities were gravel, but the sun had been very indiscriminate this particular year and the entire northern region of the state was searing in a Chinese wok.

It was the kind of summer that kept old timers in their screened-in porches arguing about which summer had been the worst, (1961 had been a bad one) how hot it had actually been and for how long, all the while cursing that *godawful* humidity that could choke a horse to its death. Which was kind of odd for a town that usually got five or six months of snow so deep that an entire network of tunnels had to be created to make driving a car fifteen minutes to the Cheboygan McDonald's possible. Well, maybe *that's* a bit of a stretch, but the fact is that north of Clare (James Arbelle, the retired Courville postmaster, always said that if Michigan had a belly button, it would be Clare. Look on the map for a place you think Michigan's navel should be, and there's Clare) all the way up through the upper peninsula *(say yah! to da yoo pee, eh?)* and into the Great White North of Canada got hit with shitloads of snow, which made all the snowmobile and snow blower dealers and ski resorts pretty dad-blummed happy. Folks who didn't partake in outdoor activities during the winter months prayed from January to April for warm weather, and by golly this year the Good Lord probably got tired of hearing all of them and decided He'd *really* give them something to whine about. The snow had melted early, right around mid-March, and by the first week of May every conversation on either the telephone or over the cedar hedge began with something like *'gee, can you believe how hot it is?'* or the ever popular but very over used *'hottunufforya?'*

June arrived, served right out of the microwave after being cooked on button number six for ten minutes. The meat and poultry button. June's serving had so far been a disappointing one, as what most people really wanted was a nice helping of Borden's ice cream, any flavor please, served fresh from the freezer. Even at night most folks were sadly disappointed that the temperature was only dropping a few degrees cooler than the daytime highs, which made you wonder just how much the Big D had been shelling out every month to pay the heating bill. The night air was warm and damp and sticky and the whirring hum of fans could be heard from house to house, apartment to apartment, morning, noon and night throughout the small lakeside community.

Electric fans had become a pretty high commodity (air conditioners too, but they cost so damned much) and most had sold out at stores early in the year. Even the department stores had trouble keeping their shelves stocked with fans as northern Michigan wasn't the only place in the state that was frying like the unfortunate guest of honor at the county pig roast. Fred Deering, owner of *Courville Hardware and Small Engine Repair,* was making a proverbial *killing* off the abnormal heat. Of course, Deering always found a way to make something out of nothing, and this year it was fans, of all things. Every day his son Lawrence would drive to junkyards from Traverse City to Alpena and pay a buck or two for broken fans. Larry was only fifteen and didn't have a license but Fred had lost *his* automobile privileges due to a second drunk driving conviction, so having his son on the highway was just the lesser of two evils. Larry would return with a pickup truck filled with broken fans and old man Deering repaired them. He turned them all on and displayed them in the front window of his shop, which was conveniently located right on Old US-27 (as opposed to 'New' US-27, which was now a major highway). When folks drove by and saw all those fan blades spinning round and round in the daytime heat it was enough to make them drool right then and there. Deering sold them for twenty dollars each which wasn't bad for a used fan considering he himself couldn't get any *new* fans in stock. And son of a gun, it looked like he was going to be able to buy that used 1978 International Harvester after all. Candy Apple red, except where the rust had eaten away at the bottom of the doors and quarter panels. For the past two months Deering had eyed the vehicle proudly displayed in Darrel Petty's (no relation to the stock car driver, but don't ask Darrel because he'll tell you he *is*) front lawn with a big '4 SALE BY OWNER' sign in the cracked front windshield. Of course, Deering had no way of knowing that the two-thousand pound jacked-up four wheel drive of his dreams had a cracked block, but he'd find out soon enough. Fifteen-hundred bucks and oh, what a deal, *yessiree*. Just six more fans out the door and he'd have himself a pink slip. Maybe even by tomorrow afternoon.

Yep, it sure was hot, but for the most part, people were getting by just fine. The heat in Courville didn't pose a problem like it did in Chicago where folks were getting heat stroke and dropping like flies. Hell, they were dropping *faster* than flies, and they hit a lot harder when they smacked the ground. And night time in Courville, even though it was still warm and humid, brought at least a *little* reprieve from the searing daytime heat. Night time enticed folks out onto their lawns to have a cold Budweiser or a Captain Morgan and Coke (with lime, thank you very much) or a Country Time Lemonade with neighbors after the kids were tucked in bed and the dishes were put away.

And night time seduced many folks into taking refreshing dips in Mullett Lake where, if for only a few minutes, one could escape the feeling of living in a crock pot that someone had carelessly turned on high, forgot, and left for vacation.

Vacation. That was another reason why so many people flocked to the lake in the summer.

Vacation. A time to just kick back, relax, and get away for a while.

✳ ✳ ✳ ✳

Brad Herrick swerved to miss the deer, grasping the wheel tightly with both hands and careening into the opposite lane. The animal had bounded across the highway at a full run, thundering up from the ditch so quickly that Brad hadn't seen the animal until it was almost too late. The white flank whirled just inches from the front of the car and the deer ran by, escaping death by a mere split second. Brad corrected the vehicle, quickly jerking the wheel to the right to get the car back into his own lane. The animal had caught him off guard, but he glanced in the rearview mirror to see the hind quarters of the deer disappearing safely into the thick brush.

Lucky for you, he thought, shaking his head. *And lucky for me too. If a car had been coming from the other direction, it would have been all over for all of us.*

He was feeling better by the hour and except for the quick adrenaline rush when the deer had charged across the highway, the trip had been smooth and calm and relaxed. Carefree. He hadn't felt that way in a long time. Well . . . not a *long* time, he reminded himself. Long enough, though. The further north he pushed, the more at ease he felt, the more comfortable he became. He had the feeling that he was somehow really *escaping,* really getting away this time.

Maybe he could finally just put everything behind him and really enjoy himself after all.

He stopped at a small roadside market to grab a snack. The store was empty of customers. Behind the counter, a heavy-set woman with incredibly short, jet-black hair, managed a smile with some effort and quickly returned her attention to the black and white Zenith television set that hung from a corner behind the counter. The talk show host on the TV was trying to keep a

CHRISTOPHER KNIGHT

debate from becoming less than civil, which didn't seem to be an easy task. The topic of the show was *women who've slept with their best friend's man,* and the store clerk was as attentive as a cat at a can of tuna fish. Her eyes bulged when a rude comment was made by one of the guests on the show, and a thundering roar of applause and shouts came from the TV set.

"Can you believe that shit?" she asked incredulously as she shook her head, her eyes not leaving the TV. Brad assumed the question had been directed toward him but he said nothing, rounding the corner of an aisle and inspecting the items along the shelves.

When he returned to the counter the woman rang up a coffee and a bag of pretzels, every few seconds turning her gaze to the TV screen, mindful of the raging debate that, in her eyes at least, was most certainly an issue of national security.

"I just don't know what this world is coming to," she exclaimed, shaking her head. Her short, black hair was stiff and frozen and looked painted on her head. Large pink plastic loop earrings slapped her cheeks as her head turned from side to side. "That's two-ninety."

Brad handed her some bills.

"Outta three," she continued, placing the ones into the register with one hand and expertly snapping out a dime with the other. More cheering and applause came from the TV and the woman turned, gazing at the set, holding the dime in the air as if she were teasing a dog with a biscuit. Brad held his hand out patiently for a moment and waited until the woman finally returned her attention To him.

"He shoulda left'er," she sneered, dropping the dime into Brad's palm and glancing back at the television. "Long time ago. *Nobody* should be puttin' up with that bullshit."

CHRISTOPHER KNIGHT

"Nobody," Brad muttered, smiling. For a split second the woman gave Brad her complete attention . . . but *only* for a split second.

"You have a good day, all right?" was all she said, and in the next instant her head snapped back around again, fixated on the TV. She never saw Brad as he nodded, smiled, turned, and walked out the door.

He opened the bag of pretzels and stuffed a few into his mouth before reaching the beat up Cutlass Cierra. The car wasn't all that old, but Brad had taken rather poor care of it and had packed on the miles over the past few years. When little things had broken, he hadn't taken the time to fix them. But what the hell. That's why they were called *little things*.

He hopped back in the car, setting the foam cup of coffee on the dash as the vehicle swerved back on the road. Old US-27 was quiet at this early hour, and he'd encountered relatively few cars since he started his journey at three in the morning. An odd time to begin a vacation, but then again this wasn't one of those 'planned' vacations. He hadn't met with any travel agents to find out the 'prime tourist attractions' or any of those *'perfect northern getaways.'* No, Brad had awoken at three a.m. to take a leak, his mind still cluttered from months of anxiety and stress.

Of course, he hadn't *always* been that way. Until his girlfriend had left him last year, he'd been pretty happy. Happy, fun-loving, free-wheeling Brad Herrick. That was, of course, until the day she had told him that the fire just wasn't there anymore. The Five-Alarmer just died out. No fire trucks, no sirens. It just went out. It wasn't someone else, she had said. But of course there was. There *always* was. When you were told up front and ahead of time that *'it's not you, it's me,'* it was usually followed up with *'and there's nobody else, I swear.'* Zits and an eighth-grade education gave you the wisdom to see through *that* line like Saran Wrap.

And it probably hurt a little worse when he found out the 'someone else' happened to be a friend he worked with.

But that was last year . . . he should have been over it long ago. Even his lab supervisor, Frank Girard, had told him so, which, in a very direct way, was why Brad had been in his car for the past seven hours, heading north.

He chuckled at the thought, the fact that he had actually taken such a suggestion from Frank. Actually what began as a suggestion became an absolute ultimatum. Not that he didn't like Girard; quite the opposite. Frank was a bald, bespectacled man with a tiny round face and sloping, droopy shoulders. He said he'd been a state swim champion for the Ohio State Buckeyes in his day, and coming from Frank Girard you probably believe it. Old Frank was about as genuine as they come, and Brad got along great with him from day one, as did most of the others at the lab. It was just that, well, a *vacation* was the last thing Brad thought he needed. He liked his job, liked where he lived. *Hell,* he thought. *I'm on vacation all the time.*

Up ahead on the highway a cop suddenly appeared from around a turn, coming toward him in the opposite lane. Brad glanced down at the speedometer and lifted his foot off the gas. Sixty-three in a fifty-five: some cops would, some cops wouldn't. This one didn't, and Brad allowed the car to coast to a safe fifty-six miles an hour before resuming acceleration.

A vacation. Wow.

Bradley Andrew Herrick (as his mother called him when she *really* meant business) was a marine biologist at a small university in Lorain Ohio, on the shores of Lake Erie. It wasn't a great job, but it wasn't a bad one either. It was in his field of interest, but the pay was sadly well below what one would imagine an assistant lab tech would or should be paid. The trade-off was that he pretty much got to do what he wanted, and that made up for a lot. He couldn't see himself behind a desk wearing a suit and tie. Nor could he imagine himself on the line screwing in bolts five days a week. His father had done that for thirty years and loved it, and made a very good living doing so. *UNION AND PROUD* was the bumper sticker that graced the right rear fender of every vehicle the Herrick family had ever owned. Much to the dismay of the elder Herrick, Brad wouldn't be following in his father's proverbial footsteps, or fitting into his shoes, or carrying on the torch or however you wanted to describe it. Brad could have had a good-paying job at the factory, thanks to his father, but he had opted for college instead, accepting an assistant's position at yet another college after he'd graduated in 1989. And for the past six years he had been the proverbial 'model' employee. He worked a lot and got along with everyone. Girard trusted him implicitly and Brad had a lot of freedom, even if it didn't do much for his paycheck. He worked hard and threw himself into various projects aligned with his field. When asked what field that was, Brad usually just smiled and said that he played in the water a lot.

And in essence, that was what he did. He and he alone had been instrumental in getting a government grant to study zebra mussels, a small clam-like creature that had been invading the lakes and wreaking havoc within the past few years. The little buggers attached themselves to the hulls of boats, to intakes of large freighters, everywhere they could, coating and covering just about everything beneath the surface like flies on dog shit. Zebra mussels were considered at one time to be one of the greatest threats to the ecosystem of the Great Lakes, simply because there was just no way of getting rid of the damn things. There had been *some* benefits, however. Zebra mussels filtered and cleaned the water and were helpful in cleaning up Lake Erie to a quality not seen in decades. Progress was being made to strike a balance, but any real solution was years away.

Brad had worked on other projects as well but within the last year, (since his break-up) things had begun to change. He found himself frustrated all the time. No matter how much or how hard he worked, he felt it wasn't enough. He preferred to work alone and spent most of his spare time in the office or in the field doing research. He *told* himself he didn't know why, but he knew. And it all had to do with Jennifer Whatsername. (Brad obviously knew her last name but was convinced that he could forget about her completely if he didn't use her full name when he thought about her.) Being dumped was nothing new for anyone, but Brad had never even seen it coming. He'd put some money down on a ring and was going to ask Jennifer to marry him. He had big dreams and plans and made reservations at an exclusive restaurant in Cleveland, where he had planned to pop the question and present the ring.

It never got that far.

By this time, obviously unknown to Brad, Jennifer was headfirst into another relationship, and had been for quite some time. Maybe she suspected what Brad was up to and figured she'd better do something first. She had no intention of marrying Brad, or even continuing the relationship. She finally just came right out and told him that things had changed, things weren't the same, that she just needed a break for a while.

Right.

In hindsight it was more ridiculous now than it seemed at the time. Brad went into a depression, becoming quiet and withdrawn and into himself. Soon people began to notice the change. Brad's temper had become shorter. He became discouraged easier. When things weren't going his way, hopelessness set in, clinging to his soul the way a pit bull locks onto its prey. Brad even started seeing a shrink, which he felt didn't seem to help much. Not for seventy-five bucks an hour, anyway. Brad usually felt worse going out than he did coming in, so he knocked *that* shit off after seven sessions.

By this time, his supervisor at the lab had become more *concerned* than angry. He tried to talk to Brad but Brad denied there was anything wrong, claiming he was fine. *Couldn't be better, thank you very much,* Brad always told him.

Then, just yesterday, came the day at the lab. Or, *The* Day at the Lab, with the emphasis on *The.*

Yesterday morning another assistant at the lab had accidentally taken some of Brad's paperwork home. When Brad arrived and found his work missing he flew into a rage, throwing a glass beaker across the room. The beaker shattered on the wall, sending an explosion of glass shards to the floor . . . just as Frank Girard walked into the room. A piece of glass caught Girard right in the temple, creating a two-inch gash that required stitches.

Girard did nothing when the glass hit him. He had just stood there, looking at Brad, blood dripping down his cheek and dripping onto his white lab coat.

Brad felt *awful.* He felt foolish for executing such a childish reaction, and he felt even worse that he'd hurt someone. Someone that was his boss . . . and his *friend.* He was certain he would be fired, but that didn't bother him as much as knowing that he was responsible for the gaping wound on the side of Girard's head.

Brad, it's time for a vacation, was all Frank had said as he turned and walked out of the lab.

When he returned from the hospital with a square white bandage on the side of his head, he called Brad into his office. Brad was sure that this was *it.* Walking papers. So long, Brad.

Been fun.

But that's not what happened. Frank decided that Brad needed a break. A mandatory vacation. He hadn't taken any extended time off in over three years, and now it was time to unwind a bit. *Two weeks, longer if you want, paid,* Frank told him. Brad protested, But Frank Girard had made it clear: take a two-week paid leave of absence and get your shit together, or take the rest of your life off, unpaid.

And Brad, Girard had told him, *don't call my bluff.*

There had been something in Frank's eyes that told Brad that his supervisor was more than serious. It was a strong warning from a kind, caring man. If it would have been anyone else, he would have been shit-canned for sure.

A vacation, Brad. Some time off to get it together. And don't call my bluff.

Brad put on his best poker face, looked at his own cards, and folded. He wasn't going to win with this hand. Not today.

✳ ✳ ✳ ✳

He rolled down the window and Girard's words were drowned by the rush of passing wind. The fresh air whirling within the car was fresh and invigorating and he sped up a bit, beginning to like the idea of a vacation more and more.

A getaway, he had thought at three that morning. Maybe that's really what he needed. Maybe that was *it*. To take some time off and get away from all the people who kept telling him he needed time off.

He had been standing over the toilet when the thought struck him, thinking about how nice it would be to just leave town. To just go somewhere where no one knew him. To travel to a quiet town, a small community on a lake. A place to buy a good twenty-nine ninety-five fishing rig like the Zebco outfit that he had growing up. He would rent a small rowboat, do a little fishing. *Bass* fishing. Hell . . . *any* kind of fishing. He'd been working in and around water for years, but he hadn't been fishing since he was ten. He'd enjoyed it then, and he had the yearning for the past few seasons to wet a line or two.

And a place where maybe . . . just *maybe* . . . he could finally just forget about Whatsername.

So at exactly three-twelve that morning he had flipped open his *Rand McNally*, opened it up to the state of Michigan, closed his eyes, and plopped his index finger on the small, sleepy community of—

—Detroit? No, something a bit tamer. A little quieter than the Motor City, he thought. He tried again, cheating a little by slightly opening one eye as his finger darted toward the paper. After all, he wanted to make sure he would wind up at least *close* to water. His eye caught a small dot of blue and he aimed for it, closing both eyes tightly so it wouldn't *really* be like he was cheating. His finger fell forward, and Brad opened both eyes and strained to read the tiny letters.

Mullett Lake. The jagged blue splotch on the paper didn't look like much. And it was 'Mullett', not 'Mullet.' Two t's, not one. Just another of Michigan's hundreds of lakes that were scattered about the lower and upper peninsula. Mullett Lake, from what he could gather, appeared to be connected to another lake or lakes through a series of small rivers and streams. The chain of lakes stretched northeast from Petoskey on the northwestern side of the state, to Cheboygan, where the river finally flowed into the massive expanse of Lake Huron. Mullett Lake and Burt Lake (one of the adjacent lakes) seemed to be rather large. Certainly larger than any of the lakes in Ohio. A few tiny villages and towns dotted the shores of both watersheds, and once again Brad had swept his finger over the map, half closing his eyes, looking for a final destination, which was going to be–

Plop.

–*Courville.*

It seemed as good of a place as any.

✳ ✳ ✳ ✳

Seven hours and seven cups of coffee. He hadn't planned it like that; it just worked out that way. The highway continued rushing toward him, and broken slabs of sunlight broke through the treetops, jabbing at his eyes and causing him to squint.

He glanced in the rearview mirror, looking disdainfully at his reflection. Dark rings had formed under his eyes from lack of sleep, making the few wrinkles around his eyes appear even more prevalent. His short blonde hair was uncombed but not entirely unkempt. Years ago when he'd had longer hair he resembled more of a gangly rock star than a marine biologist. But in his early twenties his hair began to thin rather quickly, and he had cut it off in fear that he was going to lose it all. Now, at twenty-nine, his hair was much shorter and conservative. He had only the beginning of a receding hairline, for which he felt fortunate: his father had lost most of *his* hair by the time he reached the age of twenty-six. And back in those days you couldn't just run to the drugstore for your kit of Rogaine, either. When it was gone, it was gone, just like that.

Kind of like Whatsername.

Poof.

He picked up the tattered map that lay unfolded in the passenger seat, retracing his long journey north. Coffee stains had smeared a few cities, and he mused that with just a few short careless drips he had created some of the largest mud holes in the state.

Courville lay between the village of Somerville and the small town of Cheboygan. Old US-27 wound around the western shore of Mullett Lake and Brad put the map down and slowed, mindful of his nearing destination. He gazed out over the lake and a large osprey soared over the water, its gray and white feathers gleaming majestically in the morning sun. A few small fishing boats were on the lake, and Brad passed a long dock that extended quite a distance out from the shore like a long, bony finger. Silhouetted in the sun at the end of the dock sat three shadows, enjoying coffee in the stillness of the morning. It was the land of dreams and fairy tales, where *real* homemade pumpkin pie was made and parents walked their kids to meet the school bus and fourteen-year-old boys made extra money by delivering papers and mowing lawns. The pace was slow; much slower than most cities, and you couldn't be in a hurry if you tried. You couldn't even hurry *slowly,* the pace was that slow. And those who felt that Courville was *too* slow needed Courville more than those in *Courville* needed Courville.

"You people don't know how lucky you have it," he said aloud. Then, glancing back at the three silhouettes at the end of the dock: *"Well . . . maybe you do. Maybe you do know how lucky you have it, because* you *live here and* I *don't."*

CHRISTOPHER KNIGHT

If he hadn't turned his gaze back to the highway at that exact moment, he would have missed it. An old green and white sign blankly stated *COURVILLE-POPULATION 204*. A few inches beneath the white letters an old campaign sticker showed the face of some smiling candidate. *Re-Elect Mayor Fer–* was all it said. The rest had been worn and torn away. And, in typical Michigan nobility, someone had been rather accurate with a deer rifle, as evident by the seven or eight crater-like dents that nearly perforated the heavy steel. He had seen a number of such signs on his trip north, and Brad wondered jokingly if they *made* the signs that way. Or maybe there was a state regulated sign hunting program. Maybe you were allowed something like five signs per day during sign season. It was also quite possible that the signs were divided up into categories, like big and small game. Maybe stop signs and speed limit signs were big game; street signs and yield signs could be small game. Or vice versa. It was a novel thought, and Brad smiled as he pulled into the single coffee house/gas station/grocery store/post office.

The outside of the building was clean and well-maintained. The parking lot was gravel, and there were two other vehicles parked, both unoccupied with their engines running. Brad had encountered this phenomenon more frequently the farther north he traveled. There was a strange absence of paranoia and distrust, as if people didn't seem at all concerned about leaving a twenty-five thousand dollar vehicle unlocked and running. Brad killed the engine of his own car and walked inside the small store.

✳ ✳ ✳ ✳

On a small cork board inside he found just what he was looking for. Dozens of hand written signs touted everything for sale from lawnmowers to sport utilities to sailboats. There were hundreds of such notices, some carelessly scribbled on lined note paper, others typed on small note cards. A small church poster announced the arrival of an evangelist from Maui, appearing at the Life in Truth Chapel on February 14, 1999 . . . four months previous. A girl named Carol was offering babysitting services for a dollar-fifty an hour. Brad had no idea how much babysitting costs these days but he figured that a buck and a half an hour was probably a good deal. Other advertisements offered services such as lawn care, horse shoeing, and snow plowing.

Lord knows, Brad thought, shaking his head and wiping a bead of sweat from his temple. *Gotta watch out for those Killer June Blizzards.*

Beneath the snow plowing card was an advertisement he had been hoping to find. On a letter-sized piece of paper someone had hastily written:

Cottages 4 Rent
1 and 2 bedroom
Daily-Weekly-Monthly/Reasonable Rates

Beneath the ad a row of identical telephone numbers had been scribbled vertically on the bottom one-inch of the page. A few of the numbers had been torn off by other interested persons. Brad tugged at a piece and tore it away, reading the number as he walked toward the pay phone.

✳ ✳ ✳ ✳

CHRISTOPHER KNIGHT

The cottage certainly wasn't anything spectacular; three hundred-fifty dollars a week didn't buy much, even in the village of Courville. It didn't buy a pool or hot tub, and it sure as heck didn't buy valet parking. The rooms were small, about the size they give you at Motel 6, but they were comfortable. And the cabin was neat and clean, even if the accommodations were meager at best. His three-fifty per week bought a few huge oak and willow trees to shade him from the hot summer sun. It bought a small, sandy beach and a forty-foot long dock that suspended out over the water. And it bought a small hummingbird feeder that hung from a tree branch just outside the door of the cabin, should Brad ever take an interest in bird watching. The grass was as lush and thick and green as a golf course, and various birds flitted among large birch trees that edged close to the cabins. A hundred feet away, a group of children played in the shallows, splashing and laughing. The resort was more of a glorified campground with only a dozen single units or so, but it was un-cluttered and well kept, and that suited Brad just dandy.

It was noon. The day was already hot, and the sun danced within tiny glittering diamonds on the surface of Mullett Lake. The enormous weeping willows swayed easily in the breeze like big olive mops, their long, stringy spines shuddering gently in the light wind. A blue jay whisked by over head, lighting on a large feeder in front of the next cabin. There were already a number of sparrows and warblers on the feeder, and the arrival of the jay caused screeches of panic and indignation from the smaller, more numerous birds. The blue jay, as if taunting the smaller birds, quickly snared a sunflower seed in its beak and was off again, darting over the hedges and disappearing. The warblers and sparrows angrily voiced their opinions, but they quickly forgot about the intruder and went back to their business of pecking at seeds.

Brad walked down the sloping grass and over a short sandy beach to the water line. A small frog panicked and leapt to the safety of the lake, plopping beneath the surface to find a more secure hiding place. The shallow water near the shore was filled with tiny fish, and every time Brad made a move the entire school of minnows darted in a thousand different directions. Beneath the surface, the bottom was sandy and clean and every few feet a small stone or snail spoiled the perfect underwater desert. An old, graying dock protruded out from the shore, and, according to a new hand-painted sign, was intended for use by *Resort Guests Only, Please.*

He leaned over and placed his hand in the water, swishing it back and forth and bringing his wet palms up to wipe his face. Brad felt clammy and stuffy from the ride north, and the clear blue water was just too inviting to ignore.

A swim, he thought. *A nice cool swim should be the first order of business today.*

He turned and walked back up the creeping slope and looked around, taking a long, sweeping look at the village of Courville. Old US-27 wound behind the cottages, and a large field opened up on the other side of the highway. Most of the homes and cabins were on the lake side, of course. In one yard a man with blue jeans and no shirt pushed a lawnmower over the grass. In the same yard, a woman in her fifties trimmed an absolutely stunning bed of flowers. They boasted colors of all sorts and Brad was sure he could smell them from where he stood. He turned slowly, surveying the small town.

Clear water. Blue skies. Clean air, flowers, noisy children and buzzing lawnmowers and the scent of freshly-mowed grass in the air. Prickly green blades beneath his bare feet, water-wings, wading pools, frogs and turtles. The stuff summer dreams were made of. Bottle it all up and put it on the shelves boys . . . we got ourselves a *winner*. Won't even be able to keep it in stock. Call it a 'Courville Cooler'. All natural ingredients, no artificial sweeteners, no preservatives added. One week supply: just three hundred and fifty dollars.

Even Fred Deering didn't have a deal going like that.

✳ ✳ ✳ ✳

Brad returned to cottage number 12, lakeside. Actually, *all* of the cottages were lakeside. It just looked better on the brochures if potential guests had a choice. Marketing *is* everything, as they say.

He emptied the contents of his suitcase on the small bed and found his trunks, draped a towel over his shoulder and exited the cottage, leaving only the screen door closed. The blue jay had returned to the bird feeder but when Brad stepped off the porch the bird made a hasty departure, sending tiny seeds spraying into the grass below. The jay flew to a branch high in a birch tree and screeched at the intruder before it leapt from its perch and swooped into the yard where a half-dozen children were still playing in the back. Parental Guidance was just a few feet away in the form of a rather large, sunglass-clad woman wearing a black one-piece suit. It is said that the color black, when worn, has certain slimming qualities. Not true in this case, and Parental Guidance was living proof. She was reclining in a lounge chair, reading one of those romance novels that you can buy from the metal spindle at the *Courville Partee-Mart* . . . the kind of novel that featured stone-faced, bare-chested, long-haired mastodons of masculinity emblazoned colorfully on the cover, ready to whisk the reader away to a foreign land for a dangerous adventure and fleeting affair. Something for everyone in Courville, Michigan, population two-oh-four.

Brad strode across the grass and down the slope, over the sand, past the *Resort Guests Only, Please* sign, and plodded down the old wooden dock.

✳ ✳ ✳ ✳

The rage was immediate and certain. The fish had been sleeping, tucked within dense reeds and tangled underwater vegetation. The sudden, unexpected splash from the surface was disturbing, and the huge muskie snapped around, looking to see where the noise had come from. It moved slowly, cruising effortlessly over the leafy green weeds that grew up from the bottom of the lake. Were it not for its enormous size of twelve feet, the muskie would be well hidden among the thick aquatic shrubbery. In the depths, it could bury itself within the dense vegetation and lay in wait for hours without being detected.

It wasn't hungry. Often times the fish ate regardless of its appetite, as was customary with most muskies. Many times a muskie would snare a large fish or a duck or other animal simply because it was there and the opportunity presented itself. A muskie could and would eat much more than it could swallow and would have to carry its prey in its mouth, swallowing it portion by portion as it slowly digested.

The fish moved quicker as the splashing grew louder. Its eyesight was keen, but it was still too far from the disturbance to see it. It glided faster through the water, its burning eyes darting from side to side, back and forth, scanning the surface and the green-yellow waters. Smaller fish skirted quickly out of its way, seeking shelter within the thick seaweed.

The muskie was in shallow water now, about ten feet deep. It didn't care to be in such shallow water during the day, as there wasn't much cover provided and certainly no place to hide. It wasn't that the fish was afraid; indeed, it wasn't afraid of *anything* in the lake. It was just that it relied on the element of surprise in so many situations. It needed to stalk its prey without being seen.

But the muskie was far too angry this time. It had been disturbed and surprised, and its anger seethed beneath its thick scales. Massive, four-inch razor sharp teeth clenched within powerful jaws. The splashing was continuing, and the fish, its temper building, moved faster toward the noise.

✳ ✳ ✳ ✳

The water felt wonderful. It was cool and intoxicating, and Brad lay on his back for a moment, kicking lazily with his feet and staring up at the perfect blue sky. There were no clouds, not one single white wisp. A few seagulls screamed overhead and a warm breeze rippled the lake. The children were still playing near the shore, their laughter echoing out over the water. The woman in the lounge chair was still completely engrossed in her novel, only in one hand she now held a large glass of iced tea just below her chin and a plastic straw dripped mindlessly from her lips. Brad mused that maybe she was probably at one of the good chapters.

He began to think about his job and Frank, and his know-it-all shrink. And whatser–

He caught himself before his mind ventured further.

"Nope," he insisted to the blue sky above. *"Not gonna do that. Not even gonna think about that crap today."* He shook the thoughts aside as he turned over in the water and began to crawl, arm over arm, back to the dock.

✱ ✱ ✱ ✱

There. The muskie could see the disturbed water on the surface. Its anger grew to an intense fire that boiled from within. The eruption on the surface was moving, heading back toward the shore. The fish moved faster through the water, fueled by a strong, powerful tail and a burning desire to kill. Hunger played no part in this attack, as the muskie was still full from an earlier meal consisting of three unsuspecting Canadian geese and a large snapping turtle that was just unlucky enough to swim by that morning. The fish had swallowed the big turtle whole, and followed it up by chasing down and devouring numerous other fish.

The muskie was now just a dozen yards from its prey. The fish began to open its mouth as it moved closer, displaying rows upon rows of ugly knives that would rip its prey into pieces.

Now only a few feet away, it lunged forward for the kill, opening its mouth to its full extension.

✳ ✳ ✳ ✳

Brad grasped the old wood support posts at the edge of the dock and pulled himself up. Or rather, *tried* to pull himself up. There was no ladder, and nothing to slip his foot into. He fell back into the water, his head bobbing beneath the surface. He shook his hair to the side as his head broke water. Placing his palms on the edge of the dock, he lowered himself in the water, just a few inches, then sprang and pulled with all his might. Struggling and kicking the water to boost himself upward, he fell forward on the dock and pulled himself the rest of the way up. His hand caught a sharp portion of the dock, and he winced in pain as an inch-long sliver of wood drove into his palm.

"Shit," he cursed beneath his breath as he stood up. A small bead of blood formed and ran down his arm, and Brad turned and bent down to rinse his hand in the lake. A large shadow—a movement behind him out of the corner of his eye—caught him off guard and he jumped, snapping his head around.

There was nothing there.

He was certain there had been *something* there, however, just beneath the surface. Water churned and boiled, evidence that there *had* been something there. A fish, obviously, but what kind? They were often curious, and sometimes a swimmer would be within just a few feet of a bass or carp or some other freshwater fish and not even know it. As soon as they were spotted or a safe distance had been jeopardized, the fish would turn and take off like a rocket. Fish, although quite curious, were spooked easily.

Brad continued to search the clear waters. A few clumps of lime-colored seaweed splotched here and there along the bottom, and a broken cement block lay tipped on its side, green and slimy with algae from years of being submerged undisturbed. Dusty brown silt had been kicked up from the bottom, and the cloud began to grow larger as Brad searched the depths. If he was lucky, he might get a glimpse of the bass or whatever it was that had ventured to the dock.

He leaned over the water and looked under the dock, once again finding nothing but the dull sandy bottom and sporadic clumps of seaweed some nine or ten feet below him. He shrugged, turning around. Whatever it had been was now long gone.

Oh well, he thought, starting back up the dock. *Nice to know that there's some fish in here anyway.*

He glanced down, noticing his hand. He had forgotten about the splinter, and part of his hand was now drenched in blood. A few dark red drops fell from his fingertips, splattering the gray boards beneath his feet. And he had carelessly wiped his trunks with his injured hand, staining the yellow nylon with dark, dirty crimson blotches. He knelt down, rinsed his bloodied hand in the water, and continued down the dock and back to shore.

✸ ✸ ✸ ✸

The huge fish had turned at the last instant, closing its

enormous jaws. Its prey had escaped by leaving the surface of the water. The muskie had been just *inches* away . . . just a mere few *inches* . . . but at the final moment . . . *a warning*. Not fear, not hesitation, but *warning*. Instinct. Like a stop sign on the highway or a flashing red light. A very simple, plain alarm to alert the fish to danger. The fish didn't reason, didn't weigh the pros and cons. It simply followed its instinct.

With one powerful swish of its tail it was gone, heading back to deeper water, back to the depths, unheard and unseen.

TWO

Amy Hunter was extremely attractive, she just didn't know it. Which was probably best, because she had eyes that could turn away a hurricane and a body that could sink a ship. She had a petite frame and long, honey-wheat colored hair. Her teeth were as white as paper. Amy thought that her breasts were too small and wished they were larger and fuller like the women she'd seen in magazines and on TV. But if you'd ask any of the single men around Mullett Lake, well . . . Amy Hunter was *perfect*. If you asked any married men the same question, they'd think the same thing, but they'd lie to you. But Amy was clueless as to how beautiful she really was, and that was a good thing. Women who are that attractive and know it have a false sense of physical security; Amy had none of that and wouldn't know what to do with it if she did. Oh, she *hoped* that she was attractive, but she wasn't so caught up in the glitz and the glam that it interfered with who Amy Hunter really was.

Of course, one doesn't find much glitz and glam in

Courville, but if there was, Amy Hunter was the best thing going. Sweet and secure for a twenty-three year old. She'd grown up in Courville but moved away to attend college, and now that she had graduated with her business degree she had returned for the summer to stay in one of her uncle's cottages on Mullett Lake, earning her keep by doing light housework for the cabins. The work could be tedious, but she'd live rent-free as long as she wanted. She planned to stay in Courville through September. Then, who knows. Who *really* knew what you did with a business degree, anyway. Amy wasn't sure what field of interest she would pursue, and that was just fine for now. Four years of collegiate studies had been rewarded with a degree, and now it was time for a short break. A summer's rest, that's what it was. She still had several thousand dollars in the bank, and that would suit her needs for the summer at least. Besides . . . there were any number of restaurants or bars where she could waitress, an occupation that went well with her natural easy-going charm. She'd put herself through college by waitressing at an exclusive golf club in Brighton. First year earnings: just over forty-thousand dollars, most of which was in tips. Not bad for a young college student right out of high school. A lot of people would be tempted to stick with the waitress gigs, but Amy knew that the pace (along with the endless supply of rude remarks, drunks trying to fondle her breasts, or out-of-town businessmen trying to take her home) would take its toll in the long run. Being a waitress had paid the bills, and that was it: Amy had no intention of making a career out of it.

When she moved back to Courville she was the obvious target for all young, testosterone-charged, mentally under-developed males. Billy Reppler, a rather rude individual who certainly didn't deserve the opportunity to date her (he did so once, not again) dreamily said that she could derail a train with one glance of her green eyes. Amy had struggled through three torturous hours at a restaurant in Cheboygan. While the food was good, it was the only positive note during the evening. Amy was doomed to listen to Billy theorize for twenty minutes about why Polaris made *'the best fuckin' snowmobile on the planet'*, as he put it plainly. And no, she had told him, she did not want to go *'mudding'* with him through the trails. Whatever the hell that was. She was sure it had something to do with his jacked up yellow truck (which he had picked her up in) parked in the restaurant's lot. While an adventure of that sort wouldn't necessarily be out of line, she had no desire to wind up in the forest at night watching Reppler swig Molsen beer with that *I wanna screw your brains out* twinkle in his eye. After dinner he cruised her around Cheboygan in the truck, bumping into his friends who were easy to find: most had trucks or other SUV's parked in parking lots, engines running with windows rolled down, occupants talking to one another and sneaking sips of beer from cans hidden between their legs while they discussed the world's problems. Like Dave Miller's new Bronco (which wasn't really new, it was what the dealerships called 'pre-owned') that he'd wrapped around a tree last night. Later, when he took Amy home he had tried to kiss her good night but she was able to expertly bypass it with a quick hug and an even quicker half step back.

Wanna go out tomorrow night? he had stammered before Amy closed the door of her cottage.

No, she had said, smiling. She offered no explanation and closed the door before one was requested.

The following day, *'didjagitteny'* was the sixty-four thousand dollar question posed to Billy Reppler by his cohorts, to which he grinned and told everyone *shit yes, you betcherass I fucked her. And let me tellya—she was incredible. In-fuckin'-credible.*

It was for liars like Reppler that hell was created bottomless.

* * * *

With most of the housekeeping duties complete, Amy walked to the mailbox and picked up the daily stack of bills, credit card offers (*you've been pre-approved for up to $100,000!*) and the usual assortment of junk mail. And a letter from her parents, letting her know that all was well and Alaska was wonderful. They'd left six weeks ago to travel and see the U.S., and weren't expected back to their home in Petoskey until sometime in September.

She tossed all of the unwanted mail into a large drum near the front office and waved to her uncle inside. He was seated at his desk, talking on the phone. He waved back, blowing her a silent kiss. Jim was her father's brother, and he was also more of a brother than an uncle to Amy, who had more than once confided in him when she had the urge to do so. He was patient and kind; just the kind of uncle everyone wanted. Jim's wife was killed in a car accident in 1987, and now it was he and he alone who ran the cabins. Except, of course, this summer. This summer Amy moved into one of the cabins and worked part-time. He was happy to have the help.

She returned to her cabin to find Pepper, her golden retriever, waiting patiently on the porch, basking in the morning sun. He thumped his tail happily as she returned, and Amy bent over to scratch his creamy belly.

"Good boy," she said. "You're a good boy." She patted his stomach then stood up, gazing out over the lake.

There were dozens of boats on the water, as well as a few

jet-skis and sailboarders. On the other side of the cedar hedge the group of neighborhood children were hard at play, splashing one another and frolicking in the cool water. A woman was in a lounge chair with a book, where she had been the day previous and the day before that, and the day before that as well. Seemed like everyone was taking advantage of the prevalent sunshine, being that they couldn't take refuge from the stifling heat.

She went around the cottage and opened the windows wide and tried the fan again. No luck. Amy had purchased a used fan for twenty dollars at the *Courville Hardware and Small Engine repair,* but it had broken yesterday and now when she turned it on it simply made a loud buzzing noise; the blades remained frozen and useless. She'd have to take it back and hope that they'd repair it or replace it.

A splash diverted her attention from the broken fan and she turned her head in time to see a man pulling himself up at the end of the private dock. Amy made another mental note to tell her uncle that the ladder had broken and she'd pulled it out the other day. The *last* thing they needed was someone getting hurt on a broken ladder. Without the ladder, however, it was difficult to pull yourself up and out of the water.

The man struggled a bit but didn't seem to have too much of a problem, until she noticed him staring at his hand as he stood at the end of the dock. Even from where she was she could see the blood begin to drip down his arm.

Wonderful, she thought, turning and walking into her cabin. *Just what we need. A lawsuit.* She scurried back into the cottage and returned with a hand towel.

❋ ❋ ❋ ❋

CHRISTOPHER KNIGHT

"I thought you might need this."

The woman's voice surprised Brad, and he looked up from where he stood on the sloping grass, squinting in the sun as he stared in the direction of the voice. The woman emerged from the doorway of one of the cabins, walking toward him carrying a green hand towel. Faded cutoff denims clung tightly to her hips, and a plain white cotton T-shirt, probably a size too big, draped over her shoulders and tucked beneath her shorts. Long, blonde-brown hair tied in a ponytail fell between her shoulder blades. She wore a baseball cap that had a small caricature of a squirrel holding a hockey stick over-looking the bill. Soft green eyes smiled back at him, and Brad guessed the woman to be eighteen . . . nineteen tops.

A *sport model*, as Billy Reppler had described her. She was slim and her body was firm and tight, and Brad, sensing his initial inspection had already dragged on far too long, glanced down at his hand and spoke.

"Yeah. Not as bad as it looks, though. Just a splinter."

He raised his hand and watched her as she approached. Her legs were tan and toned: the legs of a runner, or at least the legs of someone who was in the habit of taking care of herself.

She wrapped the towel over his palm carefully and inspected his hand.

"That's a nasty splinter. Hold on . . . I have a pair of tweezers in my purse."

She left Brad holding the towel over his right hand and he watched her walk quickly back to the house. Again he caught himself staring longer than he should.

At least, longer than he wanted to get *caught* at.

CHRISTOPHER KNIGHT

She returned after a moment with a pair of tweezers. She took his hand in hers and looked again at the wound. The skin around the buried sliver was swollen and pink, and blood continued to ooze from the cut. The splinter was at least an inch long, and Brad had driven it deep into his hand. A small corner of the wood protruded, and the woman pinched it with the tweezers. Brad gave his best *'it don't hurt a bit'* look, but he wasn't sure if he was succeeding. It was quite painful. Gradually, the dark purple form beneath the skin began to shorten as she gently pulled.

"Half way there," she said, glancing up at him with a quick smile. Blood continued to trickle from around the cut, and finally the sliver was removed. She held it firmly in the tweezers for a moment then tossed it aside, wiping the metal utensil on the towel.

"Thank you," Brad said, hyper-extending his fingers and then clenching his fist. "I guess I wasn't watching."

"There was a ladder there until last week, but I pulled it out," Amy responded. "Two of the rungs had broken and I was afraid someone would get hurt. I guess pulling it out didn't help much."

Brad chuckled. "I think I'll live," he said, smiling warmly.

Amy was relieved. *Thank God he's not one of those sue-happy litigation lizards,* she thought. She extended her right hand, then, realizing that a towel covered Brad's right hand, switched and extended her left.

"Amy Hunter. You met my Uncle Jim this morning. He owns the resort."

"Brad," he responded, briefly taking her hand in his. "Brad Herrick. Nice to meet you."

"Come on," she offered. "You need to wash that out with soap." Brad followed her across the thick lawn to her cabin.

✳ ✳ ✳ ✳

At twenty-three, Amy was older than Brad had thought. She was just out of college and living in one of her uncle's cottages for the summer. It was a great deal, she told him. It took her only a few hours a day to clean the cabins, leaving her free for the rest of the day. She had thought about taking a job as a waitress or a bartender a couple nights a week, but she said that at the moment she was in no hurry. She was going to take it easy for the summer and just relax. She had a soft, pleasant voice, and there was a constant hint of a smile on her lips as she spoke. The two sat at a table in her cabin and Amy offered Brad a beer. He declined, settling for a cold lemonade instead.

"So . . . what was your major in college?" Brad asked, setting his glass back on the table. The conversation had been light, and that was fine with both. Although Amy was very attractive, Brad had come to Courville to get away, not to start a relationship. And Amy had come to Courville for convenience; the living was cheap and the lifestyle was casual . . . she intended to keep it that way.

"Business administration," Amy answered. "I have a bachelors degree. I just haven't quite figured out how I want to use it yet."

"There's not much around here?" Brad wondered aloud. He was curious as to how anyone would make a living in northern Michigan. There certainly weren't many factories to attract a large working class, and tourism seemed to be the biggest industry north of Michigan's navel.

"Actually there's quite a bit of work, if you know where to

look. It's just that a lot of work is seasonal, you know?" Her voice was soft and she smiled as she spoke. "I mean . . . there's a lot of work available . . . but lots of businesses are only open three or four months out of the year. If you're trying to build a career, it can be tough. It's a great way to put yourself through college, though. Besides . . . the area is growing fast. There's a lot of opportunity if you look hard and are willing to work."

Brad looked at his hand. She had bandaged up the wound and it still throbbed a bit, but it would heal fine. He shook his head and spoke.

"Thank you again. I guess I better be more careful."

Amy smiled and got up to re-fill their glasses of lemonade. "Well," she said, opening up the refrigerator, "besides the fact that the ladder is down, that dock *really* needs to be replaced. It's been there since I was a kid. Most of the boards are too old. Some of them are on their last legs. I carved my initials in one of the planks when I was eight years old. It's still there."

"You know," Brad said, recalling the incident on the dock, "I was just about to wash my hand off and I think I–"

He paused for just an instant, wondering if he was being too trivial. After all, seeing a fish in a lake wouldn't be out of the ordinary. It was just that . . . well, the disturbance beneath the surface *had* been rather large . . . certainly larger than most fish could create.

He continued, perhaps thinking that the risk of being trivial outweighed the risk of having nothing more important to say. "I saw something in the water. A fish, I think. Actually, I didn't even *see* anything. Just a quick shadow, and some churning where the water had been disturbed."

"Probably a bass or maybe a walleye, Amy responded. They get pretty big. I don't know much about fishing, but Jim fishes quite a bit and does pretty good."

"Well, this was pretty good size, whatever it was. But I didn't get a look at it. Just a shadow."

"It might have been a sturgeon, too. They get huge."

"A *what?*" Brad asked. Although he was well aware of what a sturgeon was, it surprised him that they were in Mullett Lake. Sturgeons were prehistoric fish left over from the dinosaur era.

"A sturgeon. Ugly things. Some get up to six or seven feet long. I guess about twenty years ago someone caught one in Burt Lake that was almost nine feet long."

"They're in *Mullett Lake?*" Brad asked curiously. He had studied a number of sturgeons that had come from the Great Lakes. They were large, docile fish that fed on plankton and other small aquatic life. True, he knew that they inhabited many freshwater lakes throughout the Midwest and Canada, but he always was just a bit surprised to find sturgeon in any lake that had a large influx of people. Sturgeon were shy fish, and usually their population suffered when the number of human invaders rose. Sturgeon, among other aquatic life, didn't adapt well to human infiltration.

The conversation continued for nearly an hour. A pleasant hour, at that. Once again Brad found himself immersed in something that had completely taken away all thoughts of the lab and all of life's other trappings that had ensnared him back home in Lorain. This was going to be a good thing, he told himself as he got up to leave. By tomorrow he would have forgotten about everything, he was sure. When he returned from vacation he would have to re-introduce himself at the lab and learn everybody's names all over again.

Amy promised that she would show him around Courville, which, she assured him, would take a whopping three minutes. Brad bid good-bye, grateful for the first-aid and the lemonade, and maybe a little bit grateful for the fact that he was certain to see her again. She would be living only three cabins away which pretty much *guaranteed* he would bump into her on a daily basis, and frankly, he found himself not minding that a bit.

✳ ✳ ✳ ✳

The cabin was cozy and surprisingly cool despite the heat. Brad hit the sack early, his lack of sleep finally catching up with him even before the sun had set. He lay back in bed listening to the echoes of distant laughter, the dwindling sounds of children as they played in backyards, and the frequent splashing of water made by those escaping the constant, stifling heat. The faint smell of freshly mowed lawns, flower gardens, campfires, and roasted marshmallows drifted in and out of the cottage. A small fan whirred at the foot of the bed, rotating slowly and blowing soothing air around the small bedroom. Brad fell asleep quickly; he slept soundly.

He awoke at six the next morning and walked over to the Courville *Partee-Mart* for a coffee and a copy of the *Indian River Daily*. He returned with the paper beneath his arm, walking slowly, taking in the sights and sounds of the new day. Now he sat on the porch of his cabin, admiring the early morning sunrise as the big yellow ball crept up over the eastern tree line on the other side of the lake. A small group of sparrows feasted at the bird feeder without the annoying interruptions of any scrounging blue jays. There were no boats on the water and the lake was perfect, shining in the morning sun like smooth, glossy glass.

Brad sipped his coffee and plopped the paper open on his

lap and began reading.

DROWNING PUZZLES AUTHORITIES, the headline read. Beneath the big block letters was a black and white picture of two sheriff deputies in a marine patrol boat, scanning the water around them. Craig Allen Sheldon, 32, was missing and presumed drowned. He was last seen by some friends and co-workers at the bar where he was employed. Sheldon had told them that he was going to stop by Mullett Lake on his way home and go for a late night swim to cool off. Yesterday a state trooper had found his car parked at Courville's roadside park, and the jeans and shirt found on the dock had been positively identified as the clothes Sheldon had been wearing the night he disappeared. Deputies from the Cheboygan County Sheriff Department as well as the Michigan State Police had searched and searched, but couldn't find the body—if the man had indeed drowned.

But that's what puzzled the divers. While Mullett Lake was a big lake, it shouldn't be that hard to find a drowning victim. There wasn't any strong underwater current to pull the body any great distance. Usually when someone had drowned in an inland lake, the body was recovered within a few hours at the most. Or some unsuspecting swimmer came across it by accident, in which case they'd scream, splash frantically, and make a quick beeline to the shore while the bloated corpse bobbed innocently beneath the surface.

Whoops, here I am. Sorry ta bother ya like that. Probably scared the shit outta ya, huh?

The story of the missing man took up a good portion of the front page. Brad imagined that something like this was probably pretty big news around here.

He put the paper down and again gazed out over the pristine lake. A half dozen ducks skirted the shoreline, bobbing beneath the surface in search of their morning meal. Soon Brad began to hear faint noises and shuffling in the other cabins around him. Far out into the lake a small aluminum boat was speeding across the smooth surface, traveling either to or from a favorite fishing spot. The temperature was beginning to rise; not gradually, as one would expect, but rapidly. The day was going to be another Xerox copy of yesterday, that was for sure.

A car drove by on Old US-27 and another one slowed, pulling into a driveway next to the resort. The small village of Courville was beginning to wake up.

And beneath the tiny ripples of Mullett Lake, something else had awoken.

✳ ✳ ✳ ✳

Slow. The fish moved slowly, watching intently, its eyes keenly adjusted to the dim, murky light of the depths. An unsuspecting sucker had lumbered along and was instantly devoured, but the meal was hardly filling. Such food was eaten merely out of anger and frustration. The lake was too small, too confining, and it didn't provide the tremendous depths or the ample availability of food that the Great Lakes had supplied. Here, the fish had to be more careful. There weren't near as many fish to eat, and the muskie had resorted to many other creatures, first out of hunger, then out of rage. It didn't like its new surroundings. The muskie hadn't had a good meal since a few nights previous, and that meal had been a very fortunate find. A large, filling meal that had put a taste in its mouth for more.

CHRISTOPHER KNIGHT

The huge black form slipped effortlessly over the bottom, then stopped.

A noise.

It began very faintly and grew louder, alarming the fish. A steady drone that drew closer and closer. The muskie stopped, alert, its bulging eyes darting madly about. The sound was annoying, and getting worse. It grew closer still, louder, and the fish's rage intensified. It began to move toward the sound, first cautiously, then faster as the drone filled the water.

There. On the surface. The fish had seen this before, but it usually could slink away to deeper water where the incessant humming couldn't penetrate. But here in the shallower water of Mullett Lake the fish couldn't escape the gnawing, intrusive ringing.

The object on the surface above passed directly overhead. The intense droning sound peaked and began to fade, but the fish challenged the intruder with sadistic fury. It paced beneath the object, growing closer, ready to strike.

✳ ✳ ✳ ✳

For John Crenshaw, the morning had already been bad.

It was about to get a lot worse.

He held the throttle of the outboard motor wide open, skimming across the lake as fast as the small aluminum boat would take him. He was tired and sleepy, and he wondered why in the hell he had gotten up so early anyway. He'd had a vicious headache since yesterday, but he had dragged himself out of bed

CHRISTOPHER KNIGHT

regardless, threw the small boat into the back of his pickup, and headed for the lake.

It was still dark when he launched the boat, and he clumsily dropped his flashlight in the water where it was immediately extinguished. He retrieved it and tried clicking it on and off a few times before giving up in disgust and throwing it in the bed of the truck.

Then he had sped across the dark lake to a deep hole where he'd been having some good luck as of late. Unfortunately, fishing had been a waste of time, as he hadn't even seen so much as a fish, nor did he even get so much as a strike. He repeated the flashlight fiasco by dropping his thermos overboard and could do nothing but watch as the red and black canister disappeared into the depths below. Not twenty minutes later, when he stood up to take a leak off the side of the boat he stepped on his fiberglass spinning rod, snapping it in two. No, things were not going well for John Crenshaw. His head still pounded, he was tired and felt sluggish, and he wished he was home in bed. With his rod snapped and his spirit broken, it was time to call it a day.

One short pull and the Evinrude outboard roared to life. John pointed the bow toward the other side of the lake. The boat skimmed easily across the smooth surface. The sun had risen above the trees and the air rushing at his face was fresh and warm. Crenshaw shook his head again as he recalled the flashlight, Thermos, and spinning rod incidents. He twisted the throttle further to increase his speed. The whining motor raised in pitch, but the boat was already traveling as fast as it would go.

His flannel shirt sat on the seat in front of him. He had taken it off as the morning grew warmer, but now the force of the wind flipped it over. John saw it tumble and tried to reach for it, but it was too late. The wind had already picked it up and the shirt rolled over the edge of the boat, slipping into the water.

For cryin' out loud, he thought as he turned the boat around in a wide circle. *What the hell else is going to go wrong?*

＊＊＊＊

The muskie was just beneath the boat. Suddenly the dark shadow on the surface swerved, changing its course. The fish followed it from a distance, guarded and cautious, burning with fury. The object slowed, the noise faded to just a gentle rumble then ceased altogether, and the fish approached warily, watching.

＊＊＊＊

Crenshaw killed the motor as the small craft glided toward the floating shirt. Given a few minutes the shirt would sink, and it was already almost entirely beneath the surface by the time he reached it. The small craft slowed to a stop and John knelt down, leaning over the side of the boat to retrieve the sopping flannel. His hand grasped the shirt.

Suddenly, the water exploded with such force that the boat came fully out of the water, flipped end over end, and landed capsized. John found himself in the water, gasping in terror. He had only caught a glimpse, just an enormous dark shadow lunging upwards, but in that split second all of his childhood nightmares and fears had come true. Horrible, piercing eyes. Rows of incisors, each the size of steak knives. The beast had attacked with a savage, violent rage, and John knew instantly that he had just been given a glimpse of a terrible demon straight from the bowels of hell. The boat had been literally blown out from beneath him. His entire right arm was severed at the shoulder and blood spewed in pulsating spurts, staining the water a thin, runny crimson. Torn flesh and mangled tissue dangled from a bloody stump. He screamed, kicking with his feet and clumsily trying to tread water with one arm.

The boat was upside down in the water, twenty feet away. Crenshaw began kicking frantically toward the boat. The pain in his arm—or, where his arm *should* have been—was numbing. And as if playing some sort of cruel trick, his brain was trying to use the limb that wasn't there. John swung his shoulder thinking his right arm was still attached and would sweep the surface and help him float.

Moving through the water was difficult and clumsy and the pain was numbing. He kept screaming, howling at the top of his lungs, hoping that someone . . . *somewhere* . . . would hear. He was still way out in the lake and his voice would carry . . . but then again, that was pretty wishful thinking at best. He continued thrashing wildly but his progress was slow.

When he was just a few feet from the boat, John Crenshaw's entire body snapped beneath the surface with such force that his neck was broken instantly. Water swirled and churned and boiled the surface, but within seconds the disturbance had vanished. The boat bobbed aimlessly, the belly of its aluminum hull shining brightly in the morning sun. Crenshaw's flannel shirt, now completely soaked with water, heaved its own final breath, and sank slowly to the bottom of Mullett Lake.

CHRISTOPHER KNIGHT

THREE

Again the day was hot (although not quite as humid as it had been), and Amy and Brad rode about the village in her black Jeep Wrangler, minus its canvas top. She wheeled the vehicle to a stop in a small gravel parking lot.

"And this is the fire department," she said, pointing to an old building with two large steel garage doors. "One truck, two volunteers. My uncle Jim is one of them."

"Probably not too busy, huh?" Brad asked.

"Actually, probably busier than you think. But not much happens here in the village. We did have one fire last year, but that was started when Geraldine Miller's cat knocked over a candle. A drape caught fire, and she doused it with two fire extinguishers. Then, just to make sure it was out, she called the fire department. She had tea and cookies waiting for them when they came through the door."

Brad laughed, and Amy glanced up at the rearview mirror

through her sunglasses and turned the Jeep back onto the road and headed south. She looked over at Brad, who seemed to be enjoying the nickel tour.

"So . . . you never did say what brought you here," she continued. "I mean, Courville isn't the *only* vacation Mecca of the north. Most people head for the more well-known places where there's a bit more to see and do."

"Oh, I don't know," he replied. "I guess I just thought I was due for a vacation. I was—"

He stopped in mid-sentence. Amy saw the disturbance as well, and she slowed the Jeep. A Michigan State Police Suburban with an empty boat trailer attached was parked in Courville's only roadside park. Two other Michigan State Trooper cars were parked nearby, along with two black and white Cheboygan County Sheriff cars. Out on the lake the marine patrol boat appeared to be towing another boat in. Four uniformed officers stood at the shoreline, watching.

"Maybe they found that guy I read about in the paper," Brad wondered.

"I don't know," Amy responded, shaking her head and taking off her sunglasses. "I don't think so, though. It looks like they're pulling in a boat or something. The guy that drowned the other day was swimming off a dock from a roadside park about a mile south of here. I don't think he had a boat. I think he was just out swimming. Boy . . . Mullett Lake has sure seen its share of action over the past couple weeks. First that poor woman, then some guy drowns at the park. It's going to be—"

"What woman was that?" Brad interrupted. "What happened to her?"

"Oh, that's right. You weren't here. About a week ago. A woman from . . . oh heck, I forget now. Anyway, She was swimming down near Mullett Heights. I guess someone didn't see her, and she got hit by a boat propeller. Cut her completely in two."

"Doesn't sound like a fun way to go," Brad winced.

"No, I imagine not. Odd thing was, they only found her *upper* body. Below the waist . . . *gone.* And no one has come forward to admit that they were the ones who hit her."

"How can you hit someone in the water with a boat and not know it?" Brad wondered aloud.

"You can't, unless your half in the bag. Which is what the cops think. They think someone hit her, got scared, and took off."

Amy sped up and headed south on Old US-27 to the village of Somerville. There was a post office, a grocery store, a library and two hotels. The amenities of the small town were common and consistent with the many other villages that dotted northern Michigan. Brad had passed dozens of towns just like Somerville and Courville on his trek north.

"Probably no *Gap* stores around, huh?" he asked, smiling. Amy laughed.

"Sure there is," she replied, still chuckling. "Right next to *Nieman-Marcus.*" Brad himself now laughed and shook his head as Amy continued. "It's actually pretty cool. There's not a lot of the options that you'd have in a larger city, but then again you don't have the crime or the pollution. It's not a bad trade-off. And you're not going to find cleaner water in the world."

"Speaking of which," Brad interjected as he spied *Breakers* bar coming into view. "I'm kind of thirsty. You wanna grab a beer?" Amy let off the accelerator and began to pull off to the side of the road.

"I'll tell you what," she said, stopping the Jeep and waiting for a car to pass before wheeling the Wrangler around. "Let's grab a six at the store and kick back at the cottages. I am in desperate need of some sun."

"That'll work," Brad agreed. Amy spun the vehicle around and headed back to Courville.

✳ ✳ ✳ ✳

Sam McAllister was pissed, and he gripped the phone tightly as he spoke.

"All this bad publicity is not going to be good for business. Especially in a town like Courville."

On the other end of the line the editor of the *Indian River Daily* listened to Sam's complaint, giving him the usual 'freedom of the press' and 'First Amendment' bullshit.

"Look. I don't give a rat's ass about your 'freedom of the press.' But why do all of you make everything sound worse than it is?!?!?" He paused, listened to the editor's response, then spoke harshly again.

"Look. You can run your paper any damn way you please. But you are part of this community. *Our* community. All this garbage you're printing isn't doing anything to help out any businesses or anyone who's trying to attract tourist dollars. In one week, Courville is going to have its one hundred year centennial celebration. Fireworks, games, bake sales . . . *and* a half mile swim competition. Nobody's gonna want to go near the water if they think they're going to bump into a dead body the first time they jump off the dock."

The editor tried to respond, but Sam interrupted again.

"I don't care! Listen to me! *I don't give a rat's ass!* What I

want to know is why you gotta drag it out in *every* paper!?!? Phil
Hartnell runs a *weekly* paper and he doesn't print garbage like this!
Now I'm not tryin' to be insensitive, but people drown *every day*.
They're gone. Who cares if they find the bodies or not?!?! Just
give it a rest, wouldja?!?! That's not too much to ask. Just give it
a rest for a few days. This town *depends* on tourists . . . especially
this weekend. Try not to scare the hell out of everyone with your
goddamn ten-cent fish-rag newspaper!"

He shook his head in disgust and slammed the receiver
down before the editor had a chance to respond. He had a right
to be mad, at least in *his* mind. He was in charge of putting on
this whole centennial celebration . . . lock, stock, and barrel.
There was a lot at stake. Courville was small, but it brought a lot
of influential people in from all across the country. *Wealthy*
influential people. Sam always described Courville as a 'cross
between Never-Never Land and Mayberry R.F.D.'. Some of the
wealthiest people in the country owned summer homes in and
around Courville.   True, the population was just over two
hundred . . . but during the summer months, Courville and the
immediate surrounding areas swelled to nearly three thousand.
Summer residents brought a lot of money in to the few local
businesses. But the summer residents also wanted Courville to
stay that way. *'Gate Closers'* is what Sam called them. People that
came up north, slammed the gate closed, and said *'Okay . . . nobody
else.'* Those people demanded a lifestyle and a laid-back pace that
they couldn't find in New York or Los Angeles or Chicago.
That's why they came to Courville. They came to unwind, to
relax, to forget about everything else. They came to get away
from murder and death and all those things that are just a fact of
life in larger metropolitan areas. And the *last* thing that Sam
McAllister needed was some wanna-be-big-time small town
newspaper editor printing front-page garbage about drownings

and people getting hacked in half by boat propellers. It wasn't good for the Mullett Lake image. It wasn't good for Courville. And it wasn't going to be good for his centennial celebration.

But then again, Sam had another motive altogether, and it had nothing to do with anybody else but him.

When it really came down to it, he couldn't care less about Courville, the centennial celebration, the people. None of it.

Screw'em all he thought. *Screw'em all and shoot'em if they get pregnant.*

But he needed the weekend to go smoothly, regardless. He had *bigger* plans. *Much* bigger plans.

Then I can get out of this goddamn two-bit hobo town, he told himself.

"Let's just pray that people use some common sense on the water this week," he said aloud to no one. He was the only person in the office; actually it was *his* office, and there were no employees. He shook his head. "One more death in this fucking lake and I'm going to go bananas."

He pulled open a drawer and found the pint bottle of vodka stashed neatly beneath a stack of papers. Sam took a long, lasting swig and stared out his office window overlooking the water. He was a bulldoggish-type man, unusually stocky for a man his size. Sam McAllister looked like he could have been a marine at one time with an enormous, powerful chest and large, brawny arms. A popcorn bowl sized potbelly sagged tiredly over his belt, making it difficult to keep his shirts tucked in properly. He had thick gray hair that always seemed to be out of place, and large fuzzy sideburns that dipped down below the front of each ear. His forehead was big and round and his eyebrows were gray and equally matched to the hair on his head: thick, gray, and unkept. He had a glare in his eyes that made him look like he was always squinting or annoyed at something. His cheeks were almost always flush red, regardless of how many or few beers or shots of vodka he'd had the night before.

Sam had moved to Courville after his third divorce from the *'Tyrannical Bitch from Hell'* as he affectionately referred to her these days. In actuality, the term should have been turned around. Sam had used his third wife as a virtual punching bag, as he had done with his second wife as well as his first. During the course of it all, he had spent a year in jail for aggravated assault, second offense. Upon his parole he decided that he needed to just get the hell outta Dodge . . . which is how he landed in Courville. It was an easy escape as it almost always is in a small town. People knew everyone, and if they don't know much about you, there were those who would just make something up. Nobody knew who Sam was, nobody knew where he came from, but he was friendly—overly friendly, mostly—but it still got him the thing he needed most: cover. He lied about his age, he lied about where he was from . . . he even lied about his name. 'Murray' was his legal last name. But upon his arrival in Courville he changed it to McAllister. Anything to disguise who he really was or where he'd been. He lied on a job resume, filling in nonexistent jobs that he'd had over the past few years, and even gave an impressive list of references (a bit less impressive if you knew that they were all bogus). The former Courville Chamber of Commerce president had been on his way out and never bothered to make any phone calls or check up on McAllister's resume. He hired Sam on the first interview.

You'll do fine, just fine, he told Sam. *It's a cakewalk. Just be nice to people and bring in business.*

Sam took another long swig of vodka and held the bottle at his waist, staring out at the pristine blue waters of Mullett Lake.

Just be nice to people and bring in business.

"Yeah, well . . . to hell with all you people and all your

businesses," he said softly.

He took one more short drink, screwed the lid back on, and replaced the bottle. His desk was messy and cluttered and the garbage can was overflowing, but he'd get to that tomorrow. It was five o'clock; the workday was over. He closed the door of the Courville Chamber of Commerce, locked it, and left.

✸✸✸✸

Brad lay back on his towel, his eyes shaded by a pair of three-dollar sunglasses he had purchased at the *Courville Partee-Mart*. He raised the bottle of beer to his lips and set it back down in the grass, swallowing slowly as he gazed up at a single, billowing white cloud. The afternoon was perfect . . . almost *too* perfect, he had told himself. Truly, Mullett Lake was more relaxing than he could have ever dreamed.

He suddenly realized that it had been hours since he'd had his last thoughts about the lab or other details that no doubt waited for him in Lorain. He'd forgotten about bills, work, flying beakers, stress, even whatsername . . . .

All I need is a week of this and I'll be fine, he thought.

Of course, there *was* another reason for his positive outlook. And she had just emerged from her cabin and was walking toward him, carrying a bucket of ice and another blanket. Brad stared at her freely, his eyes hidden by the reflective mirror of his sunglasses, and he acknowledged to himself once again that she was beautiful. She wore a black two piece bikini that fitted every curve of her body. The top was clinched by a small knot between her breasts and the fabric was thin, showing the tips of her nipples through the dark material. Her hair was down and it swirled about gently as she walked, falling over her shoulders and cascading down her back. Brad became aroused as he watched her, and he rolled over on his stomach to conceal his excitement.

"More ice," she said, setting the bucket down and unfolding her towel. "This heat is melting it faster than my fridge can make it." She spread the blanket out on the grass next to Brad and sat down with her legs crossed, facing the lake.

"Good thing you've got those glasses," she said, opening a beer for herself. "Or I'd have thought you were staring." She smiled and looked at Brad. He was still laying on his stomach and he turned his head away in embarrassment, then shrugged it off.

"Was it that obvious?" he replied sheepishly, taking another sip of beer.

"Quite," Amy replied. "But that's okay. You didn't make a complete fool of yourself."

"Complete?"

"Complete. Care to roll over on your back?"

Whoops.

"Ummm . . . not at the moment, thank you," he laughed nervously. Amy just laughed and sipped her beer.

"So just what *does* a marine biologist do?" she asked.

Brad was thankful that she had changed the subject.

"Well, for the most part," he began, "it's the study of aquatic life. Anything and everything in the water. My supervisor is an instructor at the college, and I'm kind of his assistant. When he's gone, I fill in. Otherwise, I'm pretty much stuck with the task of research."

"Stuck? You mean, you don't like it?"

"Oh, not at all," he answered quickly. "I *love* it. It's just that the state regulates most of what we research. They spend a ton of money on things that have no bearing on the aquatic ecosystem. They spent three million dollars last year to find out where pollution in the lake was coming from. Three *million* dollars. For a good Margarita and five bucks I could've told'em that they might want to check some of the chemical plants along the shoreline."

Amy laughed in agreement and rolled over onto her stomach setting her beer in the grass. From there the conversation flowed to and from a variety of different topics, from theories about why it was so hot to what concerts each had seen and who had been the best performers. Brad took great interest in the conversation, but struggled to keep from staring at the dark shadow between Amy's breasts every time she tipped her head back and sipped her beer.

Shit, he thought. *Maybe it* has *been too long.*

✳ ✳ ✳ ✳

Brad heard a distant splash and awoke, disoriented. The searing sun baked his skin, and he raised his hand to shield his eyes from the intense glare. He knocked his beer over in the process but quickly grabbed it, preventing the entire bottle from emptying into the grass. Creamy foam spewed from the top and Brad placed his mouth over it.

Mullett Lake, he recalled finally. *Oh yeah.* He had fallen asleep on his back, soaking up the sun's hot, soothing rays. His body was drenched in oily sweat. He propped himself up on one elbow, still shielding his eyes with one hand, and looked out over the water.

The lake was abuzz with activity. Ski boats, aluminum fishing boats, sailboards and other small vessels dotted the lake. Most were quite a ways out, far from shore and shallow water. A few scattered, high clouds hung lazily, suspended beneath a brilliant blue canopy. The breeze had died completely and the giant weeping willows near the shoreline stood unmoving and still like huge olive statues.

Ripples expanded in the water around the end of the dock, and Amy's head popped up a moment later.

"Come on in!" she hollered. *"The water's great!"* The offer was inviting, but Brad shook his head. A swim would feel good, but he needed to wake up a bit first.

"Oh, come *on!*" Amy shouted. She splashed water playfully in his direction. *"Come on!"* she begged again. "What are ya . . . *afraid of the water?"*

FOUR

Brad arose before dawn, went for a walk, and on his way back to his cabin the market was just opening. A sprightly dressed man wearing khakis and a yellow golf shirt recommended a bagel (Brad declined) and an orange juice (he accepted). He also bought the day's paper, rolled it under his arm, and returned to the cottage for some coffee. Last night Amy had managed to find an old coffee percolator, and Brad was one of the few guests living in complete luxury with his own in-room coffee, which was bound to make the other guests drool if they only knew. By the time he had returned to the cottage the coffee was done brewing, and he relaxed in an old wicker chair and opened up the paper.

The headline on the front page of the *Indian River Daily* told the story. There was yet another person missing in Mullett Lake. A capsized boat had been spotted by someone on shore and by the time someone had motored out to it, there was no sign of anyone. The man was identified as John Crenshaw, 37, from

Indian River. Or at least, that is who they *assumed* it was. Can't be sure until you have a body, as the cops say. Crenshaw's wife, however, identified the boat as belonging to him. Once again, divers had spent the entire day searching for a body, but to no avail. Crenshaw had vanished, just like Craig Sheldon had a few nights previous.

He picked up his coffee and looked out the window.

The sun was absent, and a thick, gray sheet of clouds had slipped in overnight. The forecast, according to the paper, called for rain for the next two days. But the heat wave showed no signs of letting up, with temperatures expected up in the nineties and maybe even one hundred degrees by the coming weekend.

Brad returned to reading the paper. He flipped the page and scanned the usual small town stuff: 4-H meeting announcements, a half-dozen alcoholics anonymous meeting locations, four obituaries, and one birth announcement. The following page drew a bit more interest.

COURVILLE CENTENNIAL EXPECTED
TO DRAW THOUSANDS

the headline read. Brad scanned the article. The centennial was going to be quite a celebration, according to some Sam McAllister, the head of the Courville Chamber of Commerce. McAllister said that the celebration would be unlike any other ever seen on Mullett Lake . . . complete with a parade, fireworks, an art fair, a swimming competition, bake sales . . . the list went on and on. He was quoted as saying that most of the events, of course, had been *his* ideas . . . and that he'd been working on this event for the past year. But the highlight, he went on to say, was the fact that a former resident who was now deceased but wanted to remain un-named had donated nearly fifteen-thousand dollars for a pyrotechnics show. That would mean that Courville would have one of the biggest fireworks displays in the state, and that fact alone had begun to attract regional attention to the small community. Nearly three thousand people were expected for the coming weekend, twice what the usual annual celebrations drew.

But it was the adjacent page that attracted Brad's attention. A blurry, black and white aerial photograph showed a portion of the lake and the shoreline. A few houses were cropped close to the top of the picture, but near the center was a long, dark form beneath the water.

AERIAL PHOTOGRAPHER CAPTURES GIANT STURGEON ON FILM

There really wasn't much to see except a dark, oblong-shaped shadow in the water. The photographer claimed that the fish was swimming so quickly that he only had the time to snap the single photo. He had made several passes over the area looking for the fish again, but the search proved unfruitful.

Brad stared at the photo with more amusement than interest. The picture reminded him of some of those old UFO photos that were always out of focus. You never really could tell what they were, and the power of suggestion came into play in most scenarios. Most, if not *all* UFO photos, probably were just Frisbees or pie tins tossed into the air and photographed with a cheap camera. The photograph in the paper could easily have been a picture of an old, submerged log.

But if it were indeed a sturgeon, it would probably be a record. It looked to be as long or longer than a car and at least half as wide. A sturgeon that size would easily earn a spot in the *Guinness Book of World Records* and probably in *Ripley's Believe it or Not!* as well.

Yet it was more than doubtful that the object in the picture was a fish of any kind. While a sturgeon *can* grow to enormous

CHRISTOPHER KNIGHT

size, they didn't grow *that* big. Somebody had been smoking jumbo-sized bowls of hash for this one.

Still, the photo fascinated Brad. He'd always been interested in stories of mysterious giant sea creatures, the Loch Ness monster, bigfoot, the devil's triangle, the abominable snowman . . . whatever. Two years ago there had been reported sightings of some half-man, half ape creature not far from where he lived in Lorain. There was even a name for it . . . *Chupakabra.* None of the stories ever panned out and pretty soon the whole thing just died off, like most hoaxes. It was oddly coincidental that every single photo of ghosts, UFOs, sea creatures, bigfoot . . . every single photo on record was blurry and out of focus. It seemed to Brad that most 'flying saucers' had been witnessed by someone on a farm that spoke with a broken, southern lisp. No one had one inkling of proof that any of these phenomena existed, except in the out-of-focus, amateur pictures from a twenty dollar off-brand camera.

Probably just drumming up some extra interest for the centennial, Brad thought, turning the page.

He poured another cup of coffee and sat back down in the chair when a scratching at the door surprised him and he jumped a bit, spilling a small amount of coffee over the edge of the cup, dripping it on the wood floor.

Shit, he thought, wiping his hand on a napkin. The scratching continued. Whatever the noise was, it was coming from below the screen, below the door handle. He stood up to investigate and as he drew closer to the door, his suspicions were confirmed.

"And just where did you come from?" he said aloud to the young golden retriever. The dog responded by scratching the door again and wagging its tail with glee. It wasn't very old, maybe eight months or so. He was still a bit small to be full grown but his feet were big and he seemed a little clumsy, as if he had grown too fast too soon and didn't know how to compensate for the additional weight and size.

Brad opened the door and the dog bounded inside, first checking out Brad's crotch with an innocent but direct poke and then bounding through the cabin, sniffing everything in sight. There was a half-empty bag of potato chips on the table from yesterday. Brad opened the bag and the dog instinctively became Brad's best friend, plodding up to his chair and sitting down. The animal eyed the bag with passionate lust, following Brad's hand as he pulled a few chips from the bag. The dog ate hungrily, wolfing down the two chips in a split-second. Once again it froze, eyeing the bag, poised for more. Every few seconds the dog would glance quickly at Brad, pleading for more chips, then return its hungry gaze to the bag.

"When he pukes, you can clean it up."

Amy's voice had come from the doorway. Brad turned and the dog shot a quick glance for just a moment, then quickly returned to eyeing its prey in the foil bag.

"When he pukes, I hope he'll be outside," Brad responded, standing up and closing the foil bag. "Okay, you," he said, addressing the dog. "Enough chips."

Disappointed, the dog backed away from the table and headed for the door. Amy opened the screen and the dog bolted between her legs, over the porch, and into the lawn.

"That's Pepper," she said as she stepped inside.

"*Your* dog?" Brad asked, nervously glancing around to make sure the place was picked up. The past year or so he had gotten used to being a bachelor again, and it often showed by the empty wrappers and dirty dishes that piled up on the counter. Thankfully the cabin was still rather neat, except for the bag of potato chips on the table and a few glasses in the sink.

"Yeah," Amy responded. "He's pretty much still a puppy. Has the run of the resort. But junk food makes him puke. So if he pukes . . . whether it's in the yard or wherever . . . that's *your* job."

"Deal," Brad said, smiling. He glanced out the window to see the dog bobbing happily near a row of shrubs at the cabin next door. "But how did he get the name 'Pepper'?"

"Cause he loves pepper," Amy answered. "Pepper on *anything*. Dog food, biscuits, whatever. I spilled some pepper on the floor when he was a puppy, and he just sat there and licked the linoleum clean. It was the craziest thing. He's been 'Pepper' ever since."

A dog named 'Pepper' that can't eat junk food, Brad thought, rolling his eyes and smiling.

The dog was still bounding happily along the hedge when a man emerged from the house a few cabins over. Amy recognized him and quickly poked her head out the door.

"Pepper!" she shouted, with more than a hint of alarm in her voice. *"Come here!"*

The dog raced across the yard and Amy opened up the door of the cabin, allowing Pepper inside. She pointed over the yards and Brad followed her upraised arm.

"That man," she began, "is the *biggest* jackass in town. Maybe the entire state."

Brad watched the man as he walked to a car and drove off. He had a walk that was confident; a bit too confident maybe. It was an arrogant stride, slow and careless, and Brad thought that if snakes could walk, surely this was how they would do it. Slow, sure, and deliberate. Just like a snake.

"Sounds like he got on your good side early," he replied, raising his eyebrows and grinning at Amy.

"Pepper was in his yard one day and McAllister kicked him for no reason at all. Then he told Uncle Jim that if Pepper was ever in his yard again he had the right to shoot him."

"Sounds like a real social guy," Brad said, shaking his head.

"And a perverted one to boot. I've been laying out in the sun and I've caught him a half-dozen times staring at me from his living room. Once he even had a camera."

"Can't you kick him out?" Brad asked.

"No. That house over there doesn't belong to Jim. It's just on the other side of resort property. Boy, I *wish* we could kick him out. He's a complete jerk. But he's got everyone else in town believing that he's just the nicest guy in the world. He runs the Chamber of Commerce and he thinks he's King of Courville."

"Well I certainly know who the Queen is," Brad said, changing the subject. He turned and smiled at her. She smiled, and blushed a tiny bit.

"Coffee?" Brad offered. Amy said she would, and Brad poured a cup and handed it to her. She took the mug, glancing at the open newspaper on the table. It was open to the page with the photograph of the fish.

"Sturgeon, huh?" she mused.

"That's what it says. But whether this is a real picture or not . . . that's the question. I mean . . . sturgeons get big . . . but not *this* big."

"A little skepticism, maybe?" Amy smirked.

"Call it common sense. I've studied enough at the lab. Freshwater fish don't grow to be that big. And I've seen some *big* ones. We get guys all the time who've been out fishing. They call the college, telling us they've caught the biggest fish they've ever seen and it must be some sort of mutant. Usually they've caught a big lake trout or a salmon or something. But this–" He tapped the paper as he spoke. "It sure makes a good story. I think it's a neat photo for the third page of a small town daily. It'll give folks something to talk about."

"As if they need help," Amy replied, smiling.

They both laughed. She was beginning to like Brad. He was

nice. Quiet, and maybe a bit distant at times, but certainly nice. Polite and fun-loving. He was genuine and had just enough confidence to make him comfortable but not too much as to make him arrogant.

Likewise, Brad was certainly taking more than an interest in Amy. She was always happy and smiling and was pleasant just to be around. And more than once he had seen past her trademark white T-shirt and denim shorts. He was certain that she would be an absolute knockout in a dress.

Hell . . . she's an absolute knockout in a pair of shorts, he thought.

And then, to his own disbelief:

"You, ah . . . *you wanna have dinner tonight?*"

He was surprised to hear himself speak those words. The voice echoed in his head and he wasn't even sure if it was *he* who had said it. He hadn't been on a date since he'd split with whatsername. Brad suddenly felt sixteen again, awkward and embarrassed like when he'd asked Sharon Mallory to the prom. He had been shocked when Sharon had said yes, and actually asked her to repeat herself.

"I'm sorry," Amy replied with a hint of disappointment in her face. "It's against company policy to date guests of the cottages."

Brad tried to read her expression. She was serious . . . or at least she played it very well. But he refused to believe that being a guest at a cottage in Courville completely nixed any chance of a date. He studied her face for another instant and picked something up in her eyes that hadn't been there before. Or, if it had, he hadn't noticed it until now. A certain comfortable playfulness that was only recognizable with time and trust.

"Well then . . . how about if I pack up and stay at that motel down the street?" he said smiling, calling her bluff. "Then I wouldn't be a guest."

A long, frolicsome grin came over Amy's face as she spoke.

"I think I could change company policy for one evening."

* * * *

Disgusted, Sam McAllister threw the paper down on the kitchen table. He thought seriously about calling the editor again. He thought about paying him a personal visit and showing him a thing or two about promotions. Didn't he know how hard Sam had worked for this? And he still was printing all this nonsensical garbage. All right, so maybe there *had* been some freak accidents over the past few weeks, but they didn't have to put it on the cover of the paper every single day. It didn't look good. It was going to screw everything up for the weekend. No one was going to come to Courville if there was a chance that the first time they set foot in the water they'd run smack into a decomposing dead body.

And it wasn't just bad for Courville, either. There were other towns to consider. Aloha, Indian River, Somerville, Mullett Heights, Cheboygan . . . they were all affected by the tourism around both Mullett and Burt Lakes.

McAllister pulled another beer from the fridge, opened it, and tossed the lid in the garbage. He took a long swig and looked out over the lake.

Throughout the afternoon, a light mist fell and the temperature had dropped a few degrees just within the past hour. It was only early evening, but Mullett Lake was void of any boating activity.

Beautiful, he thought. *Just fucking beautiful. Just what we need for a perfect weekend. Crappy weather and some bloated stiff popping up for the party at the Courville Township Beach. Fucking beautiful.*

Sam heard the rumbling of a vehicle close by and walked to the screen porch to investigate. A forest green Chevy truck with a boat trailer was backing over the grass along side of his house. Although it was a legitimate non-private access to the lake, Sam had taken down the black and white *PUBLIC ACCESS* signs at night . . . therefore making the boat launch difficult for anyone to find. When the signs were replaced by the county, he had taken them down again. In addition, Sam had planted grass over the access, making it even more difficult to discern. It was a game that had been going on ever since Sam arrived in Courville, and he was determined to win.

He threw open the screen door and stepped out into the grass, his brow furrowed, his face twisted in anger.

"What the hell are you doing?!?!" he bellowed. *"What the hell do you think you're doing?!?!?"* He stormed across the lawn, bearing down on the green truck. The surprised driver stopped, staring in disbelief as the man with angry, bulging eyes and swinging arms quickly approached.

"Get off my property! Get off my property or I'm gonna call the cops!" The driver of the truck was perplexed and a bit taken aback by the man coming toward him. He rolled the window down and produced a black and white map, detailing all the public access points on Mullett Lake.

"But this says right here that this is a public access and–"

"I said get off my property or I'm callin' the cops."

"Look right here. It's right on the map." The man in the truck unfolded the map for him to see, but Sam drew closer and never looked away from his face, intimidating the man further. Sam had been through this dozens of times. If he just looked menacing enough—if he just looked *mean* enough—most people left. Sam McAllister really had no legal claim to the property, but the fact that he threatened to call the cops was enough for most people.

"I'm tellin' ya, this is private property. And if you don't get your goddamn ass outta here in a hurry, I'm makin' a phone call."

The driver of the truck decided that any further confrontation would do nothing except take away more valuable fishing time. He rolled up the window and left, but not before spinning his tires and ripping up a six-foot strip of grass, leaving a dark black finger to scar an otherwise perfectly maintained lawn.

"Asshole!" Sam shouted out as the truck turned onto the highway and sped out of sight. He walked back into the house, feeling smug that he had won the verbal altercation, but nonetheless pissed about the torn grass.

"Fuckin' idiot," he muttered aloud to no one.

He opened the door to a small bedroom that he'd converted into a darkroom. Developing photos himself had initially been for privacy reasons, as Sam had the peculiar habit of photographing people—women—when they weren't aware of it. This behavior had already contributed to one divorce: his second wife had found a large envelope of photos of the woman that had lived in the house next to their own. The pictures were very amateurish, and had been taken at night through a crack in a thin yellow curtain. The photos weren't anything more than blurry images of a woman with rather small breasts in various stages of dressing and undressing, but they were enough to give a bit of insight to McAllister's wife about Sam's quirky psyche.

He had a number of other such photos that hadn't been discovered by his wife, which was just as well. Many were much more explicit as Sam had managed to capture more than twenty images of the same woman next door in bed with her husband, doing things that left nothing to the imagination. Sam *did* love his visual stimulation.

His photo exploits became borderline obsessive for a while, but the thrill had worn off after a few years and Sam satisfied his sexual appetite with copies of *Hustler* or *Penthouse* magazines or the very infrequent one-night tryst with a woman he would never see again. The threat of AIDS and a host of other sexually transmitted diseases over the past decade had curtailed this activity: now it was far safer to flip open a magazine and feed earthly desires from the gamut of raunchy flesh that sprang from harmless pages. Or, of course, Sam could still take his *own* photos. But that was a little more difficult in such a sparsely populated town as Courville. Difficult, but not entirely impossible.

But now his hobby had changed. His hobby had become more respectable and even profitable, if only modestly. McAllister took pictures of the area and used his own photographs to produce color brochures to promote Courville and some of the surrounding areas. He found that if he did this he could pretty much invoice the Chamber of Commerce whatever price he wanted . . . which, of course, he did. Hell, he wrote the checks, anyway. The artwork and photography could have been done elsewhere for a lot less money, but Sam had total control of the projects and had made quite a bit of cash on the side.

No harm in a little moonlighting, he told himself. The walls of his darkroom were papered with hundreds of pictures, most of them either blurry or off-centered and not good enough to use for anything. A row of empty beer bottles lined the floor by the far wall, and a pile of bottle tops littered the waste basket. Sam scanned the room, forgetting what he'd come in to the darkroom for in the first place.

Oh yeah, he thought. He looked carefully at the wall of pictures, inspecting each one.

"There you are, you sexy thing," he said, reaching for the photo he'd been looking for. Last week, a summer resident—a *female* summer resident—had been sunbathing topless in the back yard of the home adjacent to his. Her yard was fenced in completely by thick, perfectly trimmed cedars . . . but the home sat in a low area. When the woman sat up in her lounge chair, Sam could peer out his dining room window and over the trees. He'd gotten several shots with a telephoto lens. Most were out of focus and too fuzzy to make anything out, but one turned out great: crystal clear and a full shot from her waist up, exposing delicious, golden-tanned breasts lavished with oil, shining like polished chrome in the afternoon sun. He didn't know what her name was. The home was a summer residence, and Sam rarely saw its occupants. The only thing he did know about her was that she was from Birmingham, so that's what he called her. Or, at least, that's what he called the picture. *Miss Busty Birmingham.*

He held the picture in his hands and stared at it a moment before stuffing it in the top drawer of his desk. He would have visitors this weekend. *Important* visitors. Sam thought it best not to flaunt mild pornography and expose his voyeuristic tendencies, however infrequent they had become. It would be best just to keep ol' Busty and her shining melons out of sight.

He closed the door of the darkroom, took the last swig of beer from the bottle, and tossed it expertly in the garbage. Michigan had a ten-cent refund on bottles, but Sam never bothered. They *all* went in the garbage. It was a royal pain in the ass to take them back. Besides . . . no sense in giving anybody any clue about how much beer the Courville Chamber of Commerce director was putting away.

He opened up the fridge and reached for another beer and opened it. He was about to take a sip when a movement in his yard caught his attention. Sam looked through the screen toward the lake just in time to see the young golden retriever plod through his yard. It stopped to sniff a tree.

"Get outta here!" he yelled at the dog through the screen porch. The young dog, surprised and curious, bounded up to the

front steps, wagging his tail and sniffing the door.

"Git! Go on! Git home!" Sam spoke sharply. The dog, thinking that the man wanted to play, barked happily and lifted its paw to the screen. McAllister slammed his palm into the door and it burst open, catching the unwary retriever in the nose and pinching one paw beneath the bottom of the screen door. The dog yelped in pain and fled, limping slightly as it disappeared around the front of the house next door.

One more time for that little bastard and I'm gonna fix him for good, he thought. He thought about calling Amy Hunter again and complaining, as he had done last week, and the week before. Not a day went by when he wouldn't catch her dog in his yard, racing around chasing flies and whizzing on the bushes.

He picked up the phone, then slammed it back down. He didn't have time for this trivial neighbor stuff. He had a celebration to get ready for. A *big* celebration. One that would bring a lot of people and even more money into the small village. When folks from out of town came to Courville, they expected a certain flair, a certain quaintness that they didn't find in other places. And they brought *money*. It was the summer residents that kept Courville alive. And besides . . . you only celebrate a centennial once, and this was going to be Sam McAllister's only one. He wanted it perfect. Everything had to be *perfect*.

But it wasn't just the tourists Sam was interested in. A big change in his future depended on this very event. Last fall he had applied for a job as Tourism Bureau Director for Cape Touraine, a very affluent resort community on the gulf coast of Florida. And son of a gun if they didn't call. They actually called and wanted McAllister to interview. Of course, he had trumped up his credentials on his resume , but he didn't stretch the details *too* far. All of his references were legitimate people that he knew, even actual positions he'd held over the years. He just used a bit of creative doublespeak to embellish the facts. For instance Sam had managed a gas station for two years in Saginaw, so on his resume it read that he had worked for the *'Amoco Corporation'* as an *'Oil Refineries Distribution Manager.'* Likewise, the *La Forde* was an exclusive, very well-known and tremendously expensive resort hotel in Harbor Springs where he had worked as a bartender for one summer. However, on his resume, that translated into *La Forde Resort, Inc.–Public Relations Specialist.* Sam knew that not many, if not *most* people, ever bothered to check references. And if someone ever *did* check up on him and they *did* smell a rat, there were still plenty of other career opportunities. If you threw enough shit at enough people, sooner or later someone would get it smack dab over the eyes. He'd sent out over two dozen duplicate resume s since last October. One of them was bound to stick, and it happened to be Cape Touraine, Florida. The good ol' Sunshine State. Sam could see himself kicking back, enjoying the sun and living life in style. Cape Touraine was home to some of the richest people in the world. Entertainers, software developers, entrepreneurs . . . even a few United States Senators had vacation homes in Cape Touraine. Anyone whose net worth could afford the lifestyle of Cape Touraine had a place there.

And, Sam thought, *If you wanna be rich, you gotta hang out with the rich people. No . . . the* super *rich people.* He'd already flown to meet the board once, and he was able to snow them well enough for them to request a second interview.

Only this time, the board was coming to Courville.

Sam was shocked when the idea was suggested by Jack Ferguson, the mayor of Cape Touraine who would be doing the hiring. But then again, it only made good sense. When Ferguson heard that Sam was in charge of the Courville centennial, he decided that this might just be the time to see how well McAllister puts together a promotion. It would give him a first hand look at his organizational skills, his publicity skills, and overall how well of a job Sam was currently doing. Certainly

Courville was small . . . much smaller than Cape Touraine. But it was efficiency that mattered most. If Sam McAllister could work with a budget, work with the media and the people and pull off successful promotions in Courville, he could do it in Cape Touraine. And for more money, too. A *lot* more money. The position in Cape Touraine paid one hundred-twenty thousand dollars a year—ninety-five thousand more than what he was making now. Plus the job in Cape Touraine offered benefits, incentives, and housing that would value up to another hundred thousand dollars annually.

But this weekend would be it. The Courville centennial needed to go off without a hitch. No . . . *better*. It had to be *spectacular*. He needed to dazzle the people from Cape Touraine and show them that they would be making the right decision. They needed to see how smoothly everything flowed together, how perfect the planning and organization had been. They'd be watching closely to see if everything indeed was controlled and in order, that the events and festivities went off like Swiss clockwork. Cape Touraine was by no means intent on having festivals or fairs of any kind, but over the past few years the community's image had been tarnished by reports of arrogant exclusivity. Cape Touraine was becoming, in essence, a city of spoiled brats. If the trend didn't change, millionaires and billionaires would soon find other, more respectful accommodations.

So, if it was public relations they wanted, Sam McAllister wanted to be the guy. He could bullshit his way into anywhere, and the bullshit was sure going to fly this weekend. Sam was going to make sure that his guests received royal treatment, and by Sunday evening they would be praising him on such a marvelous job well done. They'd be begging him to come to work for them. Sam was sure of it. The Courville centennial was going to be better than perfect. He didn't have much control over the weather and that dismayed him a bit, but this little bit of rain was supposed to move on through by tomorrow afternoon. Everything would be perfect.

He looked over the lake through the falling mist. There was no breeze and the lake was still and gray, reflective of the sky above. He raised the beer to his lips and stopped short of a sip, holding the bottle just below his chin.

Now what in the hell, he thought. About a hundred yards off shore, a large wake had suddenly formed. The water churned a moment and the waves drifted off, and whatever it had been was gone.

Sam watched a moment longer, wondering what could have possibly made such a large disturbance beneath the surface. Whatever it was, it hadn't broken water. A sturgeon, maybe, like the one in the photograph in the paper. But they were bottom feeders and rarely came to the surface.

Finally, he took a sip of his beer and shrugged it away.

Good thing nobody from the paper saw that, he thought. *Or they'd be printing shit about giant great white sharks in Mullett Lake.* He threw the empty beer in the garbage, clicked on the television, and soon nodded off to sleep on the couch.

✳ ✳ ✳ ✳

Dinner had gone well. At Amy's suggestion, they had driven to the Douglas Lake Steakhouse about ten miles away. The two spent a few hours at the table talking about the things that most people talk about on a first date. Where each had grown up, where they had gone to school. Brad had felt a bit uneasy at first.

CHRISTOPHER KNIGHT

But if he was uncomfortable, Amy certainly didn't seem to notice, and he loosened up a bit before dinner had been served. They laughed and talked until well past sunset, and had been the last few people to leave the restaurant. She had taken him up on the offer of a nightcap on the dock at the cottages; nothing more was offered, nothing considered. After two glasses of wine, a cordial hug, and a soft kiss on the cheek, the evening was over. The two retired to their respective cabins.

Brad turned out the light in the small bedroom, listening to the crickets buzz outside his window. A car sped by on the highway and faded off into the night. He stretched and yawned as he lay back in the small bed.

Would have been nice to have some company tonight, he thought. While he had never indulged himself at all in a promiscuous lifestyle, he was becoming strongly attracted to Amy. Which, of course, didn't necessarily mean that he wanted to immediately go to bed with her; but just the thought of her in his arms so warm and close was enough to make him aroused.

He forced himself to push the thoughts away and for the first time in what seemed like weeks his thoughts returned to his job, and to a psychiatrist that he'd seen for only a brief few weeks.

Screw it all, he thought. *I don't need motivational tapes. Or anger management or whatever the class was that Frank wanted me to go to. All I needed was some time away from everything. Just some time alone, a quiet place.*

This place.

Soon the wine had done its work. His eyelids were heavy and his mind was tired. Brad's thoughts again returned to Amy as he eased into a comfortable sleep.

✳ ✳ ✳ ✳

CHRISTOPHER KNIGHT

Darkness. The fish liked night the best. It was as if it were invisible, cruising the depths slowly, warily, watching. Here it could move about unnoticed and unseen, silently stalking the deep. It cruised for hours, searching the waters for food. Here in the lake there was not such an ample supply of large fish . . . at least not as large of fish that the muskie had previously been accustomed to. Here the fish were smaller, and only once in a while did the muskie encounter a very large sturgeon which it chased down and devoured easily. The few sturgeon that the fish *did* come across provided a fairly satisfying meal . . . but nothing like the food it was becoming accustomed to. Those meals were few and far between . . . and *dangerous*. Whenever the muskie was near one of the large flailing creatures, an alarm went off inside. It was a warning, an alert that told the fish to escape, to flee and hide.

But the muskie was learning to ignore it.

The monstrous fish continued to cruise in deep water, moving slowly, watching, warily slinking through the dark depths.

Soon dawn arrived, bringing a cool green cast to the murky deep. The muskie moved silently and swiftly above weed beds and over submerged logs, watching, searching, until—

A vibration. It was a subtle disturbance in the water, a very delicate reverberation caused by something on the surface. The fish moved on and the noise became louder, clearer. Its heart pumped harder and its excitement grew as the fish drew closer and closer to the sound.

* * * *

CHRISTOPHER KNIGHT

Pepper's incessant barking awoke Brad just before ten a.m. The dog was bellowing and snarling in another yard or down by the lake; Brad couldn't tell for sure. But the dog was really going at it. He squinted his eyes a few times as he lay in bed and turned to look at the alarm clock that set on the small pine dresser. Somewhere outside Pepper's alert growling continued, louder and more ferocious than ever.

Brad got up and walked to the window. The clouds were breaking up as had been forecast, and blades of sunlight had begun to slice through the tree branches. He could see Amy's head, her hair drenched, bobbing in the water just beyond the end of the dock.

"Pepper! What's up with you?" she shouted. Pepper was standing in the shallows, barking and growling at Amy. The hair on his back flared high, and every few seconds he would dart back onto the shore, turn toward the water, and begin growling again.

"What's the matter with you?" Amy laughed. "Come here! *Come on!"* She waved a hand toward herself, motioning the dog to come to her.

Pepper bounded into the water to a depth that only reached his chest, then stopped, snarling viciously. Amy ducked her head beneath the water.

It was the last straw for the dog. Pepper bounded completely in, his legs kicking frantically beneath the surface. He continued growling as he swam, his eyes furiously darting back and forth.

Amy's head popped back up and she began to swim toward the retriever. Only Pepper's head was above the surface, frantically bobbing toward her in the water. Amy reached out her hand to pet him.

"What is wrong with you? What's—*Ow!*" She let out a yell as Pepper grabbed her arm with his teeth. It wasn't a bite to intentionally hurt her, but a tight grasp that the dog would not release. He began pulling Amy's arm, as if leading her to shore.

"Pepper! Knock it off! Let go!" Amy scolded. The teeth on her arm weren't piercing the skin, but Pepper's hold was firm and uncomfortable.

Brad had been watching the scene with amusement but now had become suspicious. He bent down to pull on his sweats and looked up.

One hundred feet behind Amy an enormous wake swirled the surface. The rest of the lake was calm and smooth, but there was something causing a large disturbance, rolling the surface as it churned toward shore.

Toward Amy and Pepper.

Brad couldn't believe what he was seeing. He didn't *know* what he was seeing. They only thing he was certain of is that there was nothing in fresh water that could create a wake that size with that much speed. Suddenly the surface broke, giving Brad a glimpse of a folded dorsal fin.

This is not real, he told himself, his mind buzzing. *This can't be. There is no fish that big in these waters.*

Suddenly he remembered the photo in the paper of the huge sturgeon. Impossible, yes . . . but whatever he was seeing in the water was real. And seeing *is* believing, as they say.

He quickly tied the draw string of his sweats and sprang.

"Amy!" he screamed. He bolted out the door and sprinted over the porch, running as fast as he could across the damp grass. *"Get out of the water! Amy! Get out!"*

Amy turned her head about in the water, wondering what all the fuss was about. First Pepper, now Brad.

The water was up to her neck and she began to tip toe on

the bottom toward the shore. Pepper was swimming at her side and pulling her along, still holding her arm in his mouth with a vice-like intensity. Amy again tried to shake his grip.

"Pepper! Knock it off, wouldja?!?! What's wrong with you!?!?!?"

Brad reached the dock and he bounded along the planks, causing the entire structure to shake. His eyes jumped back from Amy, then to the water, back to Amy, then again to the surrounding waters.

Amy was now waist deep, casually walking along side the dock. Pepper released his hold and bounded for the shore, only to turn once again and growl menacingly at the lake.

Brad grabbed Amy by the hand and pulled her up out of the water and onto the dock, his eyes still frantically darting about, scanning the waters below him, straining to see beneath the surface. His heart thumped in his chest.

"Brad . . . what in the world—"

"Shhh," he interrupted, keeping his eyes on the shimmering waters. He had watched the huge wake reach the tip of the dock and slackened. Whatever had created such a motion had stopped or slowed. Amy followed his gaze and she too searched the waters. For *what*, she didn't know.

Brad took a slow, quiet step further along the dock and Amy followed. Pepper had been growling and snarling, still raising a fuss, then he suddenly stopped. The dog yelped and turned around, bounding up to the porch of the cabin with his tail between his legs. Brad and Amy had just reached the end of the dock.

"What did you see?" she whispered. Brad paused, opened his mouth as if to explain, then stopped.

A shadow of monstrous size was approaching, low and close to the bottom.

"There," he said. *"Right there."*

Just a few feet from the dock, an immense dark shape

CHRISTOPHER KNIGHT

lumbered by. Huge wicked eyes glared up at the two forms from beneath the surface. The fish was enormous, and it was so close that Brad and Amy could see the light-green vertical stripes on its side. Black specks that were the size of quarters dotted its fins, and a large, diamond-shaped black mark stretched over the fishes' head. It continued along, seeming to take an eternity to pass.

And then it was gone, sliding off toward deeper water.

"Oh my God," Amy whispered, her voice shaking. "I have *never* seen a sturgeon that big. *Ever.*"

"That was *no* sturgeon," Brad said, his eyes still searching. They stood frozen, gazing into the waters, too afraid to move. Suddenly, about twenty yards out into the lake, the water erupted and boiled as the fish rolled the surface. A large wake moved with lightning speed for a few seconds. The wake stopped abruptly and the waves dispersed, growing smaller as they rolled away. The smooth, rich blue of the calm surface returned, shining like silver in the morning sun. The fish was gone.

❋ ❋ ❋ ❋

The muskie slid further into the depths, silently, quietly. Rarely had the fish gone hungry for more than just a few hours. Usually there was an ample supply of large fish or other aquatic life that would provide numerous meals throughout the day. But *here* . . . .

It had missed its chance, and the fish sped angrily through the underwater world, slipping back into the quiet depths. A large smallmouth bass was unfortunate enough to be in its path and the muskie easily overtook the terrified fish, swallowing it whole. It provided nothing more to the muskie than the satisfaction of a kill, as the bass provided no relief from the gnawing hunger. Fish were no longer providing a satisfactory meal. It had found much larger creatures that would satisfy its voracious appetite . . . creatures that were far easier prey than fish or other marine animals.

The fish slowed, sinking low among the weeds, remaining in the gloomy green depths where it could remain unseen and unknown. There would be other opportunities. All it had to do was wait and watch, slowly circling the depths, cruising low in the weeds along the edge of the shallows. It was still early in the day, and the fish knew that it wouldn't be long.

✳ ✳ ✳ ✳

Brad watched the lake, once again brimming with its daily dose of skiers, boaters and the like. He and Amy sat on the front porch of Brad's cottage.

"We can't just do *nothing*," Amy remarked. "I'm beginning to think that those other people—you know, the ones from the past few days—didn't drown. I'm beginning to think—"

She stopped in mid-sentence, turning to look at Brad before continuing. "Are you *sure* that thing was a tiger muskie?"

"It has to be. Or a muskie of some sort. I mean . . . I've never heard of them growing to be that size. It's impossible. It's just *not* possible. They just don't get that big. But the markings, the coloring. I'm not sure about that black spot on its head, though. I've never seen that on a tiger muskie before. Or any muskie for that sake. It could be disease, or just some type of birthmark. But that fish sure had all the markings of tiger muskie. A *huge* one."

"What's the difference between a 'tiger' muskie and A muskie? Is there any?"

"Tigers are hybrids. They're a cross between a male northern pike and a female muskellunge."

"Can they interbreed like that?" Amy asked.

"Not most fish, no. But the muskie and the pike are so closely related that it happens quite often. But again . . . they just don't grow that big. The world record is something like sixty-nine pounds. That's a big fish . . . just shy of six feet. The one we saw today was twice the length and probably would go six *hundred* pounds or more."

He glanced out at the lake and nodded his head, then looked back at Amy. "And you've been *swimming* here?" he finished.

Amy shuddered at the thought. She remembered standing neck-deep in the water, watching in amusement as Pepper stood growling menacingly from the shore. He had never acted like that before, and she should've known something was wrong. How close had she been? How close had that . . . *thing* . . . been? Brad said that he had spotted the wake moving toward her from behind, and at one point he thought that the fish's back had broken the surface.

"Well, it's only going to be a matter of time," Brad stated. "Something is going to happen. And I've got a feeling that it's not going to be good. I think we should call the police, and maybe they can keep people off the water until we know for sure what the hell it is."

Amy was quiet for a moment as she looked out over the lake. Sunlight danced on the bright blue surface, and a cool breeze shuddered through the two large weeping willows near the shore.

"There's only one problem," she said finally. Brad looked at her and didn't say anything. "Mullett Lake is part of the chain of lakes," she continued. "It's connected by the inland waterway. The fish can go through Indian River, and right into Burt Lake if it wanted to. And then even further inland to Crooked Lake. It could be long gone by now. Or at least in another lake. If we go to the police and tell them that they need to keep everyone off of *three* lakes, including the connecting rivers, they're going to think we're crazy."

"They're gonna think we're crazy anyway," Brad said. They're going to—"

He stopped himself, and his eyes widened. "Wait a minute. What about Lake Huron? Can't the fish get to Huron through the river?"

"I don't think so," Amy answered, shaking her head. "Not unless it goes through the lock, which would be impossible to do without being seen. The lock is only about thirty feet long. It's used to lower the boats to the level in Huron, so it stays closed all the time until a boat comes through. Someone would see the fish for sure and keep the lock closed."

"God, I hope so. If that thing makes it out to Lake Huron, it'll have the entire Great Lakes system to roam."

Again, Amy shuddered. She rose from the chair and stepped inside the cottage, returning a moment later with yesterday's paper. She flipped through the pages until she found what she was looking for, then pressed the open page to the table. Her finger rested below the photo that the aerial photographer had taken.

The hazy, dark form in the water had taken on a new, haunting dimension. It no longer seemed the novelty picture of someone's wild imagination. The shape and size in the photograph looked as if it could quite possibly be the exact same thing that they had seen just a few hours earlier.

Brad studied the photo closer, but there wasn't much more

he could make out. The picture was too blurry from the reproduction, and the shadow appeared to be in water too deep to make out any clear features. It could have been a log just as easily as it could have been a fish.

"We need to talk to this guy," Brad said. His finger swept the page and he found the photo credit at the corner of the caption. "Cal Rollins. We need to talk to him and find out just what he saw. Do you know him?"

"I've never met him, no. But he lives just down the road a few miles. Flies his plane from the field at his farm."

"Think he'd be around? I want to talk with him about this, the sooner the better. Maybe we should get some more concrete evidence before we start telling anybody about this and causing a big deal. And I want to call Frank down at the lab in Lorain and see what *he* says."

Amy stood up from her chair, her eyes not leaving the surface of the lake. Both she and Brad found it hard not to stare at the water, expecting at any moment to see the huge monstrosity—whatever it was—lurch to the surface.

"If that . . . *thing* . . . did kill those people," she began. "You know . . . the ones from the past couple weeks that haven't been found? How long is it going to be before it does it again?"

FIVE

Aloha State Park was teaming with activity, as was customary for most hot summer days. Kids splashing in the water, teenagers tossing a frisbee back and forth, adults relaxing on beach blankets or sitting in the shade. A volleyball game on the grass was underway with players consisting of sixteen members of the Zion Lutheran Church of Wren City. A weekend field trip, filled with fun, fellowship, and frivolity. And beer for at least two of the youths, who'd swiped a six-pack from an unattended cooler. Not a laudable testimony to the faith, but hell: they were *kids*. Besides . . . Billy Joel claimed that *only the good die young*. Maybe they just wanted a little insurance.

On the water, three jet skiers buzzed noisily past the break wall, twisting and turning recklessly as each craft jumped the others' wake. A small two-person sailboat wasn't having much luck at catching any wind, and the craft bobbed aimlessly, forced to wait out the afternoon in the doldrums.

Just beyond the swim area, twenty-two year old Steve

Hutchinson pulled the dive mask over his face and gave an 'all-okay' sign to his buddy Kurt Derry. The two men began cruising the surface, snorkeling over a thick weed bed. Mullett Lake contained a variety of freshwater fish: bass, catfish, walleye, perch, pike, muskie and the like. Often the two men saw these fish and more, along with the occasional discarded can or old tire. Once while snorkeling, Steve had even found a Rolex watch. It had been in the water a long time . . . far too long to be cleaned or repaired. But it was exciting to find things of that sort, regardless of their monetary value.

The water was ten feet deep. The visibility was good and Kurt could make out small perch on the bottom, darting in and out between the weeds. He took a long breath on the surface, held it, and used his fins to propel himself to the bottom. He'd finally spent the hundred and ten bucks on an underwater camera. It was just a simple point and click, nothing fancy, but he'd always wanted to take underwater pictures. Kurt wished he'd had one last summer, when both he and Steve had come across a big gar pike. The fish was long and snake-like, maybe four feet in length. A good size gar for *any* lake. They had been able to get within a few feet of it before it shot out of sight, returning to the safety of deeper waters.

Kurt approached the bottom. The small fish scooted out of his way at first, then, as if curious of the unknown intruder, approached with guarded caution. Seven or eight panfish filled the viewfinder, and Kurt clicked off a shot and slowly returned to the surface. He blew the water from his snorkel and, right on cue, Steve took a deep breath and descended to the bottom.

The panfish still hung in the water like a mobile, watching these strange creatures from the surface as they descended, ascended, then descended again. Steve could hold his breath much longer than Kurt, and he cruised along the bottom, turning his head from side to side, looking for anything that could possibly be of interest.

Kurt watched from the surface. It was more of a safety precaution than anything; one would dive, the other would watch. There wasn't too much trouble that they could get into in Mullett Lake, but it was still better to be safe than sorry. Last year, two men in Lake Huron drowned while snorkeling. Both were together in relatively shallow water when they became tangled in an illegally placed gill net. They weren't found until about a week later. A fishing boat found their bloated remains, still hung up in the heavy mesh net. They were gray and blue and purple and had swollen up like over-sized circus balloons. Neither Kurt nor Steve wanted to wind up like that.

Steve didn't see the fish, but Kurt did. Only a few feet from where Steve was swimming, a good size catfish . . . maybe twenty inches or so . . . chugged lazily along, searching for food among the muck and weeds. Kurt watched it stop and dig sluggishly at the mud with its bulky, wide head. Steve had passed it by unnoticed. Hopefully, it would still be there when Kurt's turn came. He waited impatiently with the camera, watching both Steve and the catfish from the surface.

Finally, Steve slowly rose to the surface, exhaling on his way up. Kurt was next, and he arched his torso forward, gliding down once again toward the thick green bed of leafy underwater vegetation. He held his camera ready, aiming at the spot where the catfish was. Or . . . *should* have been. Kurt couldn't find the fish. He found the spot where the weeds and mud had been disturbed, but there was no sign of the catfish at all. Kurt looked around, certain that it couldn't have gone far. Catfish were slow, and took their time wherever they went. Certainly it had to be within sight *somewhere*.

But it wasn't. Kurt searched and searched, but it was gone. Finally, after nearly a minute, Kurt couldn't hold his breath any longer. He turned his head toward the surface and headed up.

CHRISTOPHER KNIGHT

As he did so, he pointed to his mouth, alerting Steve to the fact that he wanted to talk. When he made it to the surface, Steve had already lifted his mask up onto his forehead and was treading water. Kurt did the same.

"Did you see that catfish?" he asked.

Steve shook his head.

"No. Big one?"

"A twenty-incher at least. Good size. But he disappeared. I wanted to get a shot of him."

"I think most of the fish are hanging in deeper water today. Notice how they're all on the bottom? Lets go out a bit to where it's about fifteen feet deep or so."

Kurt nodded in agreement and placed his mask over his face and returned the snorkel to his mouth. Steve followed suit, and the two drifted slowly over the surface into deeper water.

✳ ✳ ✳ ✳

Long before they came into vision, the fish had detected their activity. The splashing, the noise. The muskie was keenly aware of all sights and sounds and smells under water. It moved slowly along the bottom, one cautious inch at a time, alert, wary, its bulging eyes darting menacingly from side to side, watching and searching. It feared nothing. The lakes, the waters, all were its home. It was just as content in the black of night as it was in the brightness of the day. However, the day brought intrusive rays of light streaming into the depths, making the much-needed element of surprise more difficult.

During the day, the muskie stalked its prey slowly at first, waiting, often not moving for hours at a time, ensnaring its prey off guard and completely unaware. Usually, by the time its victim spotted the monstrous beast attacking (if the unfortunate prey saw the fish at all) it was far too late.

As would be the case this time.

The fish spotted the two blurry figures from a ways off. They were large, moving slowly over the surface. The muskie stopped and sank lower in the weeds, camouflaged perfectly within lush aquatic vegetation. The two creatures were still some distance away, moving slowly closer.

And the fish waited.

✳ ✳ ✳ ✳

After floating over the surface into deeper water, Kurt was the first to dive. He inhaled deeply and rolled forward, kicking his fins to propel him to the bottom. The weeds were thick but the vegetation was becoming more sporadic, leaving large gaping areas of soft brown muck.

Kurt thought he had spotted a small fish, but upon inspection it was nothing more than a dead leaf laying in the mud, half exposed. He looked around, searching the surrounding waters. There really wasn't anything to see. The yellow-green hue of the water encircled him and seemed to go on forever. Above him Steve's dark silhouette hung suspended on the surface, his dark shape every now and then blocking out the sun and casting a shadow over Kurt.

Disappointed, he rose once again toward the surface.

Steve immediately descended, quickly making it to the bottom. Kurt watched him through the camera's viewfinder, remained still for a minute, and clicked off a picture. Steve continued on, gliding easily a few feet from the bottom. Kurt held the camera to his mask and clicked off one more picture as Steve cruised over an enormous sunken log.

Suddenly Kurt stopped. He pulled the camera away from his face and froze.

The log had moved. He was sure of it.

Steve had just passed over the large shape, but Kurt was *sure* he saw the log move.

In sudden overwhelming realization of what he was seeing, Kurt became paralyzed with fear. It welled up within him like a geyser, sweeping through his body and exploding in his mind, as confusion and horror mixed like some macabre cocktail. There was no mistake. The tapered, thick head. The long, tube-shaped body. Large, wicked eyes. They were the sinister, demonic eyes of a dinosaur, like the ones he had seen in the movie *Jurassic Park*. Only that was a *movie*. The dinosaurs of Michael Crichton's imagination became the work of master illusionists and creative geniuses.

But this was *real*.

This was *real* and *alive*. No tricks of a camera, no computer-generated image. It was the biggest muskellunge Kurt had ever seen, over twice the length of a normal human. The largest one he'd seen caught was an old black and white picture of a man holding the fish up long ways toward the camera. *That* muskie was just over six feet in length, and weighed sixty-nine pounds. He remembered seeing the photos on the wall at *Breakers* bar over on the other side of the lake, and at *Paula's Cafe* in Indian River. Some of the pictures of men with their trophies were awesome sights indeed, showing off huge muskies and pike and sturgeon.

CHRISTOPHER KNIGHT

But no fish he had ever seen in his life could match the sheer size of what lay just a mere few dozen feet away. Kurt couldn't believe what he was seeing, but there it was, in Mullett Lake, in fifteen feet of water.

The fish moved again. Slow and stealth-like, it began to creep through the weeds. Steve was still ambling along, looking in front of him, side to side, below him . . . *but not behind him.* Kurt didn't know what to do. His heart was pounding and his breathing was rapid. He began to shout through his snorkel, hoping Steve would hear. Hoping he would just look up, or at least behind him. His indecipherable shouts howled through the plastic snorkel, unheard and unnoticed by Steve.

He had to warn him, somehow, in some way—*but then what?* It was obvious that the fish was stalking him. They were in the muskie's element. This was its home, this was where it lived, breathed, slept . . . *and ate.*

In a rush of horror, Kurt realized that there was nothing that he could do. He was powerless to warn Steve, let alone defend himself.

Suddenly there was an explosion of debris and water. Weeds and a cloud of silt erupted from the bottom as the fish attacked. The cloud of debris burst toward Kurt like a nuclear blast, obscuring his vision and making it impossible to see. He turned and swam away from the churning debris, and then turned back around, his eyes bulging through his face mask.

In complete terror Kurt watched as the fish emerged from the swelling cloud, carrying Steve long ways in its mouth. Steve had one arm free and he was hysterically flailing about. The muskie clamped its powerful jaws tighter and snapped its victim from side to side, causing another wave of debris to fulminate through the surrounding waters. Kurt could see the shocked, painful expression of Steve's face through his diving mask. He was wincing, struggling with all of his strength to free himself.

His eyes were bulging in disbelief and blood was pouring from his nose, splattering over the inside of the glass dive mask.

The gargantuan fish flared its gills and opened its mouth. Steve struggled harder, a tiny glimmer of hope, a long shot, an opportunity . . . .

With blinding fury, the huge fish forced its mouth closed, shaking its head sideways. In that instant, Steve disappeared. A large bulge sagged from the belly of the muskellunge.

My God! Kurt screamed in his mind. *Steve . . . that's Steve! He's inside the fish!* The bloated growth quivered for a moment, and Kurt realized that it was Steve's final attempt, his absolute *last* agonizing effort to free himself. But at this point, his situation was beyond hopeless.

The fish had won.

Kurt was still ice bound on the surface, unable to move. His body was rigid and stiff and he had the vague feeling of being frozen in some giant cube, unable to move or flex even a tiny bit. His whole body was completely immobilized by an unspeakable, unknowable terror that short circuited his nervous system, severing any possibility of moving. There was nothing he could do. If the fish wanted *him* next, Kurt would be defenseless. There was no way for him to fight, nothing he could do to protect himself. He was still way out from shore, at least fifty yards from the Aloha State Park beach. He could scream, but there would be no way anyone would hear him over the few jet skis that buzzed just outside of the swimming area. He could try to swim, but he wasn't sure if he would be able to even move a finger.

Kurt lay still in the water, completely frozen in horror. His breathing was quick and shallow, and his whole body shivered in dread. If he remained still, maybe the fish would think he was dead. Maybe the fish would leave him alone. Muskies usually wanted their prey alive, and so maybe if he stayed still long enough the fish would leave. And at the moment, remaining perfectly still was not only *easy*; it would have been impossible to do anything else. Maybe he had a chance after all.

It was his only chance.

The fish drew closer, approaching Kurt. It rose slowly, its massive fins wavering in and out, gently bringing the fish toward the surface. Like a submarine, its head began to rise higher than its body. The fish was perfectly motionless except for the methodical, calculated movements of its fins. Kurt was face to face with the most vicious, the most inherently evil face he had ever seen. It was stalking him like a cat, waiting for just the right moment to make the next cautious move forward. Inflamed, penetrating eyes glared back at him. Its mouth was open just a bit, and Kurt could see angry rows of incisors, each the size of railroad spikes, sharp as needles. A small piece of Steve's torn swim trunks dangled from the edge of its mouth, caught on a razor-sharp tooth. The fish's creamy white underbelly was grotesquely ballooned and swollen from its recent prey.

Kurt knew that this was *it*. He had seen his own future, and it was not so bright and rosy. It would be a horrible, sick way to go. He'd always hoped that when his day came, he would be lucky enough to die in his sleep. Or maybe a quick, massive heart attack after a long, good life. He never in a million years expected to go this way.

The fish inched closer and Kurt closed his eyes.

The muskie exploded and Kurt felt himself hurled upwards out of the water, then back again, plunging headlong into the lake. His mask and snorkel had been knocked off, and a terrible pain gnawed at his side. Blood poured into the water around him from a deep slash below his rib cage. The flesh above his waist was mangled and torn, and rich, red liquid gushed from the wound. Kurt began to scream, losing control, flailing his arms madly in the air.

By sheer chance the commotion attracted the attention of one of the jet skiers. Kurt became dizzy, and the fuzziness in his head welled over him. The last thing he remembered seeing were the bright white machines racing toward him.

✳ ✳ ✳ ✳

Amy saw the ambulance approaching quickly in the rear-view mirror, and she pulled over to let it by. She and Brad looked at each other, each knowing what the other was thinking. *Had it happened again? Another 'accidental' death on the lake?*

After the emergency vehicle went by, she pulled the Jeep back onto the highway. Cal Rollins had been home when she called, and he said he'd be happy to show them the picture, if they wanted to see it for themselves.

Amy turned down a well-traveled dirt road. Farms lined both sides and after they had traveled a few miles, Brad spotted a small brown and white Cessna parked next to a large out-building. An old two-story farmhouse sat majestically a few dozen yards from the barn. It was freshly painted and looked as new as the day it was built. A gargantuan maple tree with a four-foot trunk billowed up in an adjacent field. The tree itself looked to be at least a hundred fifty years old, with large, spiny branches filled with rich, new leaves. A few roosters and chickens wandered aimlessly near the enormous trunk, and a large black German shepherd slept in the shade. When the Jeep pulled into the driveway, the dog lifted its head and lazily raised its ears a moment before resting its head back on the ground, returning to sleep. If the animal was a watchdog, he either was on lunch break or had been laid off and was collecting unemployment.

"Looks like we got the right place," Brad said, pointing to the aircraft. Amy turned once again, parked the vehicle next to a rusted old Ford Granada, and shut off the engine.

Cal Rollins saw Brad and Amy coming and began to walk toward them from his barn. He was a small, wiry man, well into his seventies. Dark splotches of grease stained his faded blue overalls and a black band of oil was smeared across his forehead. He was almost completely bald except for a light dusting of gray just behind each ear. Cal wore black plastic rimmed safety glasses, and as he approached he reached up and pulled them away from his face, stuffing them into his breast pocket.

"Hello," he said pleasantly as he reached the pair.

"Hi," both Amy and Brad responded in unison.

"I'd shake hands with you," he explained, taking a stained rag from his pocket. "But this grease gets on everything. We can't have that on a pretty lady like yourself." He nodded toward Amy, smiled and winked. Amy blushed. Cal looked at Brad. "You either, fella. Come on inside and I'll get cleaned up." Brad and Amy found themselves taking an instant liking to him. He had a good-natured, easy-going character. Cal Rollins, despite his age and frail appearance and dirty overalls, had a look of prestige and confidence about him.

They followed the small man as he walked to the old farmhouse. Or rather, *jogged* to the house. Rollins' walk was quick, and he wasted no time making it over the grass and to the porch. He held the door open for them as they entered.

The farmhouse was the epitome of spotlessness, and carefully ordained with old furniture. Most of the furnishings appeared to be very old . . . most certainly all were antiques. In the kitchen beneath neatly stacked piles of papers there was an oak dining table that looked to be over a hundred years old. A large cherry wood grandfather clock stood proudly against a wall in the living room. The house had a warm, lived-in feeling: serene, homey and comfortable—but immaculate just the same.

"Give me just a second," Cal said, his shoes tapping on the wood floor as he strode down the hall. "Make yourselves at home. There's soda in the fridge, glasses are in the cupboard." Water in the bathroom sink began to run and Brad and Amy stood in the living room, gazing around the house. As if sensing their thoughts, the unseen Cal Rollins spoke loudly as he washed his hands.

"Been here all my life," he spoke loudly from the bathroom. "This was my great grandfathers' farm. He's the one who built it. Lots of the furniture in the home was hand made by him. He built all kinds of things. Except the clock, of course. Over the years a few things had to be replaced as you might expect. The couch for one. The one I got now is from 1928. Most everything else is at least that old. Some older."

Rollins emerged from the bathroom and strode back toward them, extending his hand and spoke.

"Cal Rollins."

Brad clasped the old man's hand.

"Brad Herrick. This is Amy Hunter." Cal released his grip of Brad's hand and gently took Amy's hand in his.

"The delight is all mine. You're Jim Hunters' gal, aren't you?" His eyes twinkled as he spoke, and Amy nodded her head.

"Niece," she said smiling.

"Ol' Jim's a rascal. Known him since he was this high." Cal swept his hand forward and held it out, palm down, at about waist-level. "Haven't seen him much this past year, though."

"Uncle Jim has been pretty busy this past year," Amy replied.

"Well, good. It's good to stay busy. Soda?"

"No, thanks," Brad replied. "Not for me anyway." He glanced at Amy and raised his eyebrows.

"No, thank you," she said, shaking her head.

Cal walked to the table and picked up a manilla envelope.

"I think this is what you're lookin' for here," he said, offering the envelope to Brad, who took it from Cal and opened it up.

The three carefully inspected the eight by ten photo. It was in color, and much clearer than the reproduction in the paper. Brad knew instantly that the fish in the picture was no sturgeon. Sure, the picture was taken from a distance, and it really didn't show a lot, but there was no mistaking it. The fish in the picture had to be the fish he and Amy had seen at the dock.

"Unfortunately when the paper published this picture it kind of screwed it up. Made it more blurry and less defined. Take a look here." He brought the photo closer to Brad. "See?" Cal pointed with his finger. "You can see where his tail is. And these here—" he swept his pinky along the bottom of the shadow. Cal remained silent, allowing his guests to absorb the photo for all it was worth. He looked up, glancing first at Amy, then back to Brad as he spoke.

"Fastest thing I've ever seen in my life. I've never seen a fish move so fast. The guy from the paper . . . it was *his* idea that it was a sturgeon. Ain't no sturgeon that moves that fast. No *sir-ree*."

"What do you think it is?" Amy asked.

"Got no clue. Never seen a fish like that in all my life. But a long time ago me and my brother used to spear sturgeon, over on Black River and on Black Lake. Sturgeon are slow, sure. Oh, they can really move if they *want* to . . . but not like this guy was movin'." Cal pointed to the form on the portrait and tapped the picture.

Brad's eyebrows furrowed and he squinted, gazing intently at the photo.

"And you've never seen this before?" he asked.

"Nope. Never. I'm in the air a lot, too. At least a few times a week. I know that lake like the back of my hand. Sure can see a lot from up there. Over Lake Michigan and Lake Huron you can see the shadows of shipwrecks if they're not down more than eighty feet or so. But nope. Never seen a fish like that in Mullett before. Or anywhere. Hey . . . I was just finishin' up in the shop. You guys wanna go up and look for'im?"

Brad and Amy looked at each other.

"Right now?" Amy asked.

Cal nodded. "No time like the present," he said, smiling.

"Fine with me," Brad replied, trying to contain his excitement.

"Good," Rollins said, delighted with the opportunity to fly. "I'll get my camera bag in case we see'im again."

❋ ❋ ❋ ❋

McAllister heard the first Sheriff car fly by, followed by another, then another.

All right, what now? he thought. *So help me God if some other screwball offed himself in my lake . . . .*

CHRISTOPHER KNIGHT

He hopped in his truck and sped off after the patrol cars, following them north on Old US-27, then south on M-33 to Aloha State Park. It was jammed with weekend campers and travelers, and Sam followed the winding blacktop around and through the grounds. At the beach a half dozen patrol cars were parked, as well as an ambulance. Flashing lights blinked like pinball machines, and as Sam hopped out of the truck the ambulance flared to life. Its siren screamed a single short, piercing *whoooouuup!* before the vehicle pulled out and roared on by.

Sam walked quickly toward the lake. He could see a number of boats on the water, and he knew his suspicions were about to be confirmed.

Aw hell, he thought. *Not again.*

He stopped and raised his hand to his forehead to shield his eyes from the bright sunlight. Sam recognized one of the deputies as Greg Kendall, a man he had met earlier this year. As fate had it, on the first day that Sam McAllister moved into town he'd come across a stranded motorist. In a gesture rather unlikely for Sam in the first place, he had assisted the woman by taking her to town and arranging for a tow truck himself. The woman was none other than Donna Kendall, Greg's wife. Greg had paid a personal visit to McAllister to thank him. There were, of course, a few tense moments for Sam when he looked out the window to see a Cheboygan County Sheriff Deputy vehicle in his driveway. He wasn't on parole anymore and he couldn't think of anything he had done recently that could have gotten him into trouble. He was relieved when Kendall had finally explained and Sam put two and two together. The deputy had thanked Sam for his courteousness and told Sam that if there was anything McAllister needed, to just give him a call at the Department. It was a great way to begin a new life: a new name and a justified 'in' at the Sheriff's Department.

"Hey Greg," McAllister said, extending his hand.

"Sam," the deputy responded, grasping McAllister's hand. "How are ya?"

"Fine, fine. Looks like you got your hands full here."

The deputy shook his head. "You wouldn't believe me if I told ya. I don't believe it myself."

"Try me."

"We just hauled out a kid. Well, not really a kid. About twenty-five years old or so. We just shipped him off to the hospital with half his guts ripped out. And you know what?" The deputy laughed as he spoke, shaking his head. "He says a *fish* did it."

"A *fish?!?*" Sam laughed. "Now I guess I *have* heard everything."

"Well, ya haven't heard everything yet. 'Cause he says that the same fish *ate* his buddy. He was babbling and drifting in and out of consciousness, so we're really not sure what happened. He could have been by himself for all I know. Snorkeling way out there without a flag . . . boat comes along, doesn't see him . . . *whack! That's* a little more believable."

"So'dja find anything out there?" Sam asked, nodding toward the group of boats assembled on the water.

"Nah. Nothing really. Found this guys' mask and snorkel. Oh . . . and his camera. One of these newfangled underwater ones."

The deputy held up a plastic bag containing a camera the color of a plastic banana, and he raised it up to show Sam. "We'll have to send it off to the lab to get the film developed, so we won't know much till tomorrow. But whatever's on here–" he pointed to the camera. "–I don't think it's going to help us much. Or *him* much, for that matter," he concluded, hiking his thumb in the direction of the now long-gone ambulance.

CHRISTOPHER KNIGHT

"Hell, why wait till tomorrow? I can run those for you in about an hour and drop'em off to you this evening."

The deputy snapped his head around.

"Hell, Sam . . . I forgot you do this kind of thing," he said, handing the bag to Sam. "That'd be great. But don't bother droppin' em off. I'll send somebody out to get'em, or I'll come out myself. Just don't spread it around that you're doin' it. I mean, the lab usually wants to do all the developing, but in cases like this, it's just as easy to have you do it. A lot faster too."

A Michigan state trooper popped his head out of one of the vehicles and turned toward the two men, waving at Deputy Kendall. Kendall walked over, chatted with the trooper for a moment, then returned.

"They lost'im on the way to the hospital," Kendall said somberly, shaking his head. "He lost too much blood."

"That's a damn shame," Sam said, and he meant it. There was too much bizarre shit happening in Mullett Lake. It drew too much negative attention and publicity. People were likely to think that the lake was jinxed and stay away . . . and that was *not* what Sam wanted.

The deputy spoke again.

"I gotta run. Hey . . . I appreciate you doin' this for us." He pointed to the clear plastic bag containing the camera that was now in Sam's hand.

"No problem," Sam said. "I'll have'em ready, say, eight o'clock."

"See ya then. Thanks again, Sam."

"Don't mention it." Sam walked back to his truck, gently swinging the plastic bag with one hand.

✻ ✻ ✻ ✻

The Cessna flew high above the shoreline of Mullett Lake. The small plane seated four people, and Brad sat in the passenger seat next to Cal, with Amy in the back seat behind Brad. It was early evening and from their vantage point in the sky they could see dozens of boats, water skiers, sailboarders and sailboats.

"There," Cal spoke up, pointing to a specific area below. "That's where I saw'im. Movin' so fast I only had time to get off one picture. I'm lucky I got *that*."

The water near the shore was clear and bright with a greenish cast, and Brad thought that if there was anything of that size—be it log or fish or whatever—it would certainly stand out. But farther from shore the water deepened, and the bright green faded into a rich, deep blue.

"How deep does this lake get?" Brad asked, raising his voice over the whine of the engine.

"One hundred twenty feet at its deepest," Cal answered. "There's a big hole over on the north shore that gets about that deep. But mostly, the lake averages about forty feet."

"What's going on out over there?" Amy chimed in. She had been watching a gathering of boats about a quarter mile from shore. Cal swung the plane around and circled the area.

"Well, somethin's up. That's the sheriff's boat, right there. Don't know who those other boats belong to, though. That's Aloha State Park right over there. Somethin' must be going on. Look at all the people gathered at the shore."

Five boats were anchored close together. On the shore, a long, sandy beach stretched around a small bay, and dozens of spectators had gathered to watch what was going on past the swim area.

From their vantage point in the sky it was easy to see the bottom of the lake, and the dark shapes of four or five scuba divers were visible beneath the surface of the water. Brad turned to Amy and mouthed the word *'ambulance'*, and Amy nodded her head in agreement.

"Looks like there's been another accident," Cal spoke loudly over the droning engine. He swooped the Cessna down lower but it was still impossible to make out what had happened or what the searchers were looking for. There didn't appear to be any other boats in the immediate area besides the Sheriff's Marine Unit and the rescue dive boats. Cal circled the area twice before continuing along around the rest of the lake.

The plane buzzed high over Mullett and Burt Lakes for nearly an hour before the three finally called it quits. There hadn't been anything to see besides the dozens of boats and swimmers taking advantage of the warm evening.

By the time they landed at Cal's field, the sun was going down. The blue sky faded to purple and orange as the sun set, and night's canopy was slowly creeping in overhead. The brightest stars began to twinkle in the eastern sky as it grew darker, and Brad and Amy thanked Cal and bid good bye.

"Sure thing, sure thing," Cal replied, waving to them from the porch of his house and pointing to the envelope in Brad's hand. He had loaned him the picture for Brad to send back to the lab in Lorain. "And if you need anything else, just holler." Brad thanked him again and climbed in the Jeep, and Cal watched as the Jeep backed out the driveway and disappeared down the dirt road.

✳ ✳ ✳ ✳

CHRISTOPHER KNIGHT

Frank Girard had a newspaper spread out over his kitchen table and he gazed at it intently, scouring the classifieds in section D of the *Lorain Gazette*. He was searching for a used washer and dryer, under two hundreds dollars if possible, but so far he wasn't having much luck. Girard certainly had more than enough money to purchase a new unit, but the thriftiness of his early, less financially-secure years had stayed with him through his career, plaguing him into his sixties. He had been a bit less frugal when his wife was alive, but now he was more content to get the best deal possible and keep his nest eggs growing in his retirement plans and 401k. In truth, Girard's worth was nearing a cool million. Frank had no idea what he would need it for: especially if he could still find used washers and dryers for less than two hundred bucks.

He was turning the page when the phone rang, and he let the page fall back to the table. He glanced at the clock as he reached for the phone. It was past nine . . . who could be calling at this hour?

He picked up the receiver on the third ring.

"Hello?"

"Frank." Brad didn't need to identify himself.

"Brad?" Girard responded, turning once again to look at the clock as if it was terribly out of the ordinary not only to receive a call at this hour, but a call from *Brad*.

"Yeah. I'm up in Michigan. A place called Mullett Lake."

He gave Girard a few details about the area and Frank expressed his satisfaction that Brad had indeed opted to get away for a while . . . and not just mope around his apartment in Lorain. Frank didn't know where Mullett Lake was, but Brad was in another state . . . and he sounded better. Still, there was a tone of apprehension in his voice that Frank picked up on. Brad explained the reason for his call before Frank asked.

"Frank," he began, "I know this is going to sound bizarre. Or worse. And I wouldn't be telling you this if I wasn't sure myself." He continued, explaining that he had seen what he believed to be a tiger muskie—a *large* tiger muskie—in Mullett Lake. Much larger than a muskie was expected to grow. However, he didn't mention just how long he'd estimated the fish to be. It was as if he were afraid, afraid that saying the words 'twelve feet' would somehow stir an uproar of laughter from the old supervisor. Finally, Frank just broke in and asked.

"Just how 'long' was this fish?" he asked.

Brad paused, letting Girard's words hang on the line through the miles of wires. Then:

"Twelve feet. Maybe thirteen. A girth as big around as a Volkswagon."

More silence. A *long* silence.

"You're not kidding," Frank replied, not asking a question. It was a statement. He was just re-affirming Brad vocally.

"I wish I was. But Frank, I've seen enough muskies to know. You *know* I have. What we saw was a muskie. All the colors, markings, everything . . . except–"

He explained about the dark marking on the head of the fish. "It was large. Diamond-shaped. Centered right between his eyes. Ever seen that before on a muskellunge?"

There was another long pause.

"No," Frank said finally. "No, I haven't. You sure it wasn't disease?"

"It may be, but I don't think so. It was *too* perfect. It looked more like a traditional marking, although again, I've never seen anything like that before."

The conversation ended with Frank promising to see if he could find out anything more. He hung up the phone and stared down at the paper.

Was it possible? Girard wondered. *A muskellunge twelve or thirteen feet in length?* Not now, he concluded. Not in this day and age. The way Brad had described Mullett Lake, the watershed would be too small to support any game fish of that size. Sturgeon could *possibly* grow to that length, but they were garbage feeders that didn't rely on other fish or living creatures to survive. Muskies, however, or any member of the *Esox* family of fish for that matter, were one-hundred percent pure predator. They were vicious, nasty, ornery and mean. They hunted aggressively and had an unquenchable appetite.

But they *don't* grow to twelve feet. A lake the size of Mullett couldn't support a fish of that size, even if they did. There wouldn't be enough food.

And besides, Frank told himself again as he folded up the paper and stuffed it under the counter. *Muskies don't get that big. Not anymore, anyway.*

Not anymore.

＊＊＊＊

A picture of weeds. A picture of weeds and mud. A blurry picture of some small fish. So far, there wasn't much to see in the photos, and that made Sam happy. Like Greg Kendall had speculated, the snorkeler was probably all by himself, skin diving without a dive flag outside the designated swimming area. *Hell, he was just asking to be hit by a boat,* Sam thought. And whoever hit him probably didn't even know. Probably didn't see him and sliced through his side like a knife through warm butter.

"It was too bad the guy didn't make it, though," Sam said aloud to no one. An injury didn't make the headlines like a death does. Sam could already see the headlines in the newspapers and hear the lead stories on the local radio station, and he didn't like it one bit.

"Whoops," he whispered. *"Spoke to soon."* Another photo was forming in the watery tray and Sam began to make out the shape of another snorkeler, cruising just above the weed bed on the bottom of the lake.

Son of a gun, he thought. There *were* two people. The picture was becoming clearer by the second, and Sam could make out blue trunks and yellow fins, as well as the bright neon green band of the mask strap.

Well if there were two of them, he thought, *Then what happened to this guy?*

In the next moment, he knew.

Another photo was developing, and the image of the snorkeler began to appear. But another image . . . a larger, longer image also appeared beneath the diver. At first it appeared to be nothing . . . a large strip of silt beneath the weeds, or maybe a submerged log from long ago. There were hundreds of such logs littered about the bottom of Mullett Lake, remnants of the logging days of years ago.

Sam watched, his eyes growing larger as the photo grew sharper.

"Ho-lee shit," he whispered incredulously. *"There's no way in hell. There is absolutely no way . . . ."*

He thought that the image must be some sort of trick with the camera lens, that maybe the fish was actually very close to the camera, making it appear much larger than the other objects in the background.

But the photo was unmistakable. Beneath the snorkeler

was a gargantuan . . . *thing* . . . a creature. Sam could make out its head, nearly three feet wide. The beast had the piercing, sinister eyes of an alligator. Above and between its eyes there was a large black diamond-shaped marking.

And the fish was *long*. It dwarfed the diver, and Sam wondered if the snorkeler had even seen it. He was probably swimming so close to the fish that he didn't notice it tucked within the thick weeds and leaves.

Holy shit, he thought. He stared at the photo for a long time, not believing what he was seeing. But it was right there in front of him, in the murky images from a point-and-shoot underwater camera.

Then: another thought.

This was going to mess everything up. He could kiss the centennial celebration good-bye. No one would want to set one foot even *near* the water with this thing hanging around. No doubt vacationers would cross Courville—and all the other communities on Mullett Lake—right off their list. They'd take their bags and their families and their dogs and their money and go somewhere else. There were plenty of other lakes . . . lakes without sea monsters . . . that would be safe. If people were forced to stay off the lake, they'd be forced to go elsewhere. No tourists, no vacationers, no centennial celebration, no—

—*No Cape Touraine*. He might as well kiss that job opportunity good-bye. If word got out that something like this was in the lake, the attendance at the Courville centennial would be *zero*. Oh sure, there might be a few that would show up for the festivities and the fireworks. But so much of the celebration centered around water. And that was why most people came to Mullett Lake. People weren't going to want to come to a lake that had some sea monster in it. And if no one showed up, that wasn't going to do much to display Sam's superior public relations skills to any visiting dignitaries from

Florida.

He continued staring at the photo. It was most likely . . . almost *certainly* . . . a muskellunge. The beast was the most menacing, most frightening thing he had ever seen. He didn't even think *he* would be able to go back in the water, and he'd been fishing here all summer and had even ventured out for a few swims. Never before had he heard or seen such a thing. Oh, he'd heard all the legends and the stories. Some Native Americans believed that thousands of years ago, muskies this size existed. But there was no concrete proof of that, and the biggest muskie on record was about six feet in length. Sam himself had caught a few muskies out of Mullett Lake. They were the nastiest, fiercest, ugly-tempered, bad-mannered fish he'd ever seen. A cross between a pit bull terrier and a rabid possum. When you got a muskie in the boat, the fish would often attack its captors. And when you've got a royally pissed off forty pound muskie bouncing around in your boat, you've got problems. Sam knew of more than a few fishermen that carried a big monkey wrench in their tackle box, and they used it to bash in the fish's head. Sometimes it would take three or four direct hits to finally subdue a muskie.

"Sorry fella," he said aloud to the photo. "No rain on *this* parade. Not this year." Sam finished developing the roll. He took the two photos—the one of the diver and the one of the diver and the fish—put them in an envelope, and slipped them right under his prized shot of Miss Busty Birmingham.

"You guys can enjoy each others' company," he said. He opened up the darkroom door, walked to the kitchen and dialed the phone.

"Yeah . . . this is Sam McAllister down in Courville. Is Greg around? Thanks." There was a pause for just a few seconds until Kendall answered his page.

"Hey Greg . . . Sam here. I'm fine, thanks. Look, I got

those photos developed . . . yeah, just like you thought. Some pictures of some weeds, some small fish. I don't know. You guys are more experienced with this crap than me. Maybe you can find something in'em that may give you some answers, but they just look like amateur photos by an amateur diver with an amateur camera . . . no, there's no pictures of any other snorkeler. It's probably like you said . . . he was by himself and got hit by a boat prop. Just wasn't his day. Hey . . . you and the kids gonna make it out here this weekend? We got lots of great stuff going on . . . ."

The two men chatted for a few more minutes. Finally, Sam bid good-bye and hung up the phone. He poured himself another vodka and sat on the couch to wait for the deputy to drop by to pick up the pictures.

SIX

The night was still and calm. And *hot* . . . just like it had been the day before, the day before that, and the day before that. Fred Deering had indeed sold enough fans to pay for his used four-wheel drive International Harvester, but tonight he was at a loss as to what the problem was. The vehicle made a loud clanking sound every time he started it. It was parked in front of the hardware store with the hood up and Deering's torso was arched over the engine as he carefully inspected the motor and its workings with a flashlight. His son Larry was at his side, peering into the engine. He had just returned from yet another fan scavenging adventure, and oh boy, what a day it had been. Twenty-seven broken fans . . . all purchased for less than fifty dollars. It was going to be a good week for the used fan business, but not so good in the automotive department. Especially when Fred Deering found out that his four wheel drive dream that he'd just purchased for fourteen hundred dollars (he was able to negotiate the hundred bucks by trading two used fans) was going to need a new engine.

A few other inhabitants of the adjacent cottages were out enjoying the warm evening, quietly laughing and talking, roasting hot dogs and marshmallows and doing the usual summer tourist activities, happy that the cool of the late evening had arrived, hoping that the overnight temperatures might drop just a bit more. Across Courville, the whirr of fans droned lightly from cabins and homes, and a few blocks away a dog barked continuously from somewhere unseen, its bored howls echoing between cottages and over the lake.

Brad and Amy returned from Cal Rollins' home and sat on the porch of Brad's cottage. Pepper lay at Amy's feet, tired from a hard day of chasing bugs and visiting the neighbors. The photo that Cal had loaned them lay on the table. Brad picked it up and held it closer to the outside porch light.

"That's our fish all right," he said. "Look here—" Amy slid her chair closer, and Brad continued. "Look at the tail. For one, sturgeons don't have tails like that. See this?" His finger touched the picture. "See how its tail is sort of shaped like a sideways dustpan? Sturgeons don't have tails like that. And here. The dorsal fin and the anal fin are set back toward the caudal fin. That's how—"

"What's a 'caudal' fin?" Amy interrupted.

"Tail fin. Both the dorsal and the anal fin are set very close to the caudal. That gives the fish tremendous power and speed in the water, and gives it that torpedo-like appearance. The only thing is—"

He stopped speaking, his eyes scanning the photo. "This picture still doesn't show it real well. I mean, even in this color picture the image is just a black shadow. We know it's a fish because we saw it. To a lot of people it wouldn't look any more like a fish than it would a sunken car. But after what we saw from the dock today I'm certain that this—" he tapped the picture with his finger "–is it. But I've never seen one with a black marking on its head like we saw at the dock. I was thinking that it was maybe just a growth or something, but it was too perfect. I'm sure it was part of the fish's markings."

"What did your supervisor think?" Amy asked.

"He wasn't sure. He was a bit skeptical, but he said he'd do some checking. Frank is a realist, but he didn't come right out and say that it was impossible. He said he'd give me a call tomorrow. Actually, he'll be calling *you*, being that I don't have a phone."

"We have to tell *someone*," Amy said in a voice just above a whisper. "I mean . . . I know what *I* saw. You do too. But at this point, who is going to believe us?"

She had called the State Police earlier, inquiring about the ambulance. It was just a hunch, but maybe . . . *maybe* there was some connection with what they saw in the lake earlier that day. But there wasn't. It had been an accident over by Aloha State Park. A snorkeler had been hit by a boat propeller, killing him. It was tragic, but that was bound to happen as more and more people were drawn to the lake. Especially during a summer like this, when the weather had been hot and humid.

"I never knew freshwater fish could grow to that size," Amy continued.

"They don't," Brad responded flatly. "They just *don't*. They *can't*. Sturgeon get big, and I've heard of some growing to ten or twelve feet. But they also live to be a couple hundred years old. Most sturgeon of that size have only been reported in the Great Lakes where they can live a relatively undisturbed life. Lakes like Burt and Mullet and Crooked are too small for fish to grow that size. This is some freak of nature or something. And that thing was pissed off, Amy. Did you see its eyes? Did you see the way it moved in the water? It has no fear. It *knows*. It knows that it's the most powerful thing in the lake. It *owns* the lake."

"What about this picture?" Amy offered. "Isn't that good enough to take to the police or somebody to make them believe us?"

"Unfortunately, no," Brad answered. "The picture makes sense to *us*. And it makes a great novelty photo in the papers. But as far as people believing that there's a giant muskie in Mullett Lake . . . well, I'm afraid that picture isn't going to go very far. With some imagination, it looks like a fish. But we know better because we saw it up close."

"What about those people in the last week that supposedly 'drowned'," Amy said, a hint of exasperation in her voice.

"There's no evidence to support anything different, Amy. At least, nothing that we've seen or heard."

"So what do you want to do? Just forget about it?"

"Of *course* not," Brad insisted. "But we have to be able to show some sort of evidence . . . *something* other than the word of two people and a blurry photograph from an airplane. I'd like to send this picture down to the lab to see what Frank thinks. But in the meantime, is there *anybody* that you can think of that may have seen this thing in the past? I mean . . . it couldn't just *appear* overnight. Have you ever heard of *anyone* seeing *anything* like this?"

Amy stared out over the lake, thinking.

"No," she said finally, shaking her head. "There have been some stories of big fish . . . and there *are* some big fish in this lake. But not like *this*. Not like this *at all*."

The two were silent for nearly a minute. Brad reached across the small table and grasped her hand gently.

"Well," he began quietly. "We can do one of two things. We can stay quiet, and see what happens. Or we can go to the paper. We can go to the paper and tell them what we saw."

"Why the paper?" Amy asked. "I mean . . . why not the

police or somebody?"

"Because we just saw the Loch Ness Monster in Mullett Lake. The police as well as the Michigan Department of Natural Resources will laugh their heads off. But the *papers* . . . the papers *love* shit like this. It *sells.* Regardless of whether it's true or not. And if it's in the paper, then radio and TV are likely to follow. Maybe . . . *just maybe* . . . some people will stay off the lake because of it. Of course, we risk getting laughed at by everyone. Me, I don't care. I'm a nobody marine biologist from another state. I'm anonymous. I can get back into my car and go back to Ohio and never be seen again. But *you* . . . you live here. You're the one that'll bear the brunt of any joking."

"I'm not sure I could handle a guilty conscience if we didn't try to do something about it and somebody was killed," Amy said somberly.

The sun had long ago slipped below the western tree line and the night was dark and quiet. Small lights reflected from homes on the other side of the lake, and a few yellow flickers from evening campfires danced playfully along the shores. Brad swatted a mosquito that had landed on his arm. The tiny blob exploded on his skin, creating a small splattering of blood mangled with tiny pieces of mosquito guts. He wiped it away with a napkin and reached for his ice water.

"Beer?" he asked her, after taking a long drink of water.

"No," Amy replied. "Thanks anyway."

Brad excused himself, entered the cabin and returned after a moment, carrying two beers. He opened one and set in on the table next to Amy.

"I know that you said '*no*'," he started, "But your eyes were saying '*yes.*'"

Amy turned and looked at him. He couldn't tell if she was offended or not. He had taken a chance; he really hadn't *meant*

CHRISTOPHER KNIGHT

anything by it. It was just a playful twist to lighten the mood. Amy smiled and picked up the beer.

"And what else do my eyes tell you?" she asked. The question caught Brad a bit off guard. There was an instant—only an *instant*—where he paused and raised his eyebrows.

"They tell me that I'm—"

He was interrupted by Pepper, who had been sleeping at Amy's feet. He raised his head and cocked it to the side, looking toward the lake. The dog began to growl and slowly got to his feet, standing in front of Amy. The hair on his back was raised, and he took a step forward, off the porch and into the grass.

"What is it, Pep?" Amy whispered. Pepper turned to look at her only for a moment and gave her an inquisitive *'I'm not sure what you said and why are you talking to a dog anyway'* look, then once again faced the dark lake. He stood rigid and frozen, growling, the hackles on his back raised in alarm. Both Brad and Amy searched the moonlit waters for a sign of movement on the surface, but there was nothing. Pepper stood fixed and focused for nearly a minute. Finally his hair fell flat on his back and he stopped growling, but he sat watching the lake until Brad and Amy both called it a night.

✱✱✱✱

Frank Girard awoke at four-thirty the following morning, and by five-thirty he decided that he probably wasn't going to get back to sleep. He dressed in the dark, opting for a simple pair of jeans and a T-shirt. After all, he was the lab director, and he had the luxury of dressing pretty much any way he wanted. His lab coat covered most of his clothing, anyway.

He spent a few moments organizing the counter, placing a stack of bills near the phone so he wouldn't forget to pay them, then he picked up his car keys and left for the lab.

McDonald's wasn't open yet and neither was Wendy's, so he stopped at a convenience store for a coffee and a bagel before continuing on to the university. His mind was continuously abuzz with what Brad had told him. If it had been anyone else, Girard would have told them to go fly a kite. But it was *Herrick*. Brad was no dummy, and he knew his fish. If he said he saw a muskie, regardless of the size, then there was a good chance that he had.

But a twelve-foot muskellunge?

It wasn't possible.

Or was it?

He'd had his suspicions even before he reached the lab. Oh, he was certain that he'd never seen a muskie the size that Brad had claimed to see. But something about the marking, something about the black diamond-shape on the fish's head that Brad had described. Frank *had* heard or read or seen something about that before . . . *but where?* What was it? He was sure he'd come across it somewhere. Frank could vaguely remember *something*. Something about some fish having some sort of marking like that. He just couldn't put his finger on it. If it would have been anyone else that had told him such a story, Frank probably would have just shrugged it off. *Somebody just had too much to drink,* he would have thought.

But again . . . it wasn't just anyone. It was Brad Herrick. Sure, Brad seemed to be having a tough time these past few months, but he wasn't one to stretch the truth like that. However unbelievable the story was, it was all the more believable simply because it had been Brad Herrick who had related it.

In twenty minutes he was on the campus at Lorain University. The back door of the lab was locked, and he pulled a jumbled wad of keys from his pocket and let himself in. Normally he would have arrived through the administration building but it too would be locked at this early hour, and he didn't have a key. He entered quietly, locking the door behind him.

The lab was dark except for a small flourescent lamp perched on a table on the far side of the large room. The shadows of dozens of tables and shelves lurched toward him as Frank wound through the maze and found his office . . . or what he called his 'office.' It was more of a cluttered cubicle than anything, a place where he threw unimportant papers to be looked at later. Most papers he never did inspect further, and the evidence was piling up against him. Literally. His desktop was completely covered by assorted papers, newsletters, journals and notes. Sooner or later (usually later) he would just start grabbing handfuls of papers and dropping them into the waste basket. This was a semi-annual event, and even Frank could never tell exactly when it was going to happen. Girard did know, however, that today was not the day. The pile would remain untouched.

He clicked on the small desk lamp and immediately strode to a large bookshelf adjacent to his cubicle. The shelf stretched the entire length of the wall, nearly fifty feet. He flipped four switches on the wall and the whole room was engulfed in bright white flourescent light. He held his finger out as he walked, pointing at books as he read their spines out loud.

"Nope . . . nope . . . not that one . . . nope . . . maybe that one." He pulled a book from the shelf and stuffed it under his arm, continuing his slow walk.

"Huh-uh . . . nope . . . that one . . . ." He pulled yet another book and the one that was right next to it. By the time he had reached the far wall he had an armload of books, and he carried them back to his desk, setting them on the floor.

He sat down, picking up the top book and plopping it open on a pile of papers. He flipped through the pages. Frank was looking for a study that he thought he had come across a few years ago. Actually a couple of studies. There was something about what Brad had said about the muskie that jolted Girard's memory, but he told himself that he wasn't sure exactly what it was.

In reality he knew—he just didn't want to believe it. There were theories—just *theories*—that supposed that millions of years ago, fish of enormous size reigned supreme in the Great Lakes. Actually, it would have been before the lakes were ever formed. It would have been at a time when the lakes were huge rivers, deep and long, winding from what now is New York, along the northern region of the United States and through what is now Lake Erie, through Detroit and up into what is now Lake Huron. It was only a *theory* . . . but the thought was entertained that fish from the ocean made their way up what is now the St. Lawrence seaway and up into the Laurentian Channel . . . a six-hundred foot deep river that was the beginning of Lake Huron. Somehow a few fish became trapped, or maybe even *preferred* their new surroundings, abandoning the saltwater of the ocean and adapting to freshwater. Most scientists and biologists dismissed these ideas as bunk.

But Frank remembered that something had been found earlier this century. Something that shed new light on the 'giant Great Lakes fish' theory. He just couldn't remember what it was. The only thing he *did* remember about it was that he himself had laughed and just thought that it was some kooky idea dreamed up by some college professor that had been into the happy weed.

Discovering nothing in the first book, he placed it on the floor on the other side of his chair and picked up another from the pile at his feet.

And kept looking.

* * * *

Two hours later the pile beside his chair had grown larger than the pile at his feet. He still had found nothing. He made sure that he flipped open each page individually, reading just a bit of each page and scanning the photos. The books were studies of Great Lakes and other freshwater fish, primarily the fish of the *Esox* family and related species. Most of the studies were case histories regarding the impact of one species against another, or how particular species fared in different aquatic environments. Some studies had been done on the cross-breeding of pike and muskies, which happened frequently in the wild. There were a number of studies done on the effects of PCB and other chemicals that had been found in fish in the past thirty years.

In the second to the last book, page one-hundred eighty-four, he found exactly what he was looking for.

* * * *

Brad slept until eight that morning and relaxed at the kitchen table for a while, sipping coffee. He picked up Cal's photo a half-dozen times, each time trying to make out something different, something that he hadn't seen before. He found nothing.

Pepper appeared in the yard, running down the sloping grass to the waters' edge, and Brad heard the padding of footsteps in the grass growing closer. Amy appeared at the door a moment later, wearing red sweatpants and a T-shirt, her hair tied back in a ponytail.

"Knock knock," she said, opening the door. "Phone call."

She handed Brad the portable phone and walked outside into the morning sun. Brad watched her as she made her way slowly over the dew-laden grass and down to the lake, taking in the clean air and freshness of the morning. He held the phone to his ear.

"Hello?"

"Brad. Girard here."

"Yeah, What's up? Find anything out?"

"Well, you're not going to believe it. In fact, I *myself* don't believe it. Are you absolutely *positive* that what you saw was a muskellunge?"

"Frank, I know what I saw. There's no other fish in the world that looks like that. What did you find out?"

"Did you ever hear of the *Nighthawk* expedition?"

"No, I can't say that I have."

"The *Nighthawk* was a ship that wrecked in Lake Huron," Girard continued. "I don't know the details, and that's not important. But apparently the wreck was found by some college research team. They found the vessel intact . . . but they also found something else. A fossil. I guess it was near the wreck or something. It was the fossilized remains of a jawbone

. . . a *huge* jawbone. There's a photo of it in one of the books I found today."

"Was it from a muskie?"

"It sure looks like it. But Brad . . . my God . . . it's five feet long. *The fish had to be nearly twenty-five feet in length.*"

Frank's words rung in Brad's head.

Twenty-five feet.

Twenty-five feet.

A twenty-five foot muskie? He thought. *There's no way.* Even *he* didn't believe that one.

But then again, both he and Amy had seen one that would go twelve feet. There was no way in hell a muskie could grow *that* big, either.

But one had.

"However," Frank went on, "it was a fossil. Millions of years old. There's no telling for sure what it is from. But it is believed to have been from *Esox Masquinous*, which was a prehistoric freshwater fish. The Smithsonian has an actual skull, but there's debate as to whether it was from freshwater or salt water. That particular bone was found near the mouth of the Hudson, so most tend to think it was from the ocean."

"Could it adapt?" Brad asked.

"Doubtful. I mean . . . it *could*, over thousands of years. But it's been extinct since long before humans arrived."

Brad thought about that. It seemed like every week some scientist somewhere was discovering a species that was thought to have been extinct. There were countless animals and reptiles and birds that had never been seen alive by man, hiding in the rain forests and jungles and deserts that were uninhabitable to humans. What was thought to have been extinct had just adapted to a way of life that kept it out of the way of humans.

Had it happened here? he thought. Could a muskie live, undetected, for years and years without being seen? That would depend on where it was hiding. Mullett Lake was out of the question. There was no way that the fish could go unnoticed in Mullett for very long.

But the Great Lakes . . . .

A nuclear submarine could remain undetected in any one of Michigan's five big lakes. A twelve-foot muskellunge, if it wanted, could remain completely out of site from birth until death, never being seen or noticed by humans.

Until now.

But how did it get in Mullett Lake?

"I'm going to FedEx a photocopy of this thing to you so you can see it for yourself," Girard continued. "But I'm sure you'll agree that it looks like the jawbone—and *teeth*—of a muskellunge."

"Why haven't we heard about this before? I mean . . . this fossil?"

"The area where it was found is part of what's called the Straits Area Underwater Preserve. Removing anything from a shipwreck is a felony . . . not only in the preserve, but from any shipwreck for that matter. Even though this wasn't actually *part* of the wreck, it was just a few feet away . . . which was close enough. The entire fossil . . . all three-hundred pounds of it . . . was raised to the surface secretly and taken to the University of Michigan by several students. Fearing legal problems, they kept the whole thing quiet for a while. I guess they even stashed it in some kids' dorm room for a while. Details of where it had actually come from weren't known until the following year. Even then I guess it pissed a few people off."

"So they couldn't really publicize it," Brad mused.

"Exactly. Oh, I've got it here in this research and studies book. But I doubt the story has ever really been made public."

"Did you find anything else?"

"I'm afraid that's it. So far. I'll keep looking. I have a friend at Berkley who knows a lot about this kind of stuff. I'll call him later this morning."

"Let me know if you dig up any more," Brad requested.

"Sure thing."

There was a click on the other end of the line and Girard was gone. Brad stood up and re-filled his cup of coffee and poured one for Amy as well. He carried both out the door and down the grass to the lake.

Amy was standing at the foot of the dock, watching Pepper as he ran back and forth along the edge of the lake, stopping every few feet to sniff some strange scent, then continuing on. Brad handed the cup to Amy.

"Thanks," she said, placing the cup to her lips.

"That was Frank Girard down at the lab." Brad told her what Frank had found out.

"So it's possible?"

"Well, let's just say we've found a few pieces of a puzzle. They may or may not fit. I don't know." He sipped his coffee and continued. "I mean . . . there has to be *some* explanation. What that explanation is, I just don't know. So far what Frank has found out is the only thing that would make any sense. Far-fetched, yes. Incredible, definitely. But there must be *some* reason."

Amy held her coffee cup with both hands and brought it up to her lips. Then she turned, looking out over the calm waters of Mullett Lake.

"So now what?" she asked, still facing the water.

"I'm going to go into the Department of Natural Resources field office today and talk to their director."

"What about the paper?"

"No. In hindsight, I think I'd feel better if we at least made more of an effort to do something about it. We can still go to the paper, sure. But that'll be a last resort. It would be much better if we had the backing of a state agency about this."

"They'll laugh their heads off."

"I'm afraid you're right. But I'm going to go in and talk to them anyway."

* * * *

To say Larry Richfield's position as regional director of the Michigan DNR was secure was an understatement. Larry had been with the department since 1965, and he wasn't going anywhere soon. He was fifty-five, tall, and fit. Short, quarter-inch gray hair stood stiff and on end like a scrub brush, receding only on the back of his head where a baseball-sized spot had been thinning for the past twenty years. Richfield was well-liked by those in the department, and had gained notoriety around the state years ago as 'Lock'em Up Larry,' a moniker derived from the fact that he had a knack for sniffing out poachers. In 1975, Governor Milliken had given him a special award of commendation for his work. A few years later he was promoted to the Cheboygan regional office as a supervisor, and earned the director's position a few years after that. He no longer worked in the field as much, but the job kept him busy. Especially on this particular morning.

Larry didn't know why the visitor needed to speak to him so urgently. The man didn't have an appointment, and besides . . . Richfield had to be in Gaylord in an hour. In fact, he should have been in Gaylord an hour ago but he'd had to call and say he was running late. Add to that an upset stomach that had kept him on the shitter half the night and into the morning, and you had the makings of a very ornery Larry Richfield.

The intercom buzzed again and his secretary's voice squawked through the tiny speaker box.

"He says it's very, very important, sir."

Disgusted, Richfield gave in.

"Fine, fine," he said as he pushed down the speaker button. "Send him in."

A moment later the door opened and a young man walked in. Larry figured he was twenty-nine, maybe thirty. Probably around his own sons' age. He had blond hair and wore blue jeans and an Eddie Baur khaki shirt.

"What's up?" Larry asked, trying to be polite. He stood as he spoke, indicating to the man that he did not have much time. The man held out his hand and Richfield took it.

"Brad Herrick," the man said.

"What can I do for you?" He offered no *'Hi, I'm Larry Richfield'* or anything else. A proper introduction would have taken too long.

Brad sensed the man's annoyance, and decided to get right to the point. He opened up the six inch by nine inch tan envelope and produced a photograph.

"It's about this, Mr. Richfield," reading the name on the director's badge. "This right *here*." He held out the photo and Larry took it, and Brad placed his index finger next to the shadow.

"Oh, yeah," Richfield chuckled. The 'giant sturgeon'.

Brad shook his head, took a breath, and spoke.

"Muskie."

Richfield's head remained cocked in the same direction as the photo, but he raised his eyes toward Brad.

"Right."

"I'm serious. Look." Brad pointed to the darker regions

and the outline of the shadow that he believed were the dorsal and caudal fins of the fish. His voice became more excited as he spoke, trying to hurry as he explained.

"We saw it in Courville. Yesterday, at the end of the dock by the cabins. Jim Hunter's resort. I'm staying there."

"And you saw a twelve-foot muskie." Larry spoke slowly and his voice was cynical, and Brad could tell that the director was quickly running out of patience.

"Give or take a foot, yeah."

Richfield handed the photo back to Brad, not hiding his disgust.

"Look, Mr. Herrick. I don't know what you want or what you're trying to pull. But if you think that there's a muskie that size living in Mullet Lake–"

"What about all the disappearances?" Brad interrupted.

"What about them?"

"This lake has had a number of people just 'disappear' in the past few weeks. How come they haven't been found?"

"They drowned, Mr. Herrick."

"But what if they didn't?"

Richfield was about at his breaking point.

"I can't believe I'm even standing here discussing this with some . . . *tourist* . . . or whatever the hell you are."

"I'm a marine biologist. I work for Frank Girard in the marine division at Lorain."

Brad didn't have to offer anything more. He didn't have to mention 'University' or even 'Ohio'. Richfield would be well aware of not only Lorain University, but Frank Girard as well. Brad didn't have to qualify himself any further, and he felt that the statement had earned him a bit of respect. Not much, but maybe a bit.

"And this," Brad continued, leaning forward and again pointing to the shadow with his index finger, "is a *muskellunge*.

CHRISTOPHER KNIGHT

I've seen too many to mistake it. I've dissected them, I've caught them fishing when I was a boy. This–" he tapped the photo as he spoke, *"–is a muskie.* Now I don't know how it got there, and I don't know why. But as long as this fish is in this lake, every person on or in the water is in danger. A muskie that size could easily swallow someone whole."

Richfield nodded his head down and looked again at the picture. He picked it up, bringing it closer, then handed it back to Herrick.

"Look, Mr. Herrick." His voice was a bit milder, but still a bit tense. "I agree that it might be *something.* A sturgeon . . . *possibly.* But a muskie . . . ." He shook his head as he spoke with a tone that carried a subtle hint of mockery, again handing the picture back to Brad. "I don't think so."

"So you're going to wait till something else happens before you do something about it?"

That was the last straw for the director.

"You know, I've got a lot going on today," he said angrily, raising his voice and glaring at Brad. "And I'm about to throw your goddamn ass right out of the building. Now, I've got shit to do. And that does *not* include even giving you the time of day if you're trying to give me some bullshit about a giant muskie in Mullett Lake. Go tell the *National Enquirer.*" He continued staring at Brad, and Brad knew that the director meant it. Without another word, he stuffed the photo back into the envelope and left.

✳ ✳ ✳ ✳

When he returned to the resort, Amy was busy cleaning cabins. She saw Brad's car arrive and she greeted him in the parking lot.

"Any luck?" she asked. Brad just shook his head.

"I'm afraid I struck out. I almost got tossed out of there." He slammed the car door closed. "You said you know where the newspaper office is?"

* * * *

"And that's pretty much it," Brad finished, glancing at Amy as she nodded her head in agreement.

The writer from the *Indian River Daily* looked up from his pad of paper. Brad and Amy had arrived unannounced at the paper's offices at noon, and the reporter couldn't believe the garbage they were feeding him. But it sure would make a great story. A great story indeed.

He hastily clicked off their picture, thanked them for coming in, then hurried them out the door so he could get back to more important things.

Monster muskies, he thought, as he watched the man and woman leave the small office and walk outside. *Now I've heard everything. It sure will make an interesting piece, though.* Maybe they'd be able to fit it in tomorrow's edition of the *Daily*.

* * * *

CHRISTOPHER KNIGHT

If Sam McAllister had been upset by the negative publicity so far, it was nothing like the jolt of lightning that was about to strike him square between the eyes.

The Wednesday morning paper was delivered promptly at 5:55 a.m., just like it always had been, give or take a few minutes. Sandy Whelan was the route driver; you could set a clock by her delivery if she hadn't been in a fight with her husband the night before. Both her and her husband were notorious dope smokers, and years of hemp abuse had made each other so paranoid that half the time they were afraid to leave the house. If you got within ten feet of Sandy's 1986 green Ford Bronco (her paper delivery vehicle) you couldn't help but catch the sweet, pungent odor of reefer licking at your nostrils. Sandy toked on a joint to help make her morning route a little more interesting. Those who had no clue what dope smelled like swore that her Ford was burning oil; those that knew just shook their heads and remembered their days in college.

Sam was awake and working on his second cup of coffee when he saw the Bronco round the corner, stopping to stuff the bright red boxes that sat next to various colored mailboxes along the road. He slipped his tennis shoes on and carried his cup of coffee with him during the grueling fifty-foot walk to the highway.

More of the same junk, he thought, scanning the front page as he tried to sip coffee, read, and walk at the same time. Coffee dribbled down his chin and he paid no mind to it, still going over the front page.

It was more of the same old stuff. Over in Onaway they'd finally broke up a bicycle theft ring. The Wilmont township supervisor was arrested for drunk driving, and down at the bottom of the page was a photo of some kid from Indian River who had won the Michigan spelling bee championship and was going on to the state finals. He had won by spelling the word 'impecunious'. Sam had no idea what the word meant, and he couldn't have given a rat's ass anyway.

At the table, he poured another cup of coffee and flipped the page.

Now that's more like it, he thought. Page two was devoted entirely to the Courville centennial. A complete list of events, times, shows, displays, contests and bake sales for charity was highlighted along with a half dozen black and white photos from last year's event showing smiling kids and parents, all having the time of their lives in Courville, Michigan.

Sam smiled, pleased at the media coverage. The entire page was picture perfect, one-hundred percent apple pie, car in every garage, turkey in every pot *American Dream*. Although it was a feature story, it was hands down nothing but one big full-page advertisement for the Courville centennial. He half thought about calling back the editor and apologizing for his rudeness on the phone a few days ago.

He didn't make the call, but maybe he should have. Because if he would have called the editor at that point, it might have kept Sam from turning the page. It might have kept him from seeing the large photo of the man and woman. And it might have kept him from reading the caption beneath it: a caption that set him off like a hand grenade. Large block letters beneath the photo read:

A MAN-EATING MUSKIE IN MULLETT LAKE?

Sam read the article, his face flushing red in fury. He was fuming. Two people had allegedly 'witnessed' a huge muskie—a muskie they claimed was twelve feet long or longer—pass by their dock. *In Courville.* Right in *Courville.* And what made Sam even hotter was that the girl in the photo was none other than that bitch from next door. Amy Hunter. The chick with the snoopy dog. She let it run around without a leash which was bad enough, not to mention the fact that McAllister *hated* dogs. Oh, he might have let her get away with it now and then if she'd be inclined to show a bit more skin when she laid out in the sun, but that never happened.

He continued reading, his mind filled with rage. At the bottom of the article was another photograph. It was the same photo that Sam had seen the other day in the paper. Cal Rollins had taken it, only the caption a few days ago had said it was a sturgeon. Now the picture had a crude, hand-drawn white circle drawn around the shadow. And below that, the caption read:

IS THIS THE KILLER MUSKIE?

The words *Killer Muskie* were almost more than he could bear. He swept his arm violently across the table, sending the coffee cup into the wall where it exploded into a dozen pieces. The ceramic tinkled to the floor and a dark coffee stain splattered the egg-white wall, dripping to the floor in rivers. He was enraged.

"Son of a BITCH!" he screamed. *"Son of a fucking bitch!"* He stared furiously at the photo in the paper. The story had no basis of fact . . . just the nonsensical ramblings of two people.

But there *was* a problem.

They were *right*. He had seen the fish himself. Sam knew damn well that such a fish existed. He and probably he alone had proof.

He got up from the table and opened the door to his darkroom, pulling open his desk drawer. Beneath a pile of papers the picture of Miss Busty Birmingham covered the white envelope that he'd stashed there the day before. He opened it up, half expecting the fish to be gone from the picture.

No such luck.

There it was, just as he'd remembered it. The same menacing eyes and huge body. The leering, arrogant demeanor and imperious, bold attitude. The fish indeed was King of the Lake . . . only it was supposed to be Sam's secret. It was supposed to be a secret until the centennial was over and Sam was already packing his bags for Florida.

But now someone else knew. He should have known that it would only be a matter of time. A fish that size couldn't stay hidden in an inland lake for very long.

So the situation presented a couple problems. On one hand, he had two loud mouths that may have seen *something* . . . whatever it was they saw. They had no concrete proof, they had no evidence, they had nothing.

But on the other hand—

On the other hand, *they knew*. Sam knew that *they* knew. He had a picture that could prove them right. As far as he knew, he had the *only* picture. But at this point, it didn't matter. The only thing that mattered is that people flocked to Courville for the big celebration. The only thing that mattered was that they brought their families, their dogs, their cars and their cameras . . . *and their wallets and their checkbooks and their credit cards.* Sam wanted a big show for the mayor and his assistants from Cape Touraine. He wanted them to see firsthand the huge number of people enjoying themselves, bringing their hard-earned money to spend in tiny Courville and Cheboygan and Somerville and Mullett Heights. So much depended on this weekend. *Everything* depended on this weekend, he told himself. Sam thought about going over to Amy Hunters' house right now and yanking her out of bed. That'd shake her up. But it would also piss off her uncle, and Sam got along okay with Jim

Hunter. Grabbing Jim's niece by the neck and strangling the hell out of her wouldn't solve much.

And the other idiot, Brad Herrick. Some biologist schmuck from Ohio. What the hell does he know about Michigan fish?

He had to think. What could he do? He couldn't just do *nothing*. The story was bound to cause a lot of stir. By noon today, every barber shop jury north of Gaylord would be in session, each filled with a dozen patrons that had seen the fish or at least caught it once in their lifetimes. It had broken their line and busted up their tackle, some would say. Pulitzer-prize winning stories would be created while a quarter-inch was trimmed off the sides and just a little off the top.

Sam thought about storming the offices of the paper, demanding equal time. He thought about calling the local radio stations and pretending he was this Brad Herrick character, and telling them that not only did he see a giant *muskie*, but there was a flying saucer hovering above it the whole time. And he would tell them that he *would've* got a picture, but Bigfoot stole his camera. They'd think he was a looney and never give him any more time of day.

No, that wouldn't work.

But diplomacy *would*. Good old-fashioned politics. It was the only way to get what you want. Sam knew that it would only be a matter of time before the paper called *him*.

✳ ✳ ✳ ✳

McAllister's phone rang just after nine a.m. The first call

was from Darrell Wieland, a friend and fishing buddy that lived over on Burt Lake. Had he seen the story? What did he think?

"I think it's a crock of shit, that's what I think," Sam told him.

The next call was from Mark Schaeffer, the guy in charge of vehicle parking during the centennial celebration, which was another problem altogether. With so many people showing up, parking the additional influx of vehicles was bound to be a problem. Mark said that he'd made an arrangement with old Melvin Deering, Fred Deering's father, who would allow parking in his field . . . at five dollars per car. And no profits to be shared by *anyone* . . . shrewd Melvin would get one-hundred percent of the cash. Mark wasn't in a position to bargain, so he accepted the offer. Then Mark made a crack to Sam about maybe charging to see the *'Man Eating Mullett Lake Killer Muskie'* . . . a comment that didn't sit very well with McAllister. But Sam didn't let it show. He laughed and joked, saying that during the centennial, there would be a special aquarium with the fish on display . . . and at the end of the weekend there would be a big fish fry.

The *next* phone call was from the paper. They were looking for comments about the story and how it would pertain to the weekend festivities.

"Well, myself . . . I'm just sorry it's a *rumor*," Sam chuckled. He told the reporter that the same story was around when he was just a boy, and that they used to call the fish 'Old Mullie'. It was just a legend, Sam explained, but next year he hoped to have a line of 'Old Mullie' shirts, hats, key chains and the like, all available for purchase during the annual Courville celebration. He told the reporter that it may even catch on, and you might find 'Old Mullie' wear all the way from Harbor Springs to Alpena. He was lying through his teeth, (Sam hadn't even *heard* of Mullett Lake until the past year) but sometimes playing the time-tested part of the devil's advocate could throw some extra weight into your own court.

"So . . . you don't think that there's a giant man-eating muskie in Mullett Lake?" the reporter asked.

"Well, let's just say I wish there was. It would bring some publicity to the lake, you know? Good for business. Attract sight-seers just like the Loch Ness Monster. Unfortunately, the big fish story is just that . . . a *story*."

The reporter asked a few more questions, most of them pertaining to the weekend festivities. It sounded like the reporter himself thought the idea of a giant muskie was bunk, and that fact alone pleased Sam very much. Maybe in tomorrow's paper there might be some sort of retraction. Doubtful, but maybe.

After a few minutes the conversation was over, and Sam hung up the phone.

****

Thursday's paper made no mention of the fish and only included a small section repeating the schedule of events for the Courville centennial, to which Sam was grateful. He would've liked to have seen more about the festivities that centered around the town, but the fact that there wasn't any more written about a giant muskie made him more than satisfied. By tonight, any hoopla about some over-sized fish in Mullett Lake would have died down. Although it was only Thursday, many vacationers would begin to arrive today, filling the local hotels and motels and summer cabins. Most resorts within a sixty-mile radius would be lighting up the *no vacancy* signs for the weekend. The Courville centennial was going to be a big deal: Sam had made sure of that. It was his baby. He had advertised on the radio downstate, which was where most of the tourists would be coming from. Both Detroit papers had write-ups, calling the Courville centennial celebration one that couldn't be missed.

By mid-afternoon the field across from the tiny village had already started filling with cars. Dust filled the sweltering air, and vehicles waited impatiently for the car ahead to move on, park, or just *do something*. There were a number of people that had even brought tents and campers. Courville might just turn into a mini-Woodstock, minus the free music, naked dancers, and plentiful dope. No bad brown acid in Courville.

The traffic continued to roll in throughout the day, clogging Old US-27 for nearly three miles in either direction. By dusk the area was teeming with activity. Kids with sparklers danced on the shores, adults sat in cheap lawn chairs sipping Margaritas, Mai-Tais, Pina Coladas, beers, iced teas and what not. Dozens of small crafts took advantage of the final moments of daylight, and Mullett Lake was dotted with canoes, small sailboats, and even a few kayaks. The sky was clear and beautiful and the air was hot and humid, just as forecast.

Sam nursed a beer, watching the goings-on from his waterfront lawn, the image of the terrible beast burnt into his brain. He told himself over and over again that he didn't see it, that it didn't exist, that it *couldn't* exist.

And yet, he *had* seen it. Not only had he seen it with his own eyes, but he had the picture. He found himself watching a particular boater or jet skier on the water, wondering to himself . . . *is he going to be next?* He half expected the creature to explode at any moment, its enormous body lurching out of the water, swallowing up some unsuspecting boater or swimmer without so much as a struggle. Then the cat would be out of the bag. The Courville centennial would be history. And that would mean that Sam had failed. It would mean that everyone would leave and head for Traverse City or Petoskey or somewhere . . . *anywhere* that they didn't stand a chance of being eaten alive by some monster that lived in the water. Which of course would mean that the entire centennial would be a flop, and that just might not reflect too well for his visiting guests.

Night fell, and Sam continued watching. He sat on his porch with the lights off, gazing over the darkening lake. Slowly and quietly, Mullett Lake went to sleep. The sounds of laughing children faded off, and the slightly intoxicated giggling and buzzing of adults began to fade. Soon, the night would be handed over to the crickets and the frogs and the nighthawks and the owls and the constant whirring of window fans.

Soon, it would be Friday.

In the morning, a limousine service from Cheboygan would head for the Pellston airport and bring Sam's guests of honor to Courville. It would be a guaranteed madhouse with cars, vans, trailers, trucks, and people milling about the small town. Children would be laughing and playing, adults would be smiling, the sun would be shining, and Sam would be schmoozing.

Only one day away.

✳ ✳ ✳ ✳

In the darkness of the depths, fury raged. The fish sped back and forth, up and down and across the four mile long lake. It was impossible to get away from the noise. Loud, irritating humming and buzzing filled the water, and the fish struggled to stay away from the many intruders that so often passed over him in the dim light of evening . . . some passing over within just a few feet. If it were daytime, the fish would have been spotted easily in some of the shallower regions of the lake. But the evening darkness added obscurity and shadows, and the fish could navigate its way around the lake without much of a chance of being spotted. But the *noise* . . . .

It would have been easy for the muskie to just destroy the trespassers. After all, the lake did belong to the fish. But there was that gnawing intuition . . . that *instinct* . . . that was stronger now than it ever had been, and the fish obeyed its intuition without question. It was a built in sensor, a built in early-warning system that told the fish to use caution, to be overly careful. Obeying such subconscious suspicions is what kept the muskie—indeed *all* fish, even animals—alive. It was when an animal acted against these intuitions that it found itself in trouble. And the muskie was far too smart for that. It was cautious tonight. Cautious, but arrogant and haughty nonetheless. It became frantic with anger, delirious with agitation. The fish sped at breakneck speed beneath the surface, unseen and unheard. It was careful not to make a wave, not to create a ripple, but the seething agitation only grew as the muskie felt more and more confined. The lake wasn't big enough; the fish needed more space, more area to roam, deeper depths to hide.

Finally, as it grew darker, the intrusive buzzing and annoying clamoring began to dwindle. The fish sought out the shelter of the deep, settling within a large thicket of underwater vegetation. Numerous logs scattered the bottom, adding to its cover. The fish was hungry, but it couldn't eat yet. It was not the time. The time would come soon enough.

CHRISTOPHER KNIGHT

SEVEN

Brad was awakened by a gentle knocking against the screen door. He had been sleeping soundly, and it took him a moment to realize where he was. It was morning, and the sun hadn't quite made it up over the trees. The room was bathed in a soft, misty pink, and the fresh scent of early dawn drifted through the room. The windows had been left open overnight, and the air that drifted through was fresh and cool.

The gentle tapping at the screen came again and Brad got up and opened the door.

Amy stood on the small porch in denim shorts and a white blouse, holding a Styrofoam tray containing scrambled eggs, bacon, hash browns, and two slices of toast.

"I didn't read about this in the brochure," Brad said groggily, but smiling nonetheless. "I feel like I'm getting the royal treatment."

"It was in fine print at the bottom of your receipt," Amy said with a playful grin. "It's an extra hundred dollars a day."

She placed the tray of food on the table and Brad found a pair of socks and stumbled into the kitchen. He ate hungrily while she started the coffee, then she sat at the table while Brad finished the meal. Already the adjacent cottages seemed alive with activity, their occupants getting a head start on the days' coming festivities.

"So . . . anything new in the paper?" he asked, putting his fork down and taking a sip of coffee.

"Not much. Nothing about any 'giant fish' if that's what you meant. Not even any 'letters to the editor', which kind of surprises me. I kinda figured that there'd at least be a *few* people who would get their jollies by ridiculing us in some way. So far there hasn't been anything. But I *was* able to find *this*."

She produced a good-sized book that Brad hadn't seen her lean against the old wicker chair. The book was old, and the cover was dirtied and yellowed from age. She handed it to him and he read the cover aloud.

"*Michigan Gamefish.* Hmmph. Where'd you find this?"

"It's my uncle's. He's had it for years. However, he doesn't believe our muskie story."

Brad looked up from the book and didn't say anything.

"We were talking about it last night," she continued. "He saw our picture in the paper. Jim said muskies get big, but not *that* big. He said that there was one a long time ago that was caught right out front here, right off the dock. It was six feet long. When they filleted it, they found a dog collar in its stomach."

"That's a pleasant thought for pet lovers," Brad said.

"Anyway, look at the picture on page forty-seven."

Brad turned to the page and lay the book on the table, shaking his head side to side as he stared down at the old black and white photograph in the book.

"*That's it,*" he whispered. "*Son of a gun . . . that's it.*"

CHRISTOPHER KNIGHT

The muskie in the picture was identical to the hundreds of other muskies that he'd seen—except for one minor detail. The muskie in the photo had the distinct marking of a dark diamond on its head . . . identical to the marking on the fish they'd seen. It looked very similar to the fish they saw the day before yesterday, except, of course, the muskie in the picture was only about four feet long, a size that wasn't at all out of the ordinary. It was photographed in shallow water, cruising near the surface. The fish appeared to be eyeing the photographer, as if taunting him. It displayed a confident arrogance, a boiling anger within its eyes . . . the same as the fish that they'd seen.

"But," Amy offered, "it says that the typical muskie grows to about four or five feet in length, max."

"Well, we have a very non-typical muskie," Brad said, his eyes not leaving the photograph. "And it's funny–" he turned the page and then flipped it back. "They make no mention of this marking on its head. I mean . . . that's not normal. But the fact that there's another photo of a fish with that same marking proves we're not crazy. And it also lends credibility to what Frank found, regardless of how impossible it seems."

He finished his breakfast, pushing the plate aside and re-positioning his coffee in front of him. "I mean . . . a muskie that size is just too much for people to believe. But they'll believe it, soon enough, if we're right, and I *know* we are. The question is, how soon? You said there was no way for the fish to leave the lake?"

"Well, it can travel anywhere in the chain of lakes. Burt, Mullett, Crooked Lakes. But it can't go out to Huron without going through the locks. In the spring there's a stream—actually, it's more like a river—that flows straight into Lake Huron. But the river is only filled with water during the spring run-off. You know . . . when the snow and ice melts. Then it's actually pretty deep. This year it was even deeper because of all the snow we had. Plus it got real warm real quick, so all the snow melted pretty fast. The stream has been dry since May, so the fish can't go anywhere besides the three lakes and the connecting rivers."

Brad leaned back in his chair and thought a minute, then spoke. "Which is going to make it difficult to stay hidden for much longer."

"What do you mean?" Amy replied.

"Well, the fish can't really *go* anywhere. I mean . . . it can go to other lakes and along through the rivers, but for all practical purposes, the fish is stuck here, just like you said. I find it hard to believe that a freshwater fish of that size can go much longer without being noticed by someone else besides us. I'm sure there'll be others that have run-ins with that thing real quick. The *real* question is where did it come from? *Huron?* There's no way a fish that size actually grew up in *these* inland lakes. I mean . . . it's just too big. Someone else would have had to have seen it by now."

"Maybe someone has," Amy mused. *"Maybe they're just not alive to tell about it."*

"Hold on a minute," Brad said, turning to face Amy. "Where is this spring creek you mentioned?"

"Just north of here about a half mile," she answered, pointing. "There's a bridge that you pass over on the way to Cheboygan. That's where it is. Of course, there's nothing there now. It's all dried up."

"But how deep does it get in the spring? Does it flow all the way to Lake Huron?"

"I'm sure it gets deep. Ten or twelve feet at least. And yes, it drains into Huron."

"That has to be it!" Brad exclaimed. "It *has* to be. I'll bet the fish came up the stream during the spring when the stream was high. Now the stream is gone and the fish is trapped in

Mullett Lake."

"As well as Burt and Crooked, don't forget."

"Are there any other streams that flow out from any of those lakes?" Brad asked.

"No," Amy answered. "Just small creeks that wouldn't be more than a foot deep at the most. The only way back to the Great Lakes is through the lock. At least until the spring, anyway."

Brad turned his head and looked toward the lake as he finished the last bit of toast, and Amy turned and followed his gaze. The tiny village of Courville was beginning to awaken. A few children waded in the shallows of Mullett Lake under the watchful eyes of their parents. Two men were busy at the end of a dock, working to repair a broken outboard motor. A boat, way out on the lake, pulled a skier across the smooth, glassy surface.

Neither Brad nor Amy said anything for a long time. They just watched impatiently, waiting for who knows what. It was Friday, and the Courville centennial celebration was about to begin.

✳ ✳ ✳ ✳

The cars on Old US-27 moved at a snails' pace. Or slower. People took their time wandering from the huge parking lot across to the lake side, and dozens of people were still busy putting up tents and booths. In the middle of the field, a stage was being built to host entertainers throughout the weekend.

A long white limousine slowly inched its way through the

crowd, finally pulling into the small parking lot in front of the Courville Chamber of Commerce building. Sam had been watching the big stretch Lincoln approach and he opened the office door and stepped outside to greet his visitors.

The long white vehicle stopped, and the limo driver swiftly hopped out and opened the door. A well-built man in a dark gray sport coat was the first to emerge. He had a striking appearance, with a head of tightly-cropped shiny black hair, a thick mustache, and a chiseled, masculine jaw. He moved with ease and confidence, and Sam remembered that when he had first met Jack Ferguson in Cape Touraine, he was certain that the man was some movie star. Now, he looked exactly like Sam remembered, only much more tired. Pink bags hung wearily beneath his eyes, and as he stepped from the limo he flipped open a pair of sunglasses and raised them to his face. A few passers-by stopped and looked at the man as if they were sure they recognized him from some movie or soap opera or TV show. The limo itself was enough to attract attention; it was not often that a beautiful white stretch Lincoln paid a visit to Courville. Sam strode up to the gleaming car.

"Mayor Ferguson! How are you?" He extended his hand in greeting and the mayor returned the gesture.

"Fine Sam," the mayor said smiling, shaking Sam's hand. His teeth were perfect, polished white. "Just fine. Looks like you've got a great weekend here."

"Just for our guests of honor," Sam boasted, releasing the mayor's hand.

Next out of the car was a woman—a *young* woman, at that—very lavishly dressed and decorated with jewelry. Sam guessed she was probably twenty-five. She wore diamond earrings, a diamond tennis bracelet, and a stunning diamond necklace that held a diamond so large Sam was certain that the sheer weight of it would cause the woman to stoop as she stood up. Her hair was long and blonde and she wore a low-cut blue dress . . . perhaps a bit too low-cut for conservative Courville. Like Ferguson, the woman also moved with an arrogant assurance as if she and she alone hung the moon as well as the stars, and had not a care in the world. She, too, appeared tired, but was able to hide her weary appearance behind a mask of powder and cover up. The mayor introduced her to Sam.

"This is my assistant, Miss Susan Corbin."

Sam smiled warmly and nodded.

"The pleasure is most certainly all mine, Miss Corbin," he said respectfully, bowing slightly as he spoke. Sam cautiously peered into the limo, expecting three or more people to emerge. None did.

The limo was empty.

He turned and addressed Ferguson, trying to hide his confusion. Sam had expected more than just the two to arrive.

"I trust your flight was good?" he asked. It was one of those mean-nothing questions, nothing more than a conversation starter. Sam could have just as well asked him how the weather was inside the limo.

"Yes, the flight was fine. A bit early, but good." The mayor turned his head, surveying the swarm of people that crowded the field and the waterfront. Again, Sam was struck by how fluidly Ferguson moved, how utterly in control he seemed. The mayor continued to watch the swarms of people.

"My, you certainly have brought a number of people to your event," he said, turning back and giving Sam a polite smile.

Sam, sensing the opportunity, smiled himself and spoke.

"Yes indeed. I tried a number of new positioning plans this year. Mostly in the field of relations. I believe it's good to maintain a functional working relationship with those of like interests around the country. I think a good media plan and some excellent exposure regionally has really helped out this year. You'll see people from all over the United States this weekend. Primarily most will be from Michigan, but this centennial has really attracted some terrific attention."

"It seems so," the mayor said, turning to look around.

"But you must be tired," Sam interjected. "Why don't I show you to your resort and let you freshen up a bit. Things are just getting started . . . we'll have lunch, and I'll give you a short tour of the area."

Ferguson smiled and Sam picked up on something that he cursed himself for not picking up quicker. He turned and addressed the driver who was standing expertly by the door of the limo.

"Scott," he said quietly, reaching into his pocket as he approached the driver. "Mr. Ferguson and Miss Corbin have accommodations at the Windward Resort. I'd like you to please see our guests to their rooms. We'll be dining at the Windward as well. I'd like you to come back and pick me up and take me there at noon."

"Yes sir," the driver said, nodding respectfully. Sam turned and smiled at Ferguson and the young woman.

"I'm certain you'll be comfortable at the Windward. It's right on the lake and they have a dining facility on the premises that is second to none. I will meet you in the lobby at twelve thirty."

"Splendid," the mayor said, nodding his head. "Looking forward to it."

The limo drove off slowly through the thickening crowd of people and Sam stood in the parking lot, waving as the vehicle pulled away, still a bit confused. He was *sure* that there would have been more than just two from Cape Touraine. He'd expected at least three, if not four or five. And the assistant accompanying the mayor was a different assistant than the one he'd had when Sam had visited Florida. Sam had *planned* to escort them to the Windward himself, but being there was just the two of them, he changed his mind. For their own sake of privacy, Sam thought it best to just stay away from their rooms. He'd booked five suites; he'd call later in the afternoon and cancel four.

✷ ✷ ✷ ✷

By mid-afternoon the tiny village of Courville had been transformed into a bustling metropolis. Cars lined Old US-27 for nearly a mile on both sides in both directions, and the large field that opened up on the other side of the highway was already filled with vehicles and campers. Frustrated motorists who were just passing through found that it took over a half an hour to go just two miles, as the highway was clogged with children and toddlers, parents and grandparents, all crossing the road to go to the lake side.

Nearly a hundred arts and crafts booths had been set up along the highway, displaying everything from paintings to hand-made organic clothing to hats made from beer cans. Another row of booths offered hot dogs, caramel apples, pop, nachos, and other assorted foods that typically contained the USRDA of fat and cholesterol, with some left over to spare. It was a carnival-like atmosphere, minus, of course, the large rides and colorful midways. The weather was perfect; the afternoon temperature remained steady at a pleasant eighty-two degrees—nearly ten degrees cooler than expected—and welcome just the same. Even so, Fred Deering at *Courville Hardware and Small Engine Repair* had sold every last one of his fans and had sent his son to scour the north in search of more broken ones.

Brad walked leisurely among the crowd, taking his time, watching the growing number of people filter through the village. They were literally everywhere. Hundreds lined the shore from the roadside park to the main dock, which itself was filled with people milling about and boats moored along its sides. The lake was teeming with water craft as well; some anchored just off shore, others tied together in groups of five or six or more. Brad raised his sunglasses to his forehead and watched the waters anxiously. He was apprehensive; maybe even a bit agitated. Yet so far, everything seemed to be going well. Better than well. *Perfect.* He began to think that what he'd seen was just his imagination, that there hadn't been a fish after all, that it was just something he'd dreamed up.

But Amy had been there. She had seen it, too. The fish was real, all right. It was real and it was alive, somewhere in the lake.

Somewhere.

And that was another thing. It could be in Burt Lake now for all Brad new. Or Crooked Lake. There were more people in danger besides the people here in Courville.

His eyes continued scanning the water.

If there is *any danger,* he thought. Once again he began to think that the whole notion of some giant man-eating muskie was silly, if not preposterous. After all, he wasn't *positive* if it was responsible for killing or harming anyone. That was just a guess, and it was a very speculative guess at that. But something told him that this was not the case. Not with *this* fish. There was something he had seen in those eyes, something in the way the fish moved that had removed any doubt that this beast was the most heinous creature he had ever seen.

He walked along the lake shore and onto the dock. Across

the lake, a group of sailboarders, nearly thirty in all, were beginning the return trip back to Courville.

✳ ✳ ✳ ✳

The fish wasn't sure what the sound was at first. It came from the surface, but it wasn't at all like the ceaseless buzzing it had become so annoyed with. This was more like a hiss, a continuous swishing that drew the fish nearer. It had been lying in deep water, tucked inconspicuously away in the safety of the depths. The night had been quiet, and except for a few of the noisy buzzings from the surface, the fish had remained undisturbed.

But now, its curiosity had risen. The fish was hungry. It cruised quickly toward the surface, eyes shifting back and forth, watching for movement.

As it drew nearer to the sound, dozens of shadows began to appear. All were moving in the same direction, and the fish advanced closer, pacing twenty feet beneath the group. The forms on the surface weren't moving very fast, and the muskie exhorted little effort to keep up.

It rose to within just a few feet of one of the shadows, cautious and alert, watching the board bounce across the surface. The giant fish couldn't make out exactly what it was, and the confusion brought anger. It backed off to a safer depth, following the group of shadows as they skimmed their way across the lake.

* * * *

"Gotcha."

Brad jumped, startled by the gentle poking at his ribs. He was still on the dock, lost in thought, gazing out over the lake. Amy had snuck up behind him and surprised him. She laughed, and Brad snickered a bit, finding only a little humor in the playful gesture.

"Don't worry," he smiled. "I'll get you back. When you *least* expect it."

"You *wish*," she smirked. "Here. Thought you could use one of these." She handed him a red plastic cup, the same ones being sold with pop in them at one of the booths. "Strawberry Daiquiri," she said, sipping from her straw.

"The Boy Scouts are selling *these?*" Brad asked, smiling. The local Boy Scout troop was offering cups of pop for one dollar to earn money for a field trip.

"Well, not exactly," Amy explained. "I made these up in my cabin. I did give them a buck apiece for the cups, though." She paused, sipping the drink. "I didn't want to use any of my glasses. It's better to look inconspicuous. The village has an ordinance about open beverages on public property. Nobody really obeys it, but it's better not to advertise, if you know what I mean."

"Thanks," he replied as he took a sip. Their eyes met a moment before Amy looked away, staring out over the water.

Dozens of people filled the swimming area. Kids with bright orange water-wings looped around their arms, adults standing knee-deep in the water, holding red plastic cups and chatting and laughing with other adults. Brad wondered if they had done the ol' *presto-chango* routine with their beverages as well. Other people splashed about in the water, some diving from docks, others playing frisbee or volleyball. Pepper, tail wagging like a fan, was having the time of his life. He frolicked in the water and went from person to person on the shore, hungrily accepting any and every handout that was offered.

"Looks like your dog is going to be doing some recycling today," Brad pointed out. Amy just shook her head.

"Goofy thing," she said. "You'd think he'd figure it out by now. I think he's going to—"

She stopped in mid-sentence. Pepper was on the shore chewing a discarded hot dog when he suddenly stopped, snapping around to face the lake. His head was cocked to one side as he focused intently out over the water.

"Brad," Amy whispered, pointing at the dog. *"Look."*

Brad turned.

Pepper stood rigid and firm on the shore, the hackles on his back raised in attention. His head snapped in jerky movements as he frantically looked out over the water. A couple of adults that were near him had stopped talking and they watched the dog in amusement.

Farther out into the lake, the sailboarders were completing their trek back from Aloha State Park. Pepper spotted them, watching the group intently. A low rumble began in his throat, but his mouth remained closed.

The sailboarders drew closer. The pack was pretty broken up by now, and the first ones to arrive were just getting into the shallows, expertly leaping off their boards and letting their sails fall into the water. A few had already started dragging their boards to shore. Pepper remained attentive and focused, watching the sailboarders one by one. Brad and Amy watched

CHRISTOPHER KNIGHT

restlessly from the dock, glancing at the dog and then back again to the sailboarders. The final two were almost to the swim area.

Brad looked back at Pepper. The dog was still taught and agitated, growling from the shore. Brad heard a splash come from beyond the swimming area and then heard Amy gasp.

One of the sailboarders had fallen.

That was far too much for Pepper to take. He let it all out, growling and barking and snapping furiously. People that were nearby became alarmed and stepped back from the animal. Parents grabbed their children and pulled them back away from the dog. Pepper began running back and forth in short spurts along the shoreline, still barking and snarling.

"My God . . . she can't get back on her board," Amy whispered.

A girl of about fourteen struggled to climb back on top of the sailboard, but she was too tired from the long ride across the lake and back. She gave up, found that she could touch the bottom with her tiptoes if she bounced a bit, and began the very slow process of dragging the entire sailboard in to the swim area.

Pepper had seen enough. He plunged into the water and began swimming toward her.

"Hey look everybody!" someone yelled. *"The dog's gonna save her!"* The girl was in no danger of drowning, and the crowd of people, unaware of any real threat, watched in amusement as the retriever swam toward the girl.

＊ ＊ ＊ ＊

The fish followed the cluster of dark silhouettes as they approached shallower water. They had moved rather slowly over the lake, and the muskie trailed beneath and behind, mindful of any other approaching intruders. Hunger burned, but the fish was tense and agitated. There was too much commotion, too much activity. In the shallow water there was too much of a chance of being seen. As it drew nearer to shore, the sounds grew louder, and the muskie's fury grew . . . but so did its sense of danger. The sensation gnawed and chewed at the fish, much like the appetite that flared from within. But there was too *much* noise . . . too *much* movement.

The huge fish turned around to head back into the depths, still hungry, its temper raging–

–*when it heard the splash.*

The muskie snapped back around and stopped, hanging motionless in mid-depth. Thirty feet away, a blurry shape had entered the water.

The enormous fish approached, slowly, very slowly, inching along, cautiously sinking deeper to slink along the sandy bottom. The presence of danger screamed at the fish but this time the warning was blindly ignored. The fish was hungry.

And *angry*.

The splashing sound drew closer. The fish had seen this kind of creature before, on more than one occasion. Four small legs pumped furiously on the surface above. There were other splashes and noises coming from all directions. The muskie could see many other creatures in the water, flailing about above and around. It was maddening. There was too much noise, too much disturbance, *too much*–

Suddenly the fish tore around and shot back, frustrated and furious, toward the comfort and safety of deeper water.

CHRISTOPHER KNIGHT

✳ ✳ ✳ ✳

Brad had already jumped into the water and began to wade toward the girl. Crowds of children still splashed playfully, with only a few people on shore watching Pepper as he paddled around the sailboarder. By now the girl had reached the swimming area, and the water only came up to her waist. One hand pulled the sailboard and its colorful sail along, the other hand extended out to pet the dog that swam at her side, escorting her back to shore.

Brad stopped. His actions had gone unnoticed, which was fine with him. Apparently nobody had paid any attention to him as he made his way toward the girl.

He looked into the water, straining through the churning debris to see anything. The water had become cloudier with so many people swimming, and it was difficult to see the bottom. He continued searching the waters but found nothing. Not that he was *hoping* to find anything. Coming across the fish while standing waste deep in the water was the last thing he wanted to do.

Finally, the girl reached the shore safely and Brad turned around, plodding through the water to where Amy stood waiting for him at the dock. Pepper bounded proudly up to them with the half-eaten hot dog in his mouth, wagging his tail as if nothing had happened.

"Nothing?" Amy asked.

"I couldn't tell. But *something* spooked him. *Something* made him act that way. Whatever it was, he seems fine now."

The dog laid down in the sand to finish his meal, seemingly

unaware of the bustle of activity around him.

"Well, maybe it was a false alarm," Brad continued. "But I sure will be glad when this weekend is over."

"You and me both," Amy responded, sipping her daiquiri. "I mean . . . normally, it's kind of fun . . . but this is just way too many people for this town. And under the circumstances—" she nodded toward the lake, "—under these circumstances, I'd just as soon see this weekend over. Come on . . . I'll buy you another cocktail, courtesy of the Scouts."

❋ ❋ ❋ ❋

The Windward Resort featured outside dining overlooking the water, and the three—Sam, the mayor, and Susan Corbin—were seated on the deck with a spectacular view of Mullett Lake as their focal point. Ferguson had met Sam in the lobby of the Windward and Susan had joined them a few minutes after the men had taken their seats. She wore a thin green cotton jumpsuit that highlighted every curve of her body, and Sam couldn't help but notice the two tiny bulges of her nipples through the fine fabric. Obviously, the relationship between the mayor and Susan Corbin was as he had suspected. There was too much of a discernable closeness, too much taut sexual energy between the two. Not that Sam cared; he didn't pay any mind either way. If Ferguson was sleeping with his 'assistant' or whoever she was, it was none of his business. He was certain that if he did get hired and relocate to Cape Touraine, he would probably never see the well-endowed Susan

Corbin again. Jack Ferguson was a man who got what he wanted when he wanted it; when he was tired of her, he would move on to more tantalizing exploits.

"So, Mr. McAllister," Jack began as he poured another glass of wine for himself and his escort. "What do you think you would like most about Cape Touraine, should the position be offered to you? What immediate needs do you see for our community?"

Sam thought about it for a moment, chewing his steak.

"I think," he said after a moment of stern contemplation. "I think that most of all I would like the challenge." As he spoke the word *challenge,* he looked Ferguson straight in the eyes and smiled. A warm breeze ruffled his graying hair. "I'm a promoter . . . and a good one at that, if you've checked my references." Ferguson nodded, but Sam knew that he hadn't even so much as picked up the phone.

He continued, smiling. "Cape Touraine would be more than just an interesting undertaking. The community has certain . . . *special* needs, if I may describe the situation in that manner. Cape Touraine isn't a Courville by a long shot. It is much more delicate. Much more refined. Therefore, I see a different approach than just a 'community friendly' tourism director. Tourism is not what Cape Touraine really needs, if my initial feelings are correct. Cape Touraine needs a *planner.* Someone that can assist in bringing in . . . *qualified* residents. Or potential residents, if that's how it should be perceived. I believe that once the proper individuals are found, they must already be considered residents, and treated accordingly. They need to feel at home, whatever the expense. Cape Touraine needs to be a safe haven, a place of rest and relaxation. A place to get away from *everything.* That is a desire that needs to be created. It's the link that Cape Touraine is lacking. Cape

Touraine, if I may be so bold, seems to have become a haven for snobby rich kids with their daddy's money. That's all fine and dandy, but those kids do one thing: *blow* their daddy's money. That's not what Cape Touraine is about. For growth and longevity, Cape Touraine needs more than just fluctuating dollars tossed into the wind by mindless spendthrifts. Cape Touraine deserves better."

He let his words hang in the air and waited for a response from Ferguson. It had been the longest, brassiest, most direct diatribe that Sam had spoken to the mayor, and he hoped it had worked. He had been trying to key in on Ferguson since he met him a few months previous, trying to figure out his hot buttons, figure out what he wanted to hear. Sam thought that a no-nonsense, cards-on-the-table approach was going to work. He *hoped* it would anyway.

A smile came to the mayor as smoothly as a passing cloud. It was a slow smile, one that began at the corner of his lips and slowly stretched wider and then wider still. Sam knew that he had guessed right.

"I like that," Ferguson began. "That's new thinking. We don't want tourists. And you're correct. Cape Touraine needs a bit of plastic surgery. Not a complete face lift, but maybe a few nips and tucks here and there. And I like what you've done with your little 'centennial' you've got here . . . it fits the small town etiquette nicely. But I don't think it would fly in a place such as Cape Touraine."

"The thought wouldn't be entertained," Sam said, shaking his head. "The situation is of entirely different necessity." Sam surprised even himself at how well he was handling the situation. The mayor genuinely liked him, and he knew it.

"You do understand that the position requires a certain . . . *'flair'* if you would. There are certain expectations that are required of this position. Would you be willing to accept those responsibilities?"

Before Sam had a chance to answer a man approached the table. Sam stood up instantly, extending his hand.

"Jonathan!" he exclaimed. "How are you?"

The young man, outfitted in a traditional black suit and tie, warmly accepted Sam's hand.

"I am well, Mr. McAllister, thank you," he replied. "And I do apologize for disturbing you, but Senator Elgin is on the phone." The man produced a small black portable phone and Sam took it.

"Thanks John," he said. Then, turning to Jack and Susan: "Excuse me a moment." He stepped away from the table and spoke into the phone.

It was nothing but a farce. Jonathan was the concierge at the Windward, and Sam had never met him before. He had phoned ahead and spoke with him, meeting him in the lobby before Ferguson arrived. Sam handed the concierge a sizable amount of cash from his wallet, asking him to interrupt lunch with an important phone call from Senator Elgin. There would be no one on the other end of the phone, let alone a United States Senator. True, Senator Elgin was expected for the opening ceremonies of the Courville centennial, but how Sam had managed that was yet another ploy altogether.

"Yes, Senator?" McAllister spoke into the phone. There was a long pause. "That's wonderful. Thank you, Senator. Glad I could help. I'll see you this evening." Sam raised his hand slightly, signaling for the concierge to retrieve the telephone.

"Sorry about that," Sam said, smiling as his eyes flickered between his two guests.

"Not at all, not at all," the mayor replied, waving it off with his hand. "This is a busy weekend."

"Yes it is. But not so busy that we can't take a short tour of this beautiful area. I'll have Scott bring the car up."

McAllister excused himself to find the driver, walking confidently across the dock and inside the Windward to the main lodge.

This is as good as done, he congratulated himself as he strolled across the main lobby and out the big, hand-carved wood doors.

The limousine driver was waiting in the parking lot, standing next to the large white stretch. Sam whistled and caught his attention, signaling the driver to ready the car. He retrieved his 35-millimeter Nikon and returned through the huge wooden doors of the resort. Sam strode through the lobby, but, before he walked back onto the outside dining deck, he caught a glimpse of Ferguson and the young woman through a large window.

Susan Corbin had been silent during lunch, and maybe a tad bit too professional and formal, despite her rather seductive attire. Sam had begun to think that maybe he was wrong, maybe Susan *was* Ferguson's assistant, nothing more. Now as he peered unnoticed through the window, he mentally congratulated himself for being correct on his first assumption.

Susan was leaning close to Ferguson, one finger on his chin. Her other hand was buried in his lap. She gave him a quick kiss on the cheek and said something to him, which sent a wave of laughter shuddering through the mayor.

"Right again, Sam," McAllister whispered to himself.

He pulled the lens cap off the camera and glanced out of the corner of his eye. There were a number of people strolling about, but none paying any particular attention, which probably wouldn't have mattered anyway. The view was spectacular from the Windward; it wouldn't be out of the ordinary for anyone to be taking photos.

Sam focused the camera and clicked off two photos before quickly replacing the lens cap. He then backed away from the window, turned and stepped through the doors and onto the sun-drenched deck, pretending to be looking in another direction. When his eyes finally turned toward the pair, they had separated a few inches and were now seated exactly as he had left them. Susan held a glass of wine in one hand and her other was resting gently on her own lap.

"All set," Sam said, smiling as he reached the table. "But if you wouldn't mind, I'd like to get a photograph of us."

"Not at all," Ferguson smiled. Sam turned and faced an adjacent table.

"Excuse me . . . but would you mind taking a photo, please?" A man seated at the table said he would be delighted to. Sam returned to the table and was about to sit when the mayor suddenly stood up, looking toward the lake.

"How about right here near the railing, Sam? That'll be a nice shot with this view."

"Great idea," Sam agreed. The two stood next to the railing with a beautiful panoramic view of Mullett Lake behind them.

Susan remained seated and out of the picture.

✳ ✳ ✳ ✳

The brief tour of Mullett Lake and the surrounding area

took them through Somerville and Mullett Heights, along through the village of Indian River, up M-33 and then back down Old US-27.

"Mullett Lake seems to be a dangerous place as of late," Jack said, relaxing in the leather seat of the limousine. Susan sat a few feet away, sipping a glass of wine. Sam responded to Ferguson's statement by cocking his head to the side as if he wasn't quite sure what the mayor had meant.

"Boating accidents," Ferguson continued. "I heard a news report on our trip from the Pellston airport. You've had quite a few in the lake here this summer."

"Unfortunately, yes," Sam confirmed, shaking his head. "You just can't get it through some folks' heads. With more and more people vacationing here, there's obviously more people in the water." Sam explained to Ferguson about the most recent mishap, the snorkeling accident near Aloha State Park. Then, sensing an opportunity to puff himself up, he made mention of the fact that the police had asked *him* to develop the photos from the victim's camera.

"The kid had one of those underwater cameras," Sam continued, "and the police gave it to me to develop the photos. I have a small darkroom in my house. Just kind of a hobby of mine. Anyway, they thought that maybe . . . just *maybe* there might be a picture that would give them a clue as to who was driving the boat. Nothing turned up, I'm afraid."

"How terrible," Susan said. She had been listening to Sam intently, thinking how awful it must be to have been run over by a boat propellor.

"Yes," Sam agreed. "It was tragic. I hope it's the last we see of accidents for a long, long time." Sam was beginning to think that her intelligence quotient and the current temperature outdoors were running about neck and neck; maybe the odds were a bit in the temperature's favor. She still hadn't spoken much, and offered nothing of noteworthiness or redeeming social value when she did. *First-class twit* was the phrase that came to his mind. *Nice tits, though,* he thought.

The limousine and its occupants returned to the centennial celebration. A welcome reception was to begin at five o'clock, followed by a cocktail hour that would probably drag on into the night. Except for the conversation in the limo regarding the snorkeler, Sam had forgotten about the carefully hidden photo of the huge fish tucked beneath the weeds. The shock and disbelief had faded, pushed away to the dark closets of his mind that were filled with odds and ends and other things he'd shoved aside over the years. At the moment, everything was splendid. Ferguson genuinely seemed to be enjoying himself, and Sam was certain that the visiting mayor was impressed at what he was seeing. And he was actually glad that there weren't more people who had made the trip. This would give Sam the opportunity to get closer to Ferguson, to give him more of a chance to be one-on-one with him. The more opportunities he had to be more personal with Jack, well, the better his chances of getting offered the job.

After winding through myriads of people and slow-moving cars the limousine pulled into the driveway of Sam's home. He invited them in for a few moments, then the three walked down the grassy slope and stood at the waters' edge.

The lake was filled with hundreds of boaters, swimmers, boardsailers . . . anything that could possibly float and carry passengers was in the water. The buzz of laughter and loud chatter filled the air from all around. Even the homeowners along the lakeshore had literally opened up their yards to the revelers, and blankets were spread out in front of every home for a half mile along the waterfront. There were so many blankets that from the air it looked like one massive quilt had been laid upon the banks.

Sam spoke to his two guests.

"Well, if you'll excuse me, I've got a few last minute preparations to make before the welcome reception. Please . . . make yourself at home and look around. Oh . . . and here—"

Sam reached into his pocket and pulled out a small, thin cellular phone, handing it to the visiting mayor. "—if you need to make any calls, please be my guest. Or if you need me within the next fifteen minutes or so, just press the 'speed dial' button, then press '1'. It'll ring right in my house. The reception starts in fifteen minutes. If you don't mind, I'd like to introduce you as a visiting dignitary and thank you for coming."

"Not at all, not at all," Ferguson replied, shaking his head and smiling with model-like quality. Sam walked back up the sloping grass and disappeared into the house.

✳ ✳ ✳ ✳

As the opening ceremonies drew near, people began gathering at the foot of the portable stage that had been assembled in the large field on the opposite side of the highway. Excited children ran under and between the legs of adults. A gentle breeze shook the huge maple trees near the stage, creating a soothing *ssshhhhh* that wasn't *heard* as much as it was *felt*. Hands clasped as friends who hadn't seen one another since last summer exchanged *goodtaseeyas* and *howyabeens*, promising one another that they'd get in touch after the weekend to get together for a burger and a beer on the lawn. Which of course, would probably never happen. Summer in northern Michigan was soccer games and 4-H competitions and swim lessons and bowling leagues and yard chores. It was hurry here, rush over there, hurry back to get ready to go somewhere else. If you managed to squeak in a bit of time here and there for a barbeque with the neighbors once or twice between June and August, you were doing pretty damn good.

Soon the entire field was packed with laughing children, chattering adults, and the smells of elephant ears and cotton candy drifting through the air. Guests began to gather behind and to the sides of the stage, including (of course) the ever-important Senator Elgin, as well as the mayor of Touraine, but just as importantly, a host of community business people and local celebrities such as Claudia Pittsman, the sixteen-year-old winner of the Miss Brookstown Pageant. Brookstown was a small, quiet community on the north side of Black Lake; as fate would have it, she was the only visiting 'Queen' that Courville could boast in attendance. She stood off to the side of the stage wearing a long pink cotton dress and a faded sash that read *Miss ookstown*. The letters had been sewn on, but the *'B'* and the *'r'* had been accidentally torn off while getting out of her boyfriend's truck. She was doing her best to greet people and wave friendly hellos, despite the fact that she and her boyfriend and his brother had just finished smoking one monster of a joint, and she was stoned out of her gourd. Claudia's eyes were the color of harvest beets and her coordination was slow and methodical, as if she were a marionette controlled by a drunk puppet master from above. She had a perpetual smile on her face and every few minutes would laugh at something funny. Or, at least something that was funny to *her*.

Soon a man wearing khaki pants and a blue blazer stepped spiritedly toward the podium. He introduced himself and said a few words, then made some announcements regarding cars that were illegally parked and vehicles with their lights on. He carefully checked his notes to make sure he'd covered everything he'd needed to, then began again.

"Ladies and Gentlemen," his voice boomed through the two loudspeakers that were situated on poles at either side of the stage. "On behalf of the village of Courville, it is my pleasure to introduce to you a man who has spent countless weeks and months to make this weekend happen. Please welcome Courville Chamber of Commerce director–" he paused as if trying to mimic the welcoming of Grand Funk Railroad to Shea Stadium. Then, in a voice that distorted the speakers and echoed over the field: "–Sam McAllister!"

The man stepped away from the microphone as he uttered the final words of the sentence. Sam stood up from the metal folding chair he was seated on at the right of the stage and walked toward the podium, extending his hand in courtesy to the man who had introduced him. The crowd roared their approval, sending cheers and whistles into the air. Not necessarily because they liked Sam or even knew him; the crowd probably would've applauded a mayonnaise jar if one happened to be introduced. It was just that type of mood. Sam smiled and waived, waited until the applause died out, then began.

"Ladies and gentlemen, it is an honor to be here today–this weekend–to celebrate a great moment in the history of a very small but very mighty community." A few claps of approval were heard and Sam continued. "This one hundred year celebration is more than just a mark on the calendar or a page in history. It is a milestone. A milestone of hard work, of achievement and advancement. It's a day of . . . ."

Sam continued with his speech, expertly grabbing the words from the air. His entire address was off the top of his head, and he hadn't even brought notes to the podium. It made for a powerful, emotionally charged speech . . . even if he was laying it on a bit heavier than he needed to. At one point he glanced into the audience and recognized his next door neighbor, Amy Hunter.

And if the bitch could keep her dog in her own yard, well, hell . . . it might live long enough for the celebration next year, Sam thought between sentences. No matter. He had a little surprise coming up in just a few minutes for Amy and her idiot boyfriend, or whoever she'd been hanging around with the past few days. The image of their picture in the paper arose in his mind and he angrily shook it away, concentrating harder on the task at hand.

He spoke about tradition, values, how Courville had changed, how pleased he was to be here to celebrate such an important day. He laid it on thick and heavy, and even brought a few of the old-timers to tears when he mentioned the fire that had almost wiped out the town in 1939. McAllister's speech went on for ten minutes until it was time to welcome a few noted special guests.

"And, ladies and gentlemen, it is my genuine privilege to introduce to you a man who has worked hard for our state . . . indeed, our *community* . . . but last time we played, I noticed that maybe he needs to work a bit harder on his golf game . . . ." This brought a roar from the crowd, and the good-natured Senator Elgin smiled and went along playfully with the ribbing, hanging his head in mock shame. Truthfully, Sam had never met Senator Elgin. McAllister simply sent a letter to his office last February saying that he was glad that the Senator had planned to participate in the festivities, and the short note included a hotel reservation with a confirmation number, as well as a few complimentary certificates at some of the finer restaurants around Cheboygan county. The ploy worked, and a few weeks after the note was sent an assistant from the Senator's office called Sam to confirm that he would indeed be at the centennial celebration. As a public figure Senator Elgin was used to attending various functions; they were mandatory requirements of the elected office. The Senator was also accustomed to a wide array of introductions, and he played along fine. As the laughter died, Sam leaned closer to the microphone and continued speaking.

"I ask you to stand and welcome United States Senator . . . Barry Elgin!" Most of the crowd was already standing, but this brought the rest to their feet in a boisterous wave of applause and cheering.

The Senator extended his hand when he reached the podium but Sam pulled one better, reaching over and embracing the Senator in a brief hug. Senator Elgin, although a bit surprised, didn't allow it to show, and reciprocated warmly. Sam slapped him on the back and then drew away, leaving the Senator alone at the podium. He turned to the microphone, made a few comments about how it was good to be here, good to be in Michigan, good to be in Courville for such a wonderful occasion. It was literally Sam's speech repeated in another's words, only the way the Senator made it sound, it was more like Martin Luther King's *I have a dream'* oration. When he was finished Sam approached the podium, and the two once again hugged briefly before the Senator returned to his seat facing the audience. McAllister was once again at the podium.

"We have yet another distinguished guest who visits us today from Cape Touraine, Florida. Let's give a big northern Michigan welcome to visiting Mayor, Jack Ferguson!" The crowd responded enthusiastically as the mayor stood and waved. Sam remained at the podium, facing Ferguson, raising his hands as he applauded. After a moment Ferguson sat down and the crowd quieted.

"And ladies and gentlemen, I'm certain that many of you have heard about the Mullett Lake 'killer' muskie by now." A rising, sarcastic groan of fear rumbled through the crowd, then faded. "Now I know that some of you may have been worried about this situation." Another sarcastic groan floated over the crowd, only louder this time. Sam searched the crowd and found Amy once again and he glared at her, smiling through his words as he continued.

"But I'm happy to report to you that there is no reason for concern. The fish has been caught, and the celebration will continue as planned!" At that moment, a skinny man wearing blue jeans and a dirty white tank top stepped up from the side of the stage holding a huge muskellunge in his arms. The fish would easily go four feet and weigh forty pounds or more.

"Ladies and gentlemen . . . the Mullett Lake 'killer' muskie!" The crowd roared and applauded and laughed and the man holding the fish took center stage, holding the fish over his chest for the entire audience to see. He was truly proud of his catch, and he struggled to hold it up higher.

By any measure it was a large fish indeed. Razor-sharp teeth could be seen jutting from the fish's mouth, and even though the muskie was dead, its eyes were open, glaring green and black in the bright sunlight. The fish had been brought to shore just a few minutes before Sam was scheduled to speak. He'd seen the man come in from the docks and asked if he wouldn't mind showing off the fish for the audience.

Finally the man made his way back to the side of the stage. Sam took one more long glance at Amy and continued speaking. He spoke about heritage, of toil, of where Courville had been and where the village was going, occasionally glancing to the side of the stage to nod his head toward Ferguson. The mayor just smiled, watching Sam and listening intently, Susan sitting a proper six inches from his chair.

God, she's even keeping her hands in her own lap, Sam thought.

He closed the address by welcoming everyone once again and inviting them to take part in the state's largest cocktail hour, beginning 'now' and lasting until 'whenever'. The crowd of several hundred shouted their heartiest approval yet, and Sam stepped back from the microphone, bowed, joined the mayor and his escort, and exited the stage.

❋ ❋ ❋ ❋

The blender in Amy's cabin whirred to life for the second time that day, and Brad looked around the room. Amy's cottage was identical to his, albeit a bit neater. Same style bed, furniture, tables, TV set . . . *everything.* Her needs seemed simple: there weren't any photos that adorned the walls except for an old watercolor painting that looked like it had been in the cabin for years. The frame looked as if it had been in water for some time, as it was warped and faded. The painting itself seemed tarnished as well, and upon closer inspection Brad found that the painting wasn't as much for decoration as it was to cover up the plate-sized hole in the wall from where an old furnace pipe had once existed. The interior walls were the same knotty pine glazed with coat after coat of varnish. The wood was old, and had faded a brown-orange over the years. The small rooms were uncluttered and tidy, as opposed to Brad's. He'd already strewn clothing over a chair and on the bed in his cabin. No sense in staying somewhere for a week and not making yourself at home.

"So . . . no boyfriend?" Brad asked after not seeing any photos anywhere. It was a subject that hadn't come up during dinner a few evenings ago.

"And where'd *that* come from?" Amy asked, setting the pitcher down and handing him the red plastic cup. He lifted the drink to his lips and spoke just before he took a sip.

"Oh, you know . . . left field, I guess. Just curious. Sorry."

"Don't be," she said. "And the answer is no. I mean, I *did*. When I was in college." She didn't volunteer any more information but instead turned the question back around. "How about you?"

"No. I had a girlfriend for a few years, but that didn't work out." He had no intention of volunteering any more information about *that* particular situation.

"Well, here's to better luck to both of us in the future," Amy said, raising her cup. Brad raised his in agreement, happy that she hadn't pressed further about the girlfriend issue, and both sipped their drinks.

"So . . . what did you think of the pervert's speech?" Amy smirked sarcastically.

"Well, he is *good*, I'll give him that," Brad responded. "He sure knows how to play the game."

"Yeah. Problem is, his game is social prostitution. And I can't believe he pulled that stunt with that fish. He looked *right at us*. Did you see that? I mean . . . he was *mocking* us."

"Amy . . . we went to the paper and reported seeing a twelve-foot muskie. We're lucky the whole *state* isn't mocking us."

Outside the cabin, the Courville centennial celebration continued. The events for the remainder of the evening included a pie eating contest, a volleyball tournament, and a community marshmallow roast at dusk. The next day, Saturday, would be the *big* day, with a five-mile foot race, assorted live entertainment on the stage, more contests, and a parade along Old US-27. The parade would consist of a few floats and the townships' two fire engines, as well as members of the local Model A club and a dozen or so of their vehicles. The usual small town, middle-of-summer festivities. The day would begin with a swim competition at ten a.m., sharp.

For some swimmers, it was to be their last.

For *all,* including the spectators on shore, it would be a day they would never, ever forget.

EIGHT

Amy awoke just before dawn to the fresh, spicy scent of wet grass and pine. A thunderstorm had rolled through during the overnight hours, but by morning the clouds had dispersed and soon the sun would be climbing over the lake, drying the grass and leaves.

She emerged from her cabin clad in black running tights and a red nylon pullover. Amy had no interest in the foot race to be held later in the morning; this was her time and her time alone. Running to Amy wasn't competition, it was the dance of one, to be enjoyed in solitude. For her, running was a time for renewal and reflection, not for competition.

The morning sky was a deep, rich butane blue. Across the lake, beyond the tree line, a bright orange band was slowly growing longer and brighter as the sun continued its never-ending trek. The village was serenely quiet at such an early hour despite the cars and tents and campers that cluttered the field on both sides of Old US-27.

Amy walked across the yard and sped up her gait, and by the time she had reached the parking lot she was at a steady jog. Her hair was tied in a ponytail and her light brown mane swished back and forth, bobbing as she ran.

A quick turn after she made it through the gravel parking area and now she was on the shoulder of the highway, her feet pounding the hard-packed ground.

She glanced over the clogged field filled with several hundred cars and campers. It was difficult for her to imagine so many people all packed into the tiny village of Courville. There was easily more people camping in the field than there was in the entire population of the village. Last year only a handful or so had camped across the street during the annual festivities. But last year hadn't been such a big *to-do* as the centennial celebration this year. It was one of those 'once in a lifetime' events that attracted so much attention . . . and *people*. Today was certain to be absolutely crazy with all of the events going on and all of the people in attendance. Poor motorists on Old US-27 that were just passing through would be caught in the middle, forced to move inches at a time while summer zombies walked back and forth across the highway without a care in the world. For them, the highway didn't exist. Not *this* weekend. There were arts and crafts booths to visit, games to be played, friends to chat with, and children to keep in line. No doubt the swim competition would draw a fair number of spectators as well.

Amy shuddered, picking up her pace along the shoulder of the highway. She had tried to put the huge fish out of her mind, tried to push it away and tell herself that she hadn't seen it. She tried to rationalize with the fact that a muskellunge *cannot* get that big. It was just not possible. Not in fresh water, not anywhere. Sharks in the ocean, maybe. Not muskies. And she didn't know what to make of Frank Girard's theories. He had told Brad that a species of muskie existing for millions of years was *almost* impossible.

Almost.

Remember, Brad had told her. *New species of plants and animals—and fish—are discovered every day.*

And Sam McAllister, that bastard. He had made fun of her and Brad by bringing that muskie out on stage. If the gag had truly been in jest without malicious intention, well, no one would have had a problem with that. But he had looked at *her*. He had caught her eye and his gaze sneered at her and rubbed her face in his mockery. No one else in the audience knew, but *she* did.

But deep down she really hoped Sam might be right. All was going to be fine, the celebration would be a tremendous success, and the only injuries suffered would be the thumping headaches of the people who stayed out a bit too late and drank a bit too much. There was no 'Monster Muskie,' as the paper had called it. No huge fish, no danger . . . .

Her lungs ached, and suddenly she realized that she had sped up to a pace much faster than normal. Two miles had gone by and she hadn't even noticed it.

She slowed to an easier, more comfortable pace and turned around, bounding over the paved highway and onto the opposite shoulder. She then cut through a yard and turned, plodded through a few more yards, and finally turned once again, following an old railroad bed that snaked along the shoreline.

The sun had risen over the lake, and birds had begun to sing in the apple trees that she passed along the route. A few early risers sipped coffee from chairs on their decks, relaxing in the pure, sweet fragrance of morning. Amy's pace was steady, a smooth, loose jog that eased her tensions and cleared her mind. Mornings such as this were her favorite part of the day. She felt refreshed and renewed after a morning run, and the feeling stayed with her from morning till dusk. If she missed more than three or four days in a row, she swore that she could literally feel her body craving exercise, pleading for a glorious heart-pumping, adrenaline-surging run. Her mind eased and for the moment she was lost in stride, soaking up the fresh fragrances and filling her lungs with crisp, refreshing air.

The euphoria didn't last long.

She looked ahead on the path and saw a figure standing in a screen porch.

"Shit," she whispered beneath her breath.

The old railroad path wound along the lakeshore, meandering right in front of Sam McAllister's house, before cutting back and threading behind the town. Sam was rarely up this early and only on very infrequent occasions had she encountered him, sipping his coffee and glaring at her as she jogged by. She always ignored him, never saying anything to him, not even a friendly *good morning.* Just being within a few feet of him gave her the creeps.

Her pace remained steady as she approached the house. Sam heard the padding of footsteps and turned. Amy kept her face straight and focused on the grassy path before her, pretending not to notice the man in the light-blue terrycloth bathrobe standing by the screen door. When she was directly in front of the house, she heard his voice.

"Careful that monster muskie don't gitcha," McAllister hissed. He let out a sneering chuckle and Amy kept running, and she didn't stop until she reached her cabin.

＊ ＊ ＊ ＊

Susan Corbin poked her head out from beneath the covers and crept up to Ferguson's chest.

"How was that?" she whispered, as she took one of his nipples in her mouth.

"Incredible," came his heaving reply. He drew in a deep breath and exhaled heavily, relaxing in the bed. The drapes were closed, and a hazy, pre-dawn gray outlined the curtains.

"I thought you'd think so," she answered, placing her hand over his groin. She bit his nipple gently, and Ferguson moaned in pleasure. They had stayed up half the night, talking, screwing, drinking wine, and blowing line after line of cocaine. Or at least, *Susan* blew line after line of coke. Ferguson didn't much care for the marching powder himself, and his intake was moderate, but Susan's appetite for the drug was voracious. She'd screw him all night if enough blow was available, so Ferguson made sure there was plenty on hand. Jack wasn't all that happy with her enormous habit; it was just too goddamn *expensive*. But what the hell . . . it was *her* life. She'd already taken a couple snorts earlier this morning when she had gotten up to go to the bathroom. He was certain that within two years she'd be found dead of an overdose in some dirty motel room somewhere.

He looked at her naked body lying next to him in bed. She was slim and fit, and her tight stomach muscles rippled beneath the skin of her belly. She had a pierced navel which was another thing Ferguson wasn't too crazy about. Tatoos, pierced body parts, branding . . . he just wasn't in to that shit. A beautiful body was just *that* . . . it didn't need to be adorned with drawings and pictures and permanent scars.

"You still got that crazy idea in your head?" he asked, kissing her forehead.

"I wouldn't miss it. Come on . . . it'll be fun."

"Not me. The only swimming I do is casual. No races."

"You're just afraid you wouldn't finish," Susan egged on. Ferguson didn't take the bait.

"Damn right," he replied. "I'd rather just stay here and screw you some more." Susan laughed and crawled on top of him, placing her hands on his chest and leaning forward. Jack reached up and gently caressed one of her breasts with the back of his hand.

"It's still early," Susan began, speaking softly. "We can do that *before*–" she leaned further toward him and kissed his chin. "*–and we can do it after.*" Her tongue found his mouth and she ran it along his lips, adjusting her hips and lowering herself on top of him. He shuddered and moaned as she drew away and leaned back, her hips gently rocking up and down over his waist.

The phone beside the bed shrilled a high-pitched, annoying ring. Ferguson paid no attention, instead reaching down to grasp Susan's hips, slowly guiding her movements. The phone rang again, and then again.

"Aren't you going to get it?" Susan panted, slowing her motions. "It's probably Sam. What time did he say he was going to call you?"

Ferguson turned his head and looked at the clock.

"Six-thirty, right on the money," he moaned, closing his eyes and coaxing her waist with his hands. He made no effort to reach for the phone.

"But aren't we meeting him for breakfast before the swim competition?"

CHRISTOPHER KNIGHT

"I couldn't care less. I'm tired of all his bullshit and phony hob-nobbing. The joke of this whole fucking thing is that he actually thinks he has a shot at getting hired. What a dumbshit. *Fuck* Sam McAllister."

Susan thrust down upon him, grinding her pelvis into his groin. Ferguson let out a moan of immense gratification, tensing his body and arching his back.

"Fuck Sam McAllister?" she repeated, leaning closer to his face.

"*Fuck* Sam McAllister," he reiterated.

"*Me first,*" Susan whispered, thrusting her tongue into his mouth.

The phone rang a few more times, then went silent.

✸ ✸ ✸ ✸

Crowds began lining the shoreline at nine a.m. Fifteen rowboats sat stationary along a straight line in the water, spaced forty to fifty feet apart. Each boat contained two people on loan from rescue facilities around the county, as well as a few off-duty paramedics. The competitors were to swim one quarter of a mile out, keeping to the right of the boats. Then, at a big orange buoy where the final boat was, the swimmers would round the boat and come back to shore on the left side of the line of boats. Each competitor wore a yellow swim cap that could be easily seen by the teams in the boats. If someone got a cramp or got into trouble, a boat would be nearby to assist.

All in all, there were nearly two hundred entrants that had signed up to compete. The race would begin with a staggered start, and the first group of fifteen would take off at the sound of the gun. Then, exactly ten seconds later, the second group of fifteen would begin, and so on, until all were in the water. A kids' swim contest for those twelve and under would be held later in the day within the confines of the swimming area.

Sam McAllister was pleased. The swim competition had been *his* idea. This was its first year, and Sam wasn't sure how many participants he'd get. He figured maybe a handful . . . twenty or thirty at the most. He was delighted that so many people had not only signed up beforehand, but quite a few had registered that morning. At fifteen dollars per competitor, Sam was going to make out quite well. The only expense incurred was the yellow rubber swim caps, and he'd been able to get a sponsor to pay for those in exchange for their company logo on the front of the caps. There was insurance, of course, but again, that was underwritten by a sponsor. That left a profit of just over twenty-five hundred dollars. And being that he was in charge of the tourism office, it was up to him to see that the funds were distributed properly, and that would probably be somewhere near the vicinity of Sam's wallet, to be deposited in the First National Bank of McAllister.

He stood on the bank watching people, scanning the growing crowd. Ferguson had stood him up. They were supposed to meet at eight-thirty for breakfast at the Windward, but when Sam had called, there was no answer, which was odd. Sam didn't know Jack Ferguson *real* well, but up till now he'd been a model of punctual perfection.

Suddenly he spotted Susan Corbin standing in knee-deep water near the shore, holding the yellow swim cap in her hands and staring out over the lake. Her hair was tied up in a knot and bunched at the back of her head. Sam walked through the crowd and stood at the waters' edge.

"Good morning Miss Corbin," he said, smiling.

Susan turned and faced him. It was an arrogant movement, as if she'd expected him to be there, knowing that she would have to face him and talk to him. She held the yellow cap in one hand and a pair of eye goggles in the other.

"Good morning, Sam," she said, her smile gleaming in the morning sun. Sam looked her up and down.

Jack sure does know how to pick'em, he thought. Most of the women competitors were wearing a one piece suit, but Susan Corbin wore a black two-piece that just barely held everything in. *One dive into that water and that top is coming off,* Sam thought. *I gotta be here when that happens.*

"Is Jack here?" he asked.

"Oh, I'm sorry. He's in his room. He has a terrible headache and said he won't make it for the swim competition. He'll be along shortly, I'm sure."

"I'm sorry to hear that he's not feeling well," Sam replied. He glanced at her swim cap and shifted his gaze to her breasts bulging out of her bikini top, then quickly shifted his eyes back to her face. "Well, I hope he's feeling better. Today's a big day. Lots of fun."

"I'm sure he'll be fine," she responded. "Just some aspirin and some rest, and he'll be fine."

Susan looked over the audience and Sam took the opportunity to look over her body once again.

"So you're gonna compete, eh?" he asked, gesturing toward the water with the bullhorn.

"Well, I'm not sure if you can call it 'compete'," Susan answered. "But it looks like a lot of fun."

"Good luck to you," Sam offered.

Susan extended her thanks and watched as Sam turned and walked back up the grassy slope.

✳ ✳ ✳ ✳

Sam surveyed the scene from the shore, carrying his bullhorn and a clipboard. He had successfully pushed the memory of the huge fish out of his mind, and the image in the photograph was the farthest thing from his thoughts. He was certain the race would go off without a hitch, that there was no 'giant' muskellunge, and that upon further inspection of the photo he would find the dark shape in the picture was indeed a log, and that maybe he'd had a little too much to drink that night and his mind was playing tricks on him. Indeed, he hadn't even *thought* about the picture since yesterday. Besides . . . there had been scores of people on the water since yesterday . . . swimming, boardsailing, fishing. Nothing had happened to *them*. The race would go *fine*, he told himself.

He was about to find out how terribly wrong he was.

✳ ✳ ✳ ✳

The blast of the starter's pistol echoed over the lake and the first heat of swimmers were off. The roar of the crowd was deafening. Spectators filled the shore and the waterfront, and the crowd swelled back up to the row of houses and cottages, spilling out onto Old US-27. The teams manning the boats were watchful and attentive, carefully eyeing each racer in the water. If necessary, one of the boats' occupants could enter the water and assist a swimmer in trouble.

Sam had been watching Susan Corbin intently, staring at her body as she stood in the shallows, waiting for the next heat. She was off in the second round, and his gaze followed her as she dove headfirst into the water and crawled out into the lake. Unfortunately for Sam, the bikini top held firmly, much to his disappointment.

Susan was a strong swimmer despite her petite size, and she moved quickly through the water, easily overtaking some of the male competitors. All around her water splashed as feet and arms flew madly about.

Within seconds the next wave was off, and then the next. By the time the first racers were reaching the half way point the starter pistol barked one final time, and the last heat was signaled to start. All the swimmers were now in the water, and the large crowd continued to roar and applaud. Spectators lining the water called out the names of competitors, urging them on. For a quarter of a mile water splashed and boiled, a mixture of flailing arms and legs and dots of yellow. The first few competitors had just rounded the final buoy and were heading back to shore. Within a few minutes, racers would begin to reach the finish line.

✳ ✳ ✳ ✳

CHRISTOPHER KNIGHT

The fish had been watching from the depths as the boats above positioned themselves in the water. It approached warily, remaining a good thirty feet below the surface, out of sight, calmly gliding effortlessly beneath the moored boats. It paced slowly, its eyes keenly aware of the distractions from the surface.

But then . . . a new sound began to filter through the deep. A distant splashing. Lots of splashing and flailing, and the fish knew instantly what it was. The sound was full and loud and overwhelming, agitating the muskie. It began to cruise faster and the noise from the swimmers became stronger, irritating the fish.

Above, a form on the surface began to take shape, then another. Then three more.

The fish angrily spun about in the water, then back again to eye the dark shadows on the surface. Again, it was faced with a deep sense of danger, a sense of impending threat, but the increasing sounds around him and the hunger that grew from within began to drown out its own instincts. Its heart pounded harder and harder as the number of forms in the water above grew. Soon the entire surface region above the enormous fish was filled with flailing shadows.

Finally, the intensity of its surrounding elements became unbearable. To the muskie, it was no longer about hunger. It was no longer about food or quenching its insatiable appetite. It was about rage, about hysterical, burning anger. Anger that grew by the second, reaching the boiling point and seething over the top. With blinding fury the beast rocketed toward the surface.

* * * *

The first victim was snatched so quickly from the surface that neither the competitors around him nor anyone in the boats saw him disappear. His head snapped beneath the splashing water, and he was gone. Then a few seconds later another swimmer was snatched violently beneath the surface, only to pop back up within seconds, screaming in agony. The commotion attracted the attention of the crowd on shore, and one of the boats began rowing toward the troubled swimmer. Within seconds another person was screaming, and then another. The muskie rolled the surface, catching two more competitors in its jaws and thrashing them wildly about. Screams of pain were heard as the fish's huge teeth tore open the flesh of its two victims. A few swimmers had caught a glimpse of the enormous monster and began swimming as fast as they could toward the shore.

Some weren't going to make it.

The fish struck in a frenzy, going from swimmer to swimmer. It wasn't hungry anymore; the first swimmer had satisfied its appetite at least for the time being. Now the fish was in a bloodthirsty hysteria, snapping and attacking every swimmer in sight. Arms and legs flailed and whirred on the surface, as swimmers frantically tried to make it to the shore. One of the men in one of the boats was yelling something about a giant fish, and he began screaming at the swimmers to swim to shore. The surrounding waters were turning a dirty crimson and the rescuers in the boats had begun to pull victims out of the lake, some missing an entire leg, others missing an arm or displaying terrible, open gashes.

Susan Corbin had just rounded the half-way buoy when she heard the first scream. It came from a few yards in front of her and she stopped swimming and watched in horror as the man snapped violently below the surface.

Oh my God, she thought. *Oh my—*

At that moment the man that had been pulled under exploded to the surface, only not by his own power. He was clamped within the mouth of some horrible animal, some ungodly beast. The swimmers' lifeless body was tossed aside like a plaything and the fish disappeared beneath the surface.

Panicking, Susan turned and began to swim to the nearest rescue boat. Other swimmers had already reached it and were struggling to climb aboard. Her arms spun through the water like wheels, pushing her body faster and faster to the boat.

Suddenly her head plunged beneath the surface, and Susan knew that it was too late. The fish had seized her leg and pulled her under, but in the next moment she was free again and she returned to the surface, sputtering and screaming in terror.

The nearest boat, filled to capacity with competitors, was only a few dozen feet away.

"There it is!" one of them yelled. *"I can see him!"*

Susan continued to swim and a sharp pain gnawed at her leg.

"Hurry! Hurry! You're almost here!" Two men stretched out their arms to grab her. Susan, only a few feet away, reached out for them.

"Watch it, watch it! Here it comes!" There was melee in the boat as the shadow of the enormous fish flew by, grabbing Susan around her torso and pulling her under. The fish had nearly come out of the water and the ensuing wave almost

capsized the small aluminum life raft.

"Jesus!" a woman in the boat screamed. *"It killed her! That thing killed her!"* She began screaming and sobbing hysterically.

The swimmers in the boat began urging the medics to head for shore. Without wasting any more time the boat began to row toward the beach.

The spectators on the shore had become more frantic. Rumors of something attacking the swimmers buzzed though the crowd, and many people began wading into the shallows to help swimmers as they reached the shore. It was pandemonium and mayhem as competitors reached the beach, relating what they'd seen. Anxious wives looked for their husbands, as did the husbands of the women competitors. Soon, all of the boats began pumping toward the shore, their occupants waving at the crowd, screaming for them to get out of the water. They had found everyone they could, and the rescuers were in a panic as well, themselves eager to get out off the lake.

In a few short minutes it was all over. A siren was heard in the distance. The crowd of people was filled with crying, sobbing, and moans of pain. The beach picnic area became a makeshift hospital with over a dozen people laying on bloodstained towels and blankets. A few swimmers had already died from loss of blood. Others were silent and quiet, frozen in shock. They stared blankly up at the blue sky, their eyes glossy and unmoving. The blood in the water began to reach shore, giving the sand a sickening pink hue, and uniformed policemen stood by lakeside, careful to keep people at their distance.

A large splash was heard out in the lake, and it caught the attention of the crowd. The large wake began to fade, and the terrible beast glided effortlessly into deeper water.

✳✳✳✳

When Sam heard the first scream, he knew. He *knew* what it was. He had turned to see what was happening, as did most other people in the crowd.

The scene was complete chaos. Flailing arms and legs in the water, screaming spectators. When things began to worsen, he quietly slipped away. He watched from behind the closed curtains in his living room where no one could see. Soon ambulances were arriving, driving over lawns and parking by the shore. Every few minutes one would race off, only to be replaced by another one. Police were talking with witnesses, there were people running about, cameras clicking away, and a van from a television station had just arrived. Sam stood back from the window, peering through a crack in the curtain, remaining out of sight.

✳✳✳✳

As fate would have it, Jack Ferguson arrived on the scene just as the first wave of ambulances did. There was chaos and confusion everywhere, and Ferguson knew instantly that something was terribly, terribly wrong. Over shouts and screams he heard something about a 'sea monster' and 'giant fish' that had attacked the swim competitors. His heart began to race as he pushed through the crowd.

The waterfront had literally been transformed into a crude morgue. People were crying and weeping uncontrollably, and others had to be restrained by grim-faced paramedics. Bodies covered with white sheets lined the shoreline, and two men were helping an injured competitor out of the water. Blood poured from the swimmer's leg where an artery had been ripped open, and there was a long gash that went from his elbow clear to the bloody stump of his wrist. His hand was completely gone.

Jack paced the shoreline frantically, calling out loud, first quietly as if just speaking her name, then, as horror began to set in and rush over him, he began shouting.

"Susan! Susan Corbin!" No one turned to look at him, nor did Susan's face appear anywhere in the crowd. Stone faced, he began looking closely at the covered bodies lined up along the shore.

The body of Susan Corbin—what was left of her, anyway—lay lifeless in the grass, covered by a blood-stained white sheet. Before one of the medical personnel had been able to stop him, he pulled back the makeshift burial shroud.

Ferguson gasped in shocked disbelief and instantly drew away. His eyes grew wide and his hands flew to his face, covering his mouth. He stared.

One of Susan's legs was missing and the other had been amputated just above her knee. Her once beautiful face had been torn open and the flesh had been peeled away like a potato skin. Her right arm was severed but it was intact, barely. It was held to her shoulder by a short, thin piece of flesh. There were deep, gaping puncture wounds over her stomach, breasts, and neck. Her skin was pale and white, and had an almost transparent appearance. Jack felt a churning in his stomach and he turned aside and knelt as he vomited.

A medical technician rushed over at that moment and he pulled the sheet back over the corpse. He consoled Jack and offered his sympathy and helped Ferguson to his feet, requesting that he remain at a distance. Jack stood staring for a long time before finally walking back up the slope and across the parking lot to the waiting limo.

✳ ✳ ✳ ✳

Amy sat in the chair across from Brad, her face streaked with tears, sobbing quietly. Brad was leaning forward, holding her hands in his.

"We could have stopped this," Amy said. "This shouldn't have happened. *This didn't have to happen . . . ."*
Brad shook his head and gripped her hands tightly.

"Amy, we tried everything. We even went to the paper. It was a pretty unbelievable story, when you think about it. We did all we could."

"But nobody listened!" she choked. *"Nobody paid any attention!"*

"I'm afraid the fish has everyone's undivided attention now," Brad replied somberly.

He turned and looked out the window of his rented cottage. The ambulances were long gone, but a few police officers remained. A yellow and black ribbon was draped near the water, closing off access to the docks and the swimming area. Two helicopters were buzzing overhead, circling the lake. The water was strangely absent of human occupation: no boats, no sailboarders, no jet skiers, no fishermen . . . *nothing*. The word had gotten out pretty fast, and now the lake was completely void of activity.

The porch moaned and creaked, and a face appeared in the screen. It was the reporter that Brad and Amy had originally told their story to a few days previous. He knocked on the screen door and asked if he could come in to ask a few questions. Brad waved his arm without speaking, indicating for him to enter.

The reporter had a saturnine, gloomy look on his face, as if he was ashamed that he hadn't really believed their original story but printed it anyway, only to find out . . . well, the same thing everyone else had.

"I . . . I guess I owe you an apology," he began, and he meant it. "When you came in with your story, I didn't really believe you. I thought it would make a good story . . . you know . . . kind of a novelty-type thing."

"No apology necessary," Brad offered, waving it off with his hand.

"I'd like to begin again where we left off. About what you saw in the lake a few days ago. And about today. I'd like to know everything about what you saw today."

The reporter asked them pretty much the same things that he had asked before, listening intently while jotting notes on a yellow legal pad. Except this time he was more attentive and respectful, carefully noting details as Brad recalled the events of the day. Amy remained silent, allowing Brad to do all of the talking. She was in no mood for conversation, much less having to recall the horrible events of the day. After an hour the reporter left, leaving Brad and Amy alone in the cabin.

It was early evening and the sun cast long, billowing shadows over the lawn and on the lake. On a normal evening, the scene would have been picture perfect. An almost cloudless blue sky . . . trees, with their leaves hanging limp in the perfectly still evening . . . and the water, with a serene, glossy surface that looked more like a hand-polished mirror than the surface of a lake. But under the present circumstances, the calm inviting appearance was shrouded with eerie silence. Mullett Lake was completely empty.

All told, nine people had died from the afternoon catastrophe. Two were missing and presumed dead, and another thirteen were still hospitalized from severe wounds ranging from severed limbs to large lacerations. Three weren't expected to make it through the night.

The story made network news around the country, with stories of the giant 'killer fish' of Mullett Lake. At this point, most experts were only guessing that the fish was a muskie or pike of some sort. All they had to rely on was the reports of witnesses, most of those being the people in the rowboats. Most swimmers didn't get a good look at the fish, and no one on shore saw anything except a lot of splashing. One person reported seeing a large tail come out of the water, and still another said the beast looked like an enormous sea snake. Depending on who you talked to, the fish—or whatever it was—was presumed to be anywhere from ten to fifty feet in length. Except, of course, at the local taverns, restaurants, and eateries. A roundtable group of retired men at the *Cafe Noka* a few miles south of Courville had agreed that the fish was somewhere in the range of twenty feet, and old Elmer Spelling, the resident fishing expert and tall-tale fabricator, said that he'd hooked into the fish last year. He claimed he'd battled the fish for eleven hours and busted his arm in doing so. He would've landed him, he assured his audience, except there was no way the fish was going to fit in the boat. He had shot the fish in the head with a .22 caliber pistol that he kept in his tool box, he claimed. But the fish's head was so hard, the bullets just bounced off. Then again, Elmer also claimed that he had helped out with the Manhattan Project during World War Two, so you had to take everything he said with a grain of salt. Hell, the whole salt shaker, for that matter.

Other stories abounded throughout the north, and aquatic specialists from around the country were all over the news, giving their opinion of what the fish really was, and what they thought should be done about it. The Michigan Department of Natural Resources had ordered everyone to stay off Mullett, Burt, and Crooked Lakes, as well as the inland waterways that connected the three. They weren't going to waste any time in trying to catch the fish, but it had taken most of the afternoon to plan just how they were going to do it. The DNR figured that the best way would be with just good old fashioned fishing tackle–in this case, of course, very *heavy* tackle–certainly much heavier tackle than Mullett Lake had ever seen before. They would be using larger boats . . . boats that were normally used for fishing the Great Lakes. Gear consisted of equipment similar to that which would have been used for sharks. Thick, cable-like wire served as line. Hooks were over a foot long, and bait was primarily large strips of red meat. Because muskies traditionally attacked their prey while it was moving, the boats would troll at a moderate speed, keeping the bait in constant motion in the water.

It was also decided to begin fishing immediately and not wait till the next morning. The sooner the fish was caught, the better. Fishing groups around the Midwest had protested, saying *they* should have the right to try and catch the fish. The Michigan DNR wouldn't budge, saying it was a far too dangerous situation to allow sport fisherman free reign to capture a fish that had already killed more than a few people. They rented boats from commercial fishermen and brought in officers from around the state to assist, and to try and figure out just what they had on their hands.

It was generally assumed the fish was a muskie, but that was only what witnesses had reported. Common sense and logic said there was absolutely no way a muskellunge could grow to such monstrous proportions—but there was at least nine people that wouldn't be able to have the satisfaction of disagreeing, and another thirteen that didn't care what it was. All they knew was that it was *real*.

So, for the time being, until the fish was caught, no one but the DNR would be allowed on Mullett Lake. And there was one person in particular who did not like *that* at all.

NINE

Sam McAllister stood in his screen porch, staring in disgust at Mullett Lake. The photo of the snorkeler and the fish sat on a folding lawn chair, and he picked it up again. The day had been a disaster. More than a disaster . . . a *calamity*. He didn't feel much in the way of remorse for those who had been killed or injured. As soon as he had heard the first few screams, he knew what had happened. Or, rather, what was *about* to happen. And it wasn't going to be good for Courville or any other community on Mullett Lake. The centennial celebration, the fireworks, the rest of the weekend festivities and activities . . . *canceled*. People had left Courville in droves.

And the newspapers and TV and radio stations weren't a lot of help. Courville certainly was getting a lot of publicity, but it wasn't the kind of publicity Sam wanted. Oh sure, there'd always be the few people that would come and see the lake where the terrible man-eating fish lived, but Sam knew that wouldn't go on for long. He knew that the DNR would be out in force, along with whoever they brought with them, to find and destroy the fish. They had already ordered the lock permanently closed until the fish was caught, not wanting to take a chance of having it escape into Lake Huron. Heavy steel pipes were driven deep into the river bottoms at the mouths of the connecting waterways, preventing the fish from roaming from lake to lake. The vertical bars were spaced only a few inches apart, creating an iron 'jail'. The fish was trapped somewhere within three lakes . . . and it was now a matter of capturing it.

But worst of all, far worse than anything else that had happened, Sam feared that his chance at the job in Cape Touraine was in jeopardy. Of course, he had no way of knowing that he hadn't been in the running in the first place: the mayor himself had decided *that* after the first interview. So Sam really had no way of knowing that Ferguson's trip to Courville was nothing more than a weekend getaway for the mayor and his Mistress of the Month. But in Sam's eyes, the job opportunity was real, and he was going to do all he could to save it.

He picked up the phone and dialed the Windward Resort. The front desk connected him to Ferguson's room and Sam heard the phone ringing on the other end of the line. It rang a few times and Sam was just about to hang up when he heard the familiar *click* on the other end as it was picked up.

"Hello?" came Jack's weary voice. He sounded distant and quiet, not at all the normal, confident Jack Ferguson that Sam was familiar with. But then again, considering the circumstances . . . .

"Mr. Ferguson . . . it's Sam McAllister."

There was a short pause before the mayor answered.

"Hi Sam," Jack responded.

"Jack, I am so sorry to hear about your assistant. I *am* so very sorry."

"Thanks, Sam," Jack replied. "Sam . . . I'm going to head back to Cape Touraine tonight. Considering everything that's happened, I think it would just be best. I've got a late flight out of Pellston at ten-thirty."

Shit, Sam thought, glancing at his watch. He was hoping he'd have a chance to talk with him one-on-one before he left. But he didn't let his disappointment show.

"I understand, Mr. Ferguson," he replied.

"I'll call you first thing in the morning from Florida and we'll proceed from there."

"That will be fine. Have a good flight." Sam said good-bye and hung up the phone.

'Proceed from there,' Sam thought. *What the hell does that mean?* Sam had been hoping to learn this weekend whether or not the job was his. Now the waiting game was set to continue . . . to *'proceed from there,'* as the mayor had said.

Proceed from there.

The thought rang through his head, and the more he heard it in his mind, the more he didn't like it. It was the tone of Ferguson's voice, something in the way it had rolled off his tongue that told Sam the worst. Certainly the mayor was under extreme duress. Maybe it was just his emotion showing through his voice. But Sam didn't think so. There was just something about how the mayor had said it, the *way* he had said it that left Sam uneasy.

He walked over to the refrigerator and found another beer, tossing the twist-off cap in the garbage as the cold bottle rim met his lips.

* * * *

Jack Ferguson hung up the phone in his suite at the Windward Resort and went over Susan's belongings one more time. He certainly didn't have a need for any of her clothing or personal items so he had requested (and received) a large black plastic bag from room service. He stuffed all of her belongings into the bag, tied it with a twist-tie, and set it by the door. After he had finished packing all of his belongings and loaded them in the limo, he would return and take the bag to the back of the hotel and deposit it in the dumpster outside.

He was still uncertain as to what happened during the swim competition. He'd watched the news reports on TV and apparently some sort of fish in Mullett Lake had been responsible. What it was they weren't sure, but they were bringing in a team of experts to find out just what was in Mullett Lake and how it got there.

And Jack didn't know who to notify regarding Susan's death. He didn't personally know any of her friends or family. He'd only started sleeping with her a few months ago, and only when a discreet opportunity presented itself. That's why this trip to Courville had been so convenient. It gave him an excuse to get away for a few days without arising the suspicions of his colleagues . . . or his *wife*. She was too busy living the jet-set life of Cape Touraine to figure anything out.

Finally he decided that he would tell no one of Susan's death. That would be the best policy. Jack Ferguson called it the *'Presidential Defense:'* If questioned, deny; if pressed, attack; if caught, *lie.* Sooner or later people would get bored with the whole thing and leave you alone. It worked well for more than a few elected officials.

And, Jack reminded himself, *I* am *an elected official.*

As he placed his suit in his garment bag, a black object fell out, bouncing off the bed and onto the floor. Jack bent down and picked it up. It was Sam McAllister's cellular phone that he had given him yesterday. Ferguson flipped it over in his hands for a moment before packing it in his suitcase. He'd mail it back to Sam when he arrived in Cape Touraine. He looked around the room and checked the bathroom to make sure he wasn't forgetting anything. As he was closing his suitcase, he saw Sam's cellular phone again and figured it would probably be easier to just drop the phone off at Sam's on his way out of town.

* * * *

Sam was in the living room of his house, sipping on a beer and watching a documentary about the Civil War on one of the cable channels. He had tried to watch the news, but he just couldn't take hearing any more about the 'Catastrophe in Courville' as the local TV stations had dubbed it. 'Mullett Lake Massacre' was another; there would most certainly be others. The war documentary was boring, but he suffered through it with the help of a twelve-ounce in his hand. After a couple beers the war documentary was actually tolerable; at least he wasn't faced with any more news reports.

Headlights shined through his window and Sam stood up, looking out into the driveway.

I swear to God if it's another reporter I'm going to kick his ass, he thought. He'd been bombarded with phone calls throughout the day, and a number of reporters from newspapers, television, and radio stations had arrived in his driveway and assaulted his home, requesting an interview. If he saw them coming in time he ducked out of site and didn't come to the door. If they saw him first, he told them he was too distraught to talk about the situation. *Maybe in time,* he'd said, *but not today.*

He walked through the kitchen and down the hall, sneaking into his bedroom without turning the light on. From here, he could safely see out the window without being seen himself. Sam pulled the drapes back a tiny bit and peered outside, seeing the long silhouette of the stretch limousine in the driveway.

Ferguson? McAllister thought. *Is it him? It has to be.* He glanced at the glowing red digits on the clock by his bed. It was nine-thirty. Ferguson must have decided to stop by before catching his plane.

He hurried out of the bedroom and back down the hall and opened up the front door.

There was no one there.

He could clearly see the headlights of the limousine in the driveway, and he thought that maybe Ferguson was still inside the vehicle. He was about to walk out to the car when he heard a voice call through the screen porch in the back.

"Sam? You home?" Sam closed the front door and spoke as he turned.

"Yeah, right here," he replied, returning through the kitchen and the living room and entering the screen porch.

Ferguson stood on the step just outside the porch and Sam flipped on a light and opened the screen door.

"I knocked once at the front," Jack began, "but I wasn't sure if you were home."

"Oh, yeah. Just in the other room. Come in, come in."

Ferguson stepped into the screen porch. He was dressed in the same suit he'd arrived in, and looked the same as he did when he had stepped out of the limousine. Except now he had a tired, aged appearance, and his usual exuberant confidence seemed to have melted away. He appeared uneasy and ill at ease, and the warm, composed smile was absent from his face.

"I can't stay," he began. "I just wanted to thank you again for your hospitality this weekend. And–" He reached into the pocket of his sport coat and produced the cellular telephone. "–I thought you might need this." He handed the phone to Sam.

"Oh, thank you, thank you," Sam offered. "I was looking for this earlier today. And again . . . I'm terribly sorry about what happened. I was–"

Sam's voice trailed off and faded until he finally stopped speaking altogether. Ferguson wasn't listening to him. Or, at least, he wasn't looking *at* him. His eyes were focused downward past McAllister. Sam turned to see what he was looking at.

Oh shit.

"What the hell is this?!?" Jack suddenly demanded, reaching past Sam and snapping up the photograph. McAllister hadn't caught Ferguson's movement until it was too late, and the mayor quickly grabbed the photograph and held it before him.

Sam had been looking at the photo earlier that day and he had forgotten to stash it back in the drawer.

CHRISTOPHER KNIGHT

"What the hell is this?!?" he repeated, his eyes bulging as he glared first at the picture, then at Sam.

"Jack, it's not what you think. It's–"

"What do you mean *'it's not what I think'*? You *knew!* You knew all along about this goddamn thing in the lake!" Sam just froze, staring at Ferguson's face, and the mayor continued. "This is from the snorkeler's camera, isn't it? *You* developed the photos! You *knew* that man wasn't killed by a boat propeller!"

Sam shook his head and began to speak, but Ferguson kept talking. "And let me guess. You just kept it a secret because it would screw up the—"

"No," Sam interrupted. He reached out and tried to take the photo from Ferguson but Jack pulled back, keeping the photo of the fish safely in his own hands.

"Give me that picture, Jack."

"And just what are you going to do, Sam? Hmm? It seems to me that you aren't in a position to do much. You *deliberately* kept this photograph from the police. You knew all along about this."

Sam stared defiantly, his hands on his hips, glaring at Ferguson. He'd been caught, and he knew it.

"Jack, let me explain," Sam reasoned.

"No. Answer me this. What do you think the police will say when they see this picture?"

Sam blinked, staring intently at Ferguson. Fury burned behind his eyes and he wished that he could just reach out and strangle Ferguson with his bare hands.

Seconds passed.

Then, ever so slowly, a sly grin formed on Sam's lips.

"I would imagine they'd be pretty upset," he said finally. *"But not near as upset as your wife when she finds out you've been banging a lingerie model all weekend."* He took a step back and picked up the pile of photos on the couch, flipped through the small stack, and produced a single photo. He turned it around, allowing Ferguson to see it.

It was the picture Sam had taken at the Windward Resort, when he had spotted the couple through the window. The photo clearly showed the late Susan Corbin leaning over Ferguson, lips on his cheek and one hand firmly planted between his legs. Very damning evidence, for sure.

The color drained from Jack Ferguson's face, replaced instantly with a raging, fire-engine red.

"You're a fucking perverted bastard," he hissed.

"They got a name for this, Jack," Sam replied curtly. "It's called a 'stalemate.' Now we can trade pictures, and we'll be all even. I give you *this* one–" he flapped the picture gently with his fingers. "–and you give me *that* one."

"Fuck you. You've got the negatives."

"And I'm keepin'em," Sam stated flatly.

"Well then I'm keeping this one. Just to be safe. And so help me if you say one word to *anyone*, this picture goes to the police. So help me God I will fuck you up for life . . . if you're lucky enough to have one after this."

Ferguson had nothing more to say. He stuffed the picture of the fish in his breast pocket and turned, opening the screen door and stepping into the grass. He walked quickly across the lawn in the darkness, not looking back. Sam watched him reach the vehicle and couldn't resist the temptation.

"About that job," he called out sarcastically in the darkness. *"When did you want me to start?"*

✳ ✳ ✳ ✳

Sam stood in the screen porch for a long time. He had turned off the TV as well as all of the lights in the house, except the small fifteen-watt bulb over the stove. He listened to the constant, distant humming of motors as the fishing boats continued through the night, the continuous droning growing louder as they drew near, then fading as they passed by. The boats had begun to appear on the lake throughout the late afternoon, and small dots of light now moved slowly over the water in the darkness. They were fishing for the muskie, trolling with big hooks and large strips of meat. No one else would be allowed on the lake until the fish was caught and until they were certain that it was the only one.

He sipped on a beer and cursed the DNR under his breath. *He* should be out there. If there was anyone who wanted that fish dead, it was Sam McAllister. He'd kill it with his bare hands. He swore he'd dive in and kill that son of a bitchin' fish with his bare hands if he had to. Sam had polished off just enough *Legal Age* beers to reach the John Wayne stage: he had grown six inches and could take on the James Gang single-handed. A fish in the lake would be no problem.

A scratching at the door startled him and he snapped around.

In the darkness, he could make out the vague shape of a dog at the door of the screen porch. His nose was pressed to the wire mesh, and he was wagging his tail in delight.

"Gowan, git outta here," Sam said harshly. The dog didn't respond and began wagging his tail faster. Sam was about to take a groggy step forward and shoo the golden retriever away when he stopped. The alcohol slithered through his bloodstream and swirled around his brain, and the John Wayne inside of him offered up a possible solution.

Now that's an idea, he thought. *Sam, that is the best idea you've had in a long, long time.* He set his beer down on the table and stood.

"Well, how are ya, fella?" he grumbled in a much sweeter tone of voice. He opened the screen door and the dog bounded happily inside, sniffing Sam's jeans and shoes. Sam bent down and scratched Pepper behind the ears.

"Good boy. You're a *good* boy. Are ya hungry? I think I might have a little something for ya."

Sam walked through the entryway and into the kitchen, followed closely by the retriever. The contents of the refrigerator were meager: an unopened two-liter bottle of Coke, seven Budweisers, a slab of butter on a saucer that hadn't been touched in nearly a month, a half-gallon of Dean's 2% milk that had expired the week previous, and a six-inch submarine sandwich wrapped in plastic that he'd brought home only a few days ago.

He unwrapped the sandwich and gave it to the dog. The retriever wolfed it down in a few quick gulps.

"There ya'r. Now . . . lessee here. Maybe we got somethin' else for ya."

He opened up a drawer and rummaged through the contents, finally pulling out a dirty nylon rope about ten feet long. He fastened the rope to the retriever's collar.

"That'll work," he said out loud to the dog. "That'll work just fine. Come on, buddy-boy. You and me . . . *we're gonna do a little fishin' together.*"

CHRISTOPHER KNIGHT

✳ ✳ ✳ ✳

The shrill chirping of the portable telephone awoke Brad and Amy. Brad jolted in his chair, disoriented. Amy lay curled on the couch, and she reached for the phone on the coffee table.

"Hello," she answered groggily, glancing at the clock. It was dark, but it was only ten-thirty; she and Brad had nodded off.

"Amy, it's Jim," her uncle's voice spoke through the phone. *"Can you run over to Brad Herrick's cottage and give him a message?"*

"Already there," she replied, glancing at Brad.

"Take down this number."

"Hold on."

Amy found a pen on the kitchen table.

"Okay," she said. Jim Hunter read off the seven digits.

"That's the number for a guy named Larry Richfield. From the DNR. He wants to talk to Brad right away."

✳ ✳ ✳ ✳

The phone buzzed once in Brad's ear before being picked up. Brad recognized Richfield's gruff voice immediately.

"Richfield."

"Yeah . . . Larry? Brad Herrick."

"Thanks for calling." His tone was calmer than he had been two days previous. And for good reason.

"Brad . . . I'm sorry about the other day. Really I am. I had a lot going on."

"No problem," Brad offered, and it wasn't. He had nothing to gain by trying to make Richfield feel like an asshole.

"Well, I guess you were right. Son of a bitch."

"I see you've got a lot of boats on the water," Brad stated.

"Yeah. We've got about fifteen in both Mullett and Burt. Eleven in Crooked. Plus we've posted some heavy pipes at the mouth of each connecting waterway to make sure the fish doesn't travel from lake to lake. We'll get him. What do you think?"

This was a change. The same guy that had threatened to toss Brad out of his office was now asking for his opinion. Brad could tell that Richfield wasn't all that certain that they *would* catch the fish. If he *had* been, he wouldn't have called.

"I think it's possible, but I doubt it," came Brad's curt reply.

There was a pause before Richfield spoke again.

"Why?"

"Too many boats, too much noise. All you're going to do is piss the fish off."

"I think that's giving the fish a little too much credit, don't you think?"

"Larry, you aren't going to catch this fish by trolling the lakes for him. It's a *muskellunge* for crying out loud."

"He's a fish."

"Then how did he survive this long without being detected?" Brad's question was sharp, and he meant it so.

Again, Richfield paused before answering.

"Got any ideas?"

"Well, a few." Brad told the director about what Girard had stumbled across, and how he thought that the muskie had originally been living in the Great Lakes where it could remain hidden for years and survive easily by eating large trout and other big fish.

"Are you saying this is some prehistoric fish?" Richfield interrupted.

"I don't know, Larry. It very well could be."

Richfield thanked him for the information and asked Brad for Girard's phone number. Larry would call Frank in the morning.

✳ ✳ ✳ ✳

It was near midnight when McAllister walked down to the lake, holding the dog by the leash. He climbed into his sixteen-foot aluminum rowboat, followed happily by the eager retriever. Sam carried a Coleman six-volt lantern in the other hand, and beneath his arm in a leather case was his Marlin 30-30 deer rifle. He hadn't used the gun in ten years–hadn't even taken it out of the case in the last five–but the gun was clean and still new looking. Both front pockets of his jeans were stuffed with ammunition, as was the breast pocket of his shirt.

The shoreline was strangely silent except for the constant trilling of crickets and the occasional car passing by on the highway on the other side of the row of houses. Considering the circumstances, one could expect it to be empty and desolate, but it seemed odd not to hear the jovial laughter of people sitting by campfires or on their porches, enjoying the warm summer night. He could hear the low humming of the DNR fishing boats on the lake, and he could spot a few tiny lights bobbing in the distance.

Sam reached into his back pocket for a half-pint of vodka, took a good slug and returned it to his pocket. The dog sat anxiously in the boat in happy anticipation, not knowing exactly what was taking place, but excited to go along for the ride just the same.

McAllister stepped off the dock and into the craft, trying to do so as silently as possible. He didn't think anyone would see him, and if they did, all they would see would be the light. If he kept the small boat at a slow, trolling pace, the tiny light would look like any other DNR fishing boat. Even the quiet electric motor would be inaudible to anyone more than seventy-five feet away.

"You and me," he spoke to the dog as the motor whirred to life. "You and me are gonna catch us a fish. A *big* fish." The dog thumped his tail happily as the boat slowly pulled away from the dock.

✳ ✳ ✳ ✳

Amy stood up and stretched, and Brad slowly did the same.

"I have to go," she said somberly, picking up the portable

phone.

Brad followed her to the screen door and they both stepped outside.

"Get a good night's sleep," Brad said.

Amy turned to face him.

"Brad . . ." she paused, as if searching for the right words. "Thanks. Thanks for being here today."

Brad reached out and slipped his arm around her waist. He leaned forward and gave her a gentle kiss on the cheek. Amy responded by giving him a brief hug, holding him tightly.

"Good night," she whispered, kissing him on the cheek before she turned and walked across the dark yard. Brad watched her disappear into the night, then turned and walked back into the cabin.

He sat at the table for a few minutes, lights off, listening to the sounds of the boats far out in Mullett Lake as they trolled the waters. After a few minutes he stood up and opened the screen door, stood for a moment in the doorway, then slowly walked down the sloping grass to the waters' edge.

A sound, somewhere in the darkness, caught his attention. The gentle hum of a battery-powered trolling motor not far off. Then: *scratching*. A light scraping noise like fingernails on aluminum. Not far off, either. Maybe fifty feet away, coming from somewhere on the water. But it was pitch black, and impossible to see anything besides the faint lights glimmering on the other side of the lake.

"Hello?" Brad called out.

There was no answer.

"Hello out there?"

No reply.

Sound probably carries a long way on the lake, he reasoned, totally unaware that Sam McAllister was only a stone's throw away. Brad turned and walked back up the slope to his darkened cabin, and climbed into bed.

✳ ✳ ✳ ✳

Sam McAllister had heard the voice calling from shore, but he said nothing. The dog was squirming about and Sam put his hands out, petting the dog on the nose.

"Sshhhhh," he whispered quietly to the retriever. The boat was on a course away from the dock and Sam kept perfectly still, allowing the craft to continue traveling farther from shore. After a few minutes he figured he was far enough out into the lake that no one could see or hear him.

"Okay," Sam said quietly, picking up the dog in his arms. *"Time to earn your keep."*

The retriever didn't resist one bit as Sam picked the dog up in his arms. Sam balanced himself carefully as he stood up, holding the dog to his chest. He stretched to one side, paused a moment, then twisted back, heaving the dog overboard.

The surprised dog splashed into the lake, plunged below the surface for an instant, then popped back up, kicking and paddling toward the boat. The nylon rope remained tied securely to his collar. Sam tied the other end to a halyard on the gunwale and then turned up the engine a notch, pulling away from the dog. Pepper struggled to catch up with the boat, and McAllister adjusted the motor to a speed that was slow enough to keep the rope taught, but fast enough so that the dog wouldn't be able to reach the boat.

"Man's best friend," Sam said cynically. *"How 'bout Man's Best Bait?"*

Behind him, the dog swam toward the boat, but wasn't making any progress. Sam posted the Coleman lantern on a metal rod. The light gave him a shadowy view of the dog, and even the waters beneath. He was still at a shallow depth, probably only ten feet or so, and he could make out thick weeds reaching up from the bottom. If the fish decided to take the bait, Sam would be able to see him clearly.

He chuckled to himself, remembering when, as a boy, he used to shoot trout with a shotgun. It had been in a small stream near his childhood home, and there wasn't much sport to it, but he sure did have fun. Sam would chum the water with pieces of bread which would attract dozens of small trout. One good blast from his Remington twenty-gauge could wipe out a half dozen fish or more. What he was going to do now wasn't all that much different . . . except the water was deeper and the fish was quite a bit bigger.

He lay his rifle on his lap, took another swig from his bottle of vodka, and waited.

"Here fishy-fishy," he slurred. "Got some food for ya. And a *surprise*. A *big* surprise. Come on fishy . . . ." The boat plodded slowly through the water, followed by the frustrated dog, still paddling furiously in an effort to make it to the boat.

✳ ✳ ✳ ✳

It had been quiet for a long time, and the fish liked that.

CHRISTOPHER KNIGHT

The muskie rested in deep water next to a pile of logs that had long ago become water-logged and sunk to the bottom. It was dark, but the fish itself looked like a log and blended in well, indistinguishable among the pile of rotting lumber. It wasn't too much longer, however, that the buzzing sound came again. Faint at first, then growing closer and closer. It was right above now, passing overhead on the surface. The fish was too deep and far away to see it, but became agitated nonetheless and began to move slowly from its resting place.

Its keen senses picked up the sounds of pushing water. Something was moving. Its eyes were adapted to the darkness, but whatever was making the sound was still too far away to be seen.

Suddenly the fish could make it out. A reddish-pink blob passed within five feet in front of the muskie. It turned and followed, picking up a delightful new odor. The fish easily kept up with the swimming object.

Again, that same warning began to boil from within. The fish became apprehensive, eyeing the prey carefully.

Something just wasn't right.

There was something wrong with this animal, something that just wasn't normal. *And the noise from the surface.* The buzzing continued and this strange animal flopped side to side, as if it were following the sound. Alarmed, the muskie backed away, allowing the large twisted ball of meat to continue through the depths. The fish finally turned and went in the opposite direction, away from the continuous droning.

The sound was soon replaced by yet another drone, and the fish moved faster through the water, becoming more and more distressed. Yet another of the reddish-pink blobs flopped past the fish and this time the muskie almost struck out of sheer anger, but at the last moment quickly turned away. The sense of danger was far too overwhelming. The enormous fish snapped around and sped off into the depths, retreating to the other side of the lake. Soon the droning ceased, and the depths were silent again.

The muskie cruised slowly, slinking through thick vegetation only a few feet from the surface. The dark waters were calm and quiet, and the fish crept through a weed bed, just barely moving.

Then: another sound.

It was very distant at first, very faint and far away. A low, steady humming. Nothing more than a whisper, but a noise nonetheless. Enough to disturb the muskie from its half-sleep state. Its eyes rolled around angrily, searching the darkness until a small disturbance on the surface appeared through the murky waters.

A large, black shadow purred above him, followed by a smaller, more frantic creature. It flopped and plodded on the surface, struggling to stay above water. The muskie approached cautiously, eyeing the creature that was now kicking and splashing harder than ever.

* * * *

Sam had just put the empty bottle of vodka on the seat beside him when he noticed it. The dog had suddenly become more panic-stricken, more determined than ever to make it back to the boat. He'd already been in the water almost two hours and the dog was tired, fighting to keep his head above water.

Now it kicked wildly, obviously in deep distress.

Sam slowly picked up his rifle, his eyes searching the waters. He could just make out the bottom in the dim light. The depth was about fifteen feet, and long, grassy weeds stretched up from the light brown silty bottom.

"Well, maybe you decided to come to the party after all," Sam whispered. The dog continued to thrash madly about, becoming more and more agitated.

Sam glanced quickly off in the distance. Most boats, evident by their tiny white lights glowing in the darkness, were some ways off. No doubt that a rifle shot would alert them of his whereabouts, but Sam was certain he could cut the light in time and hightail it back to shore without being caught.

He scoured the water for movement, and he was not disappointed.

A large dark shape suddenly loomed menacingly below. It appeared for an instant, cruising just off the bottom behind the boat. It faded from view and Sam eyed the waters cautiously, looking to and fro. His arm began to quiver in anticipation, the way it did when he hunted for deer. *'Buck Fever'* is what it was called, and it caused many hunters to become so nervous that they missed their shot. For Sam, however, the vodka was still coming to his aid, soothing his nerves and calming his muscles.

All he needed was the fish to come to the surface. Come up and just eye the bait, get close enough to get a shot off. He was sure that if he even came *close* to the fish's huge head that the concussion of water would at least knock the fish out, allowing for another, more accurate shot. He'd even thought about affixing the dog with some sort of hook apparatus, but that wouldn't work. Sam didn't have the equipment it would take to fight such a fish. His boat was no where near big enough, either. Besides . . . this would be much quicker and much more effective.

The dark shadow emerged again, coming in slowly from the side. It stopped, eyeing the dog as it splashed helplessly in the water. Sam was awestruck, breathless as he watched the huge fish.

So it *was* a muskie. It *was* the same fish he'd seen in the picture, all right. But seeing it up close and personal was a different experience altogether. Sam could see its horrible eyes watching the dog as the retriever struggled harder to return to the boat. The electric trolling motor kept the small craft at a constant speed, a few feet ahead of the dog.

The fish inched forward, and Sam slowly raised the rifle. In typical muskie fashion, the fish backed off again, content to watch and study its prey. Sam kept the 30-30 locked to his shoulder, eyeing the fish through the sights, waiting for it to rise closer to the surface. One of three things would happen. The muskie might be frightened off, in which case he would spin quickly and disappear like a torpedo, churning up the water in an explosion of weeds and silty debris. It could attack like a mad baboon, lightning fast and furious, only a dark blur as it snatched the bait and burst off. Both situations would leave Sam without a chance of a shot. But if it acted like some of the muskies he'd seen, the fish might approach slowly, cautiously, steadily eyeing its prey from a mere few inches. It may take up to fifteen minutes to strike. In which case, Sam would put a two-hundred eighty grain slug right between the fish's eyes.

The fish inched still closer toward the dog.

Sam released the safety and put his finger on the trigger. The fish was only two feet from the retriever, less than a foot from the surface.

The muskie's eyes shifted, looking directly up at McAllister. Sam stood staring, looking at the enormous beast.

There was an intensity in the fish's eyes, a ferocity that Sam had never seen before. It was anger and rage and fury that boiled from deep within. In those eyes a tempest gale of wrath burned madly out of control, and Sam knew right away why muskies were regarded as the fiercest predators in fresh water.

Suddenly a violent blast knocked him from his seat and landed him smack dab in the water. He hadn't had a chance to even think about what happened. The muskie had charged upward, capsizing the boat, and knocking Sam overboard.

* * * *

Brad lay in bed for a long time, eyes open, listening to the sounds in the darkness. He shut the fan off earlier, and only the calming chorus of crickets could be heard through the screens.

His thoughts drifted from the muskie, back to his job, and the way he'd acted that day in the lab. He was lucky to still be employed. And he was even more fortunate to have an understanding supervisor like Frank Girard.

But he thought more about the fish. How it survived, and for how long. Were there more? Could there be more? He had no answers.

The screen door rattled in the darkness and he heard it close. Soft footsteps padded across the wood floor, drawing closer.

"I couldn't sleep," Amy whispered as her dark form stood in the bedroom doorway.

"Me neither," Brad quietly responded. He stood up and

took her into his arms.

✳ ✳ ✳ ✳

In the darkness of Mullett Lake, Sam McAllister wasn't sleeping, either. He sputtered and groped in the water, frantically trying to climb aboard the overturned boat. The light had gone out and it was dark, and the electric trolling motor spun easily in the air, its blade whirring like a small fan in the darkness.

The overturned boat was impossible for Sam to climb up on. Pepper, still tied to the rope, had reached the boat and he was trying to clamber aboard as well. Neither McAllister nor the dog were having much luck.

Sam felt a bump on his right leg and he jerked around in terror, searching the dark waters for movement. He could see nothing. He splashed and fumbled his way around the side of the boat, to the back, and grabbed for the rope. He held it tightly and tried to climb up the stern, but the capsized boat tilted to the side and he slid back into the water.

Still holding the rope in front of him, he held the neck of the trolling motor and tried to break it off, in a vain attempt at possibly being able to use the aluminum stem as some sort of crude spear to keep the muskie away.

Without warning, the fish exploded in front of him, taking Sam headfirst into its powerful jaws, severing the nylon rope and plunging into the depths. For the final few seconds of his life, Sam used his last bit of air to scream in horrible agony as the muskie's iron jaws crushed him like a vice. The scream was only a muffled gurgle, and was heard by no one. With a powerful thrust of its tail the fish sped off, carrying its prey to the jet-black depths of Mullett Lake.

Pepper, freed from his tether but still unable to climb on top of the boat, began paddling furiously toward the shore.

****

Sam McAllister's capsized aluminum boat was found early the next morning by two DNR officers. It was not yet known who the small craft belonged to, as it carried no registration numbers or any other type of identification. The boat had drifted almost a mile south overnight and was towed into the public beach in Somerville. It also wasn't known if someone had been in the craft or if it perhaps drifted loose from somewhere, but the general suspicion was that someone indeed *had* been in the boat. But as of yet no one was reported missing.

Amy awoke early to the sounds of knocking on the screen door. She opened her eyes, disoriented, not immediately recognizing her surroundings. As she sat up, she realized she was in Brad's cabin. He lay next to her in the small bed, sleeping.

The knock came again, startling her and waking Brad. She jumped out of bed and peered around the bedroom door.

A uniformed conservation officer stood on the porch, politely looking out over the lake. He had an armload of papers and a copy of a newspaper. Amy pulled back from the bedroom door as another knock came.

"Just a second," Brad spoke in a raised voice. He pulled on his jeans and threw on a T-shirt and closed the bedroom door behind him.

Brad immediately recognized Larry Richfield standing on the porch. He opened the screen and invited him in.

"Hi Brad," Richfield said, extending his hand. Brad grasped it for a brief handshake.

"Good morning," Brad replied sleepily. "Sorry I don't have any coffee to offer you."

"Well, I'm sorry I came by unannounced. I just got off the phone with your supervisor."

Brad had turned to begin brewing a pot of coffee and now he stopped, looking at Richfield.

"And?" Brad asked.

"And I don't like this. Not one bit. Frank agrees with you. He doesn't think we're going to get this thing by fishing for it."

He placed the pile of papers on the table and showed Brad the front page of the morning's *Indian River Daily*. Brad's face was plastered on the front page, with the caption:

MARINE BIOLOGIST SAYS GIANT MUSKELLUNGE KILLED PEOPLE

Beneath the caption was the picture that Cal Rollins had taken from the air. Adjacent to that was a picture taken by one of the spectators at the swim competition. It showed dozens of people in a mad frantic, swimming furiously. But it also showed something else. There was a large wake in the background . . . a wake that looked very unnatural. A long, dark bar rose out of the water a few inches above the wake, showing what appeared to be a folded-back fin. It was presumed that this was a photo of the fish as it attacked swimmers on the surface.

"And that's just *one* paper," Larry said. "It's on the front page of every newspaper in the Midwest. This is a nightmare."

"What did Frank have to say?" Brad asked.

"Pretty much the same as you. He's not sure exactly what we've got here. But whatever it is . . . we've got to get it out of the lake before someone else gets killed. That's where we need some help."

Brad returned to his chair and sat quietly, not speaking. Richfield continued.

"I don't have a lot to do with the fisheries division. I mainly work in forestry and law enforcement. No offense to the guys over at fisheries, but they haven't got a damn clue about what to do, either. They insist that we just keep trolling the lake and we'll get him sooner or later."

"They'll get nothing," Brad responded. "Sure, he'll get hungry . . . just like any other fish. But a muskie can live for days—sometimes *weeks* if it needs to—without food. I don't think we can afford to wait that long."

"So . . . what do you think? How are we going to get this thing?" Richfield was almost pleading with Brad, hoping that he could offer some solution to the most bizarre problem he'd ever encountered.

"The fish wants out, Larry. It doesn't belong here. It's stuck. It wants back into Huron, which is where I'm sure he came from. A muskie has a keen sense of direction. My best guess is that the fish got into Mullett from Lake Huron. It came up through that creek that drains when the water is high during the spring. I'll bet that the fish is confused because it can't find the stream now that it's dried up. So it follows the current north through the Cheboygan river, only to find a dead end at the locks. The fish goes back into Mullett Lake, up the Indian River and into Burt Lake, only to find the same thing. The fish is trapped. He literally has no where to go. We need to trick him."

Larry said nothing, and Brad continued.

"We need to make the fish think that there is a way out."

"And how do we do that?"

"We open the lock. Opening the lock will create a stronger current upstream. You and I would never notice it, but a fish can pick it up in a heartbeat. It *might*–with the emphasis on *might*–follow the current in hopes of making it to bigger water."

Larry looked away, as if contemplating the whole idea. He was silent for a few seconds before he replied.

"So what if it works? We've got the fish in the river, then what?"

"And we keep him there. We need people to watch in some of the shallow areas . . . places where the muskie couldn't get through without being seen. Then we'd have to close the lock."

"And just how do we keep the fish in the river?" Richfield was apprehensive, not at all certain that a plan such as this would work. "More pipes?"

"Too risky. I think that the fish could push those things out of its way if it wanted to. At least we'll know that it had been there, but it's not going to hold him. We need a chain mesh net. It would be anchored with heavy blocks and strung across the river, much like a giant minnow seine. It wouldn't be foolproof, but it would be an immediate barrier that the fish couldn't penetrate. We've got a couple at the lab. They're made more for salt water, but I'm sure they would work."

"But what do we do from there? The fish is in the river—"

"The lock," Brad said, interrupting. "Once we are certain that the fish is around, we open the lock again. Just a tiny bit, creating a small current. The fish will sense it. We need to lure the fish into the lock and trap him there. Not only can we catch him, but I think we can catch him *alive.*"

The coffee pot grumbled as the final drips trickled into the decanter and Brad poured a cup for Larry and one for himself.

"It sounds too dangerous," Larry said.

"Right now, I think anything we do is dangerous. It's dangerous for your guys to be out on the lake right now. It's not a matter of what is or isn't *dangerous*—it's a matter of what's going to work."

Larry scratched his chin and looked through the screen out over the lake.

"I think we'll continue to give this a shot for a while," he said, nodding toward a boat. "At least a few more days, anyway."

Brad said nothing, neither agreeing nor disagreeing. Larry finally left to return to his office, but not before leaving Brad a whole slew of telephone numbers where he could be reached.

"Call me if you find out anything more or if you've got any other ideas," he said.

Brad said he would.

* * * *

Amy had waited until the director had left to come out of the bedroom. Now she sat at the kitchen table wearing one of Brad's shirts and her own cotton shorts.

"So . . . it sounds like you're the expert," she offered, sipping a cup of coffee.

Brad chuckled, shaking his head.

"There isn't anyone that's an expert in this field, I'm afraid. What we've got here isn't anything I've ever dealt with. I'm a marine biologist, not a monster hunter."

"Do you really think that the fish can be caught alive?"

"Tough call," Brad answered. "It's possible, yes. But they aren't going to do it out there." He motioned toward the lake. Two large fishing boats were in view, churning slowly through the water about a mile apart.

Pepper suddenly appeared on the lawn, loping slowly across the grass and stopping just in front of the screen door to lay down.

"Pepper!" Amy exclaimed. "Where have you *been?*" The dog was damp, as if he'd gone swimming sometime in the night. And a nylon rope, nearly three feet long, was tied tightly to his collar. The rope was severed and frayed at the end, as if it had been chewed.

Pepper looked up expectantly at Amy, too tired to get up. He mustered up just enough energy to thump his tail.

"Brad . . . come and look at this."

Brad got up from the table and walked to the porch. Pepper glanced at him, then back at Amy, still thumping his tail as if he might be in trouble, but he wasn't quite sure.

Brad picked up the rope and looked at it.

"Looks like someone tried to steal him," he said, rolling the nylon rope through his fingers. "Looks like they had him tied up or something, but he chewed through it."

CHRISTOPHER KNIGHT

"What kind of person would steal someone else's dog?" Amy wondered aloud.

"Hard to say. But it looks like you got away, huh boy?" Brad said, addressing the dog and scratching his ears.

"Somebody like that needs to be thrown in the lake," Amy responded in disgust.

"Careful," Brad said, standing back up and raising his eyebrows. "Throw'em in *this* lake, and they might not come back."

✳ ✳ ✳ ✳

The phone rang a few times and was picked up.

"Lorain University, administration . . . this is Jill."

"Hi Jill . . . it's Brad Herrick. Is Frank around?"

Brad waited patiently on hold listening to classical music for a moment, was bounced around to another office, put on hold again, until finally the line found its way to the office of Frank Girard. The two men spoke for nearly an hour. Then Brad shut the phone off and set it on the table, shaking his head.

It was impossible, he told himself. Frank's voice threaded through his head. *There's no way that could possibly be.* And yet, it made sense. Fantastic, yes. Incredible? That too. But it was the only answer.

Amy had returned to her cabin to shower, and Brad poured himself another cup of coffee and waited.

CHRISTOPHER KNIGHT

✳ ✳ ✳ ✳

"I don't understand," Amy said. "What's the difference between the two?" As soon as she had returned, Brad began explaining his conversation that he'd had with Frank.

"Well, actually, there's not much," he replied. "It's virtually the same fish. A muskie. But, a long time ago—1907, to be exact—a muskie was found near the shoreline in Little Traverse Bay in Petoskey. Frank's got documentation. The fish was about five feet long. A big muskie, but not unusually so. However, the fish had tried to *attack* swimmers. A few people even wound up with some pretty severe bites. Again, that's not at all uncharacteristic of a muskie, but this fish was so vicious in its attacks that it actually followed people right to the shoreline as they tried to get away."

Amy gasped, and Brad acknowledged with a nod, then continued. "Someone hit the thing with a rock, stunned it, and pulled it ashore. That fish," Brad said emphatically, "according to Frank, had a black diamond mark on its head. He said he came across it in another text book he's got at the lab. He says there's even a photo of it."

"Just like the one in Jim's *Michigan Gamefish* book," Amy offered. "But what's the difference? Why the marking on its head like that?"

"Who knows. But I think maybe this breed isn't as extinct as we thought. But there is something else." Brad paused and looked up from the table. "Frank said that a few years ago, divers over in Thunder Bay found a fossil of a fish's skull, similar to the one found by the University of Michigan divers near the wreck of the *Nighthawk*. The fossil was at first *thought* to be that of a muskie or a pike. But the teeth were so largely out of proportion with the fish's body that biologists began to rule out *most* strains of pike and muskellunge. There were also some subtle differences in portions of the jaw line and such, but it's pretty much assumed that the skull belonged to this weird prehistoric hybrid muskie. Not a tiger muskie as I had first thought. The fossil was estimated to be a few million years old, so this fish was probably around with the dinosaurs. And remember, back then, there were no Great Lakes. Back then, Lake Huron wasn't a lake, but a river. So what I think has happened is that this muskie isn't the odd one . . . all the others are. All the pike and gar and muskies . . . I think those strains are probably descendants of *this* breed of muskie. Only this particular fish was supposed to be extinct. The early Native Americans have legends about fish like this, but those stories were just kind of taken with a grain of salt. I think what we might be dealing with isn't as much a fish as it might be a living dinosaur."

"How big was the fossilized skull?" Amy asked.

"I've never seen it. Frank found a picture of it, though. He said that with a skull that size, the fish would have to have been nearly thirty feet long."

Outside on the porch, Pepper started growling. The hair on his back was raised and he went rigid, facing the lake, snarling at the water.

TEN

In a way it was a shame that Sam McAllister hadn't lived to see the goings-on in tiny Courville. Television cameras and crews, newspaper people, radio people . . . the area was teeming with media. All wanted to be the first to get footage of the big 'Killer Fish' of Mullett Lake, but the day after the swim competition catastrophe none of the DNR boats had reported any luck, and things had been pretty quiet overnight. All except for the small aluminum boat that they had found capsized. But as of yet, no one was reported missing. It would still be a few hours before someone figured out that Sam McAllister wouldn't be showing his face around town anymore, and he certainly wouldn't be in charge of any future annual celebrations in the village of Courville.

Brad found himself the unwilling center of attention. As a marine biologist, and one who had actually *seen* the fish firsthand, he was expected to be some sort of authority. He didn't like all the attention and after the ninth or tenth person knocked on the door that morning, both he and Amy decided that it was time to slip out back and sneak over to her cabin.

Brad called Larry Richfield and told him about his conversation with Frank and his suspicions of a prehistoric muskellunge of some sort.

"Well . . . do you want to try this?" he asked Larry. "I mean . . . we've gotta at least give it a shot."

There was a long pause on the other end of the line.

"No. We can't. It's too risky. If that fish somehow gets through the lock and gets into Lake Huron . . . no. We can't. Let's just give our guys in the lake a little more time."

Brad hung up the phone and returned it to its cradle.

❋ ❋ ❋ ❋

The fish stayed close to the bottom, disturbing silt and weeds as it sped through the murky depths. It couldn't get away from the noise. Every where it turned, no matter how far it went, no matter where it went, the constant buzzing filled the water. Occasionally a ball of reddish-brown flesh would stream by, and on several occasions the muskie nearly seized it out of sheer fury. But at the last moment . . . *no*. There was that distant warning, that inner alarm that went off, and the fish angrily obeyed. But it was getting hungry, and the constant drone was becoming more than irritating. It was *maddening*.

On the glowing surface above, another large shadow

appeared. The fish had seen a number of these as well, emanating a noise that had become so distasteful.

It was one too many. The muskie felt like a caged animal, being taunted and teased by its captors just beyond the bars. Only this time, there were no bars. It was the stalkers themselves that were vulnerable. They were in territory that didn't belong to them. They were out of their element, intruding in the fish's domain.

And so when the shadow loomed above, noisily disturbing the surface, all of the built up fury finally had nowhere to go.

In a seething rage the muskie shot upward, striking the object. The fiberglass shuddered and shook as a large hole was ripped open. The fish tore away and retreated, laying motionless on the bottom and watching the shadow above as it stopped, dead in the water.

✳ ✳ ✳ ✳

On the surface, pandemonium was breaking loose. The boat was occupied by two men, and they had been trolling for the fish most of the morning. The sudden jolt knocked both of them off their feet. They scrambled quickly, and one of them cut the engine and the boat sluggishly slowed to a stop. The other went below to inspect the damage.

"Oh for cryin' out loud," he said, returning to the deck. "We hit a log or something. Water's pourin' in. Better radio for somebody to tow us in."

A half mile away, another boat responded to the distress

call.

"Yeah. What's the problem?"

"We sprung a leak. Bad one. We're takin' water and we're going to need a tow. I think—"

He was interrupted by a loud thud that rocked the boat again. *"What the hell was that!?!?"*

"Did you hit another log?" came the response from the radio.

"Couldn't have. We're not movin'. I think that . . . Holy shit! You better get here! Quick!" The man was screaming now and his voice distorted and the small speaker roared liked a home town crowd at Tiger Stadium. *"Holy shiiiit!!"* he repeated. *"GET OVER HE—"*

A tremendous crashing sound was heard and the man's voice was suddenly cut short.

The radio went silent.

"Tony? Tony!?! You still there?"

✳ ✳ ✳ ✳

The fish battered at the boat in a frenzy, and fiberglass pieces fell away as the muskie ripped through the hull. It pounded at the boat with its long, rock-hard snout, splitting the fiberglass open with every savage attack. Each onslaught sent a shudder through the craft, until it had taken on so much water that it was listing badly to one side.

The fish heard a splash and turned. Another splash followed.

Two creatures had fallen into the water.

✳ ✳ ✳ ✳

By the time help arrived the boat was going down quickly. There was no sign of the two men. One of the uniformed officers from the assisting vessel bravely dove headfirst into the water and swam alongside and under the rapidly sinking boat, even venturing into the now water-filled main cabin. There was no sign of the two men. He returned to the surface.

"They're not in there," he sputtered to his partner on the boat. "They're not on board, thank God. Maybe they made it to shore." He didn't sound very convinced himself, and he quickly swam back to his boat and climbed up the ladder.

✳ ✳ ✳ ✳

"What do you see?" Brad asked. The two were at Amy's cottage, and they sat on the porch in the early evening. There was a cluster of activity a half-mile out into the lake. Three or four boats had gathered tightly, and more were racing to the scene from various points around Mullett.

"I can't tell," Amy replied, keeping the binoculars to her eyes. "Just a bunch of boats. Maybe . . . maybe they got him. Maybe it's all over." She handed the binoculars to Brad, and he raised them to his face.

"I can't tell, either. Too many boats. But maybe you're right."

Amy smacked a mosquito on her neck.

"*Ow!* Darn things! I'm going in. I'm getting eaten alive out here. You want a glass of wine?"

"No, thanks," Brad sighed. "I think I'm going to call it a night."

He got up to leave, but Amy had returned with a glass of wine in each hand.

"I know you said 'no,' but your eyes said 'yes'," she said, kissing him lightly on the lips. Brad rolled his eyes and took the glass, smiling. They watched the sun creep lower and lower until it was finally completely hidden behind the trees. After finishing the drink he kissed Amy good-night, walked back to his cabin, and fell asleep on the bed before getting out of his clothes.

Not thirty minutes after he had laid down, he was awakened by tapping on the screen door. It wasn't late, but he was exhausted nonetheless and had been sleeping soundly. He heard Amy's voice in the darkness.

"*Brad? Brad? Phone call. It's Larry Richfield. He says he needs to talk to you. Now.*"

Brad rolled out of bed and stumbled to the kitchen as Amy opened the screen door and came in. She was barefoot and her hair was down, and she wore an oversized T-shirt. It was obvious that the call had gotten her out of bed as well. She spoke again, and her voice had an urgent worried tone.

"*Those boats we saw today . . . one of them sank. Two men are missing.*" She handed him the phone.

"This is Brad."

"Brad. Larry here. Sorry to bother ya."

"No problem. What's up?"

"We gotta try it. I mean . . . what you were talkin' about."

Brad said nothing, and there was a long pause before Richfield continued.

"We lost two men today. That goddamn fish sank a boat. He sank a twenty-four foot fishing boat by smashing the hull."

"That's impossible."

"I know it is. But we've got the boat . . . or what's *left* of it. That fish must have hit the hull a dozen times. The damned thing's in shreds. You said that you've got some steel net down at your lab?"

"It's a heavy chain mesh netting. Yeah, we got it."

"How fast can you have it here?"

* * * *

It had been another short night. As soon as he had hung up with Larry Richfield, Brad called Frank at his home and explained the situation. Frank in turn called three college interns to haul five of the heavy mesh nets up to Courville in a truck.

* * * *

It was a seven-hour drive and the truck had arrived just

after eight the next morning. Brad was already up by then, and he drove into Cheboygan to meet with Larry and others with the Michigan DNR to plan a course of action. Over a dozen uniformed men met together at the offices. Larry introduced Brad to the group and they began making preparations.

It wasn't going to be easy. As soon as everyone was ready and in position, they would begin to release water through the lock, hopefully creating a stronger current to draw the fish into the river. The trick, Brad told them, was having spotters with radios at points along the river to watch for the fish. Whoever saw the fish pass by first would have to immediately radio to the others, so they could get the lock closed and the mesh nets up in time before the fish had a chance to turn around and head back into Mullett Lake. The nets were heavy, and would require eight to ten men each just to get them laid out over the river. Brad assured the men that this was not going to be easy by any means, but if they kept a good watch along the river, they could begin to move the nets further downstream toward the lock, thus trapping the fish in a confined area. That would give them time to set things up at the lock and draw the muskie in. At least, that's what Brad *hoped* would happen. It was going to be tricky, but it seemed to be the safest way of going about the seemingly impossible task of capturing the muskie.

✳ ✳ ✳ ✳

Most of the boats had been pulled off the lakes, and Brad

met Larry at the lock. Brad instructed the operator to begin releasing water, and he watched carefully to make sure there would be no place for the fish to get out.

"Are you sure the fish is going to be able to pick up this current?" Larry asked, rather skeptical. There was no visible change in the water level or current. And the mouth of Mullett Lake was over a mile away.

"Call it a sixth sense. Fish pick up on this stuff. We're still not sure how or why, but they can. But it may take a while. Maybe even a day or two. We just have to be patient and watch. We wait . . . and we watch."

"And if we don't see him?"

"Well, there's always plan B," Brad offered.

"And what's that?"

"I don't know. We may have to make up plan B as we go along."

＊ ＊ ＊ ＊

By mid-afternoon there was still no sign of the fish. The day was gray and overcast with an eerie stillness about it, and Brad drove back to the cottages to take a much-needed nap. Larry said he'd call if anyone spotted anything.

When he arrived at the cottages, Amy wasn't around. She'd left a note for him on his table that she'd be cleaning most of the cabins, being that all of the guests had left, traveling to a more safe environment. Most of the motels around the lake had begun to empty, except those that were now being filled by reporters and other media crews from out of town. One TV station had sent a team of ten people to film the story, and more were on the way. A staff from *Hard Copy* was rumored to be flying in, and CNN was even reportedly sending in a team.

Brad clicked on the television and lay back on the couch. A television station out of Traverse City was interviewing people, asking what they thought of the fish and how it should be captured or killed. One man with an enormous beard suggested a fishing competition that offered a reward. Another said that some type of exploding device rigged to some bait would do the trick. There were a number of folks who had their own ideas about what should be done. One person even said that *nothing* should be done, that the fish *deserved* to live, just as humans had a right to exist, and if we couldn't live in harmony with an animal or a fish, that certainly didn't mean we should *kill* it, for gosh sakes.

Brad clicked off the TV and within a few minutes he was fast asleep.

✳ ✳ ✳ ✳

The fish charged through the water. It was no longer hungry, but a fury raging from deep within had long since passed the boiling point. The fish wanted out. It wanted back, back to where it had been. Where the water was deep and it could hide. It could sense the movement . . . just a slight motion, a subtle feeling. There *was* a way out. Somewhere.

The muskie searched for the river that it had followed up from the big lake, but it was gone. The fish had a keen sense of orientation, and knew that it was in the right area, but the stream was gone.

The water was now only ten feet deep, but the muskie bolted through the shallows without fear of man or fish or any other creature on or around the lake. It raced at breakneck speed a hundred yards from shore, still sensing the current, looking for a way out.

Silt churned and exploded in its wake. Another large shadow suddenly appeared above the muskie and was nothing more than a blur as the enormous fish raced directly under it.

✳ ✳ ✳ ✳

"What in the hell was that?!?!"

The wake shook the boat and the man leapt to his feet, catching a glimpse of the dark shadow as it charged by. It was one of the few steel-hulled boats that remained on the lake, its two occupants watching for signs of the fish near the mouth of the Cheboygan river.

"There he is! That's it! That's it!" He picked up the mic.

"This is Hudson! I just saw it! He came right under me! I'm on the north shore . . . he's headin' right for the mouth of the river and at the rate he's going he'll be there in thirty seconds!!"

✳ ✳ ✳ ✳

The fish could feel it now. Slightly. Gently. The light pull it had felt earlier was stronger. There was a river nearby. The fish had traveled up the waterway before, late at night when it could travel through the shallows without being seen, but there was no way out.

The weeds disappeared and gave way to a sandy bottom and the lake became even more shallow, but the fish drove on, following the gentle current.

Suddenly the banks narrowed and closed in, the water deepened, and the current pulled stronger.

The muskie was in the river.

✳ ✳ ✳ ✳

Brad awoke on his own after sleeping much longer than he'd expected. He was tired and he had needed the rest, but now it was late evening. He lay on the couch for a few minutes, listening to the sounds from outside. Pepper bounded playfully through the yard without a care in the world, barked at a squirrel, and continued into the next yard.

He sat up slowly, still groggy from the long nap. He showered, shaved, hunted around for some clean clothes, and walked over to Amy's cabin. She had just finished dinner and was putting dishes away.

"Looks like I missed supper," he said through the screen. Amy turned and smiled.

"Not at all. I made enough for you and Uncle Jim."

"Speaking of which, where is he all the time?" Brad asked. "I've been here this whole time and I've only met him once when I checked in. I haven't seen him at all."

Amy laughed as she pulled a plate from the cupboard for Brad.

"And neither has anybody else. See . . . Uncle Jim is in love. He met a lady a few months ago, and he follows her around like a puppy. It's really kind of sweet. I never know when he's going to be here, except of course when he's managing the front desk. And now we don't have any guests in the cabins, and we probably won't until this whole mess is cleared up. So everyone sees less and less of Uncle Jim. He doesn't even go to the casino in Sault Sainte Marie anymore. He used to go once a week to play blackjack with a few of his friends. They've given up on him, and they–"

The phone trilled, interrupting her. Amy picked up the phone.

"Hello? Oh, hi. What!?!? . . . All right . . . okay, I'll tell him. We're on our way." She hung up the phone and turned to Brad, a look of shocked excitement on her face.

"That was Larry Richfield! He's in Cheboygan and he says that they've got the fish trapped in the backwater between Lincoln Bridge and the lock!"

ELEVEN

By the time they arrived in Cheboygan night had fallen, and the town was a madhouse. The city was one huge traffic jam with cars pulled over on the sides of the roads, parked in lawns, side streets, even the empty fairgrounds adjacent to the lock. It seemed everyone had heard about the man-eating giant killer muskie that was now trapped in the backwaters of the lock. A helicopter buzzed high overhead and even more television news crews were arriving, most forced to park blocks away and haul their gear to the lock.

The backwater was more than just a large pool. It was a very large pond, deep enough and wide enough to give the fish plenty of room to move about without being seen. Years ago during the logging days, thousands of huge logs had filled the river and it was possible to walk from one side of the river to the next simply by stepping on the enormous floating logs. Some logs had become stuck and finally sank, and the bottom of the river was littered with giant trunks that were over a hundred years old. It was hard to believe that Cheboygan was a bigger city back then than it is today.

Amy parked the Jeep in the Arby's parking lot and both she and Brad walked along the congested street and across the Lincoln Bridge to the small park. It was jammed with cars and trucks, police cars, conservation vehicles, camera crews. Police were *trying* to keep gawkers and onlookers away from the shore, but so far the authorities hadn't done very well. Everyone wanted to get a glimpse of the huge fish. So far, most had been disappointed. The backwater was about one hundred yards in diameter and depths easily reached thirty feet, providing ample space for the fish to remain unseen, especially at night.

Larry Richfield was standing by a dark green state-owned Suburban, looking at a map of the chain of lakes and the inland waterways. He saw Brad and Amy coming and put the paper on the hood of the vehicle.

"I think we got him," he offered.

"Are you sure he's in there?" Brad asked, scanning the dark waters.

"You bet. The guy working the lock called. Scared the shit right out of him. He was standing over by the edge and the fish came right up."

"Are you sure he's still here? You got the nets up in time?"

"Oh, he's here all right. We put up one of your fences under the bridge. We just got it up when two of our guys spotted the fish cruising over by that shore." He waved his arm toward the eastern side of the large pond. "Question is . . . *are we going to be able to get him into the lock without escaping into Huron?*" He looked at Brad.

"I don't think we have a choice," he answered. "But let's

put a chain mesh over the front of the lock, just in case. That will give us one more added safeguard."

Larry paused and took a long look over the water.

"Are you sure there's not an easier way of doing this, Brad?" I mean, we could set up nets, maybe, or–"

"The only problem with things like that is that it requires people to get too close to the water without being able to escape in time. I mean . . . if we start setting up things in the backwater, it's only going to increase the chance of another incident like the boat on Mullett Lake."

"Yeah, but it sounds like we're going to have to get close to the fish anyway. Over at the lock."

"Only while we get the chain mesh netting in place. And the net's only there until the lock is closed. Look Larry . . . I'm not saying this is going to be a cakewalk. But I think considering what we're dealing with here, it's our best option."

"At this point, I think it's our *only* option."

Brad surveyed the backwaters and scanned the crowd.

"Let me know when your guys are ready," he said.

"We should be finished with the preparations at the lock in a couple of hours. But I don't think it's a question of when *we're* ready." He thumbed a motion toward the dark waters. "I think it's a question of when *he's* ready," he finished.

Brad walked back over to where Amy stood. Both were silent, watching the waters and the surrounding crowd of people.

"Brad . . . what if this *doesn't* work? I mean . . . what if the fish somehow gets through the lock?"

Brad drew a deep breath and sighed.

"I've thought about that. It's possible. We're going to have to be on our toes. If he makes it through, we've lost him. He'll have the entire Great Lakes system to roam."

Amy didn't respond, and both she and Brad spent a long time watching the backwaters. Watching, wondering . . . *and waiting.*

✳ ✳ ✳ ✳

More and more spectators showed up as the night wore on. The police had finally succeeded in keeping the crowds back away from the perimeter of the backwaters, but the number of people put the small town in a stranglehold. Traffic couldn't move. Cars lined the streets on both sides. Burger King (which was conveniently located directly across from the backwaters and the lock) remained open late, and a steady stream of customers kept the restaurant busy. The large pond had become more than just an attraction. It was like an amusement park. Television crews had set up their cameras and were giving live reports, newspaper reporters dashed about with pen in hand, and the local radio station was broadcasting live from a van parked across the street.

But so far, nothing had been seen. No one saw any sign of the fish: no wake, no shadow, *nothing.* People came and went, and it wasn't long before the mood grew from enthusiastic anticipation to a party atmosphere. It was now near midnight, and many people were stopping by on their way to and from their favorite nighttime establishments. Everyone wanted to get a glimpse of the huge fish. It had been a long time since anyone had seen the muskie in the backwaters, and many were wondering if it had been contained after all.

A makeshift eight-foot chain link fence, guarded by police, surrounded the small channel to keep people from venturing too close. A few uniformed conservation officers inspected the lock, surveying the area intently. Brad was working with Larry and a few other men, continuing to make preparations. They had placed twenty, four-inch thick iron rods across the top of the lock, nearly two feet apart. Holes were drilled into the cement, and the bars were bolted down. If the fish did try to jump, which would be very probable, the rods should be strong enough to keep the fish from leaping out and over the front of the lock.

The night had been quiet (except for the hoots and howls of the gathering crowd), and the adjustments and preparations to the lock were finally finished. When the fish made a move into the lock, one of the large chain link mesh nets would be dropped behind it, containing the fish for an extra moment or two. When the fish swam over it and into the lock, men on either side would heave the heavy netting up, trapping the fish. It wouldn't hold him for long, but if they could confuse it, that may give them a few more seconds to get the back of the lock closed. It would trap the muskie, confining it to the very small area of the lock. How they would proceed to move the fish *from* the lock was anybody's guess. Some suggested poisoning the fish, killing it while it was trapped within the lock. Right now, the biggest concern was just capturing it—and keeping it out of Lake Huron.

At one a.m., nearly four-hundred people still milled about on the shores. There had been no sighting of the muskie since earlier in the day, and most began to doubt that the fish had been contained in the backwaters at all.

At exactly one-seventeen a.m., everything changed.

CHRISTOPHER KNIGHT

✳ ✳ ✳ ✳

Unknown to the spectators on shore, the fish was *furious*. More than furious. It was in an uncontrollable rage. It spun about angrily in the depths, unable to return upstream or follow the slight current flow downstream. Everywhere the fish traveled, it encountered the shallow water near a shoreline or one of those strange shiny fences that wouldn't allow any escape. The muskie kept its distance, staying close to the bottom, away from the shallower water, away from the mesh fence. It moved slowly, cautiously, watching the surface above. The fish could sense movement and motion from the shore, causing further alarm and agitation. It's frustration was growing, turning to rage and fury. The more the fish moved about, the more it was keenly aware that it could not get out into deeper, safer water. It began charging faster, churning through the depths of the backwaters, searching for a way out, looking for a means of escape.

✳ ✳ ✳ ✳

Lights had been positioned around the large pond illuminating the area brightly in the early morning hours. Suddenly a large swirl disturbed the surface. It was big, and it made a wake big enough to be seen by nearly everyone on shore. The churning water rolled away and disappeared, and the surface was calm once again. A few flashbulbs popped, but the fish had caught everyone so off guard that by the time cameras flashed the wave was long gone. The small crowd began to applaud and cheer, and then the noise died down and faded into a thick air of suspense. For the next few minutes, all eyes watched in hungry anticipation, waiting for the fish to appear again.

Without warning, the hushed silence over the gathering was rocked by an enormous explosion as the muskie, all twelve feet of it, leapt completely out of the water. It crashed into the surface once again, spraying water forty feet and sending waves rolling to the perimeter of the backwaters. The crowd cheered and roared, *aaahhhing* and *ooooohing* as the fish crashed down into the backwaters.

Brad nodded to Larry, and he in turn glanced at a few of his men around the lock.

"Okay guys," he said. *"Showtime."*

✳ ✳ ✳ ✳

The back of the lock began to swing fully open. The chain mesh netting was laid across the fifteen-foot wide opening and allowed to rest completely on the bottom, leaving plenty of room for the fish to swim over it and enter the lock. The water was murky, but the men could see the silvery chain heaped on the bottom. Once the fish was in the lock, it would take ten men—five on either side—to pull with all their might to raise the chain net and hook it to a pair of cleats on either side. When the fish found the chain mesh at the front of the lock it would turn around, and hopefully be trapped by the net at the back of the lock. If it tried to leap, it would strike the steel rods bolted to the cement. But it would take nearly thirty seconds for the back of the lock to close, and in those thirty seconds, no one knew what might happen.

"Okay!" Someone shouted from the control operators room. *"Opening the front just a bit!"*

Water could be heard trickling and then rushing from the front of the lock as it was released to fall the fifteen feet to the river below. Three men on either side of the lock held the chain netting tightly with leather gloved hands. All eyes were cast downward, searching the dark waters.

Seconds ticked by, then minutes. No one had moved. Not a flinch, not a muscle.

✳ ✳ ✳ ✳

It was gentle at first, ever so slight, but the fish could sense the movement of water. A current began to flow and the muskie snapped around, heading in the direction of the subtle motion. The water became shallower and bright lights lit up the waters but the muskie rocketed forward, bolting through the depths, heading in the direction of the flow.

✳ ✳ ✳ ✳

"There he is!"

The black shape rocketed into the lock, churning up debris and silt. The men heaved with all their might, pulling the chain mesh netting up, closing off the fish's escape.

"Hurry up! Hurry up!" someone shouted. The door of the lock began to close, and the men quickly fastened the chain links to the cleats on either side. A buzz went through the crowded shoreline as people tried to edge closer to the lock, trying to get a better view of what was going on. Cameras flashed in the night and people squeezed together near the shore, straining their necks to see inside the lock.

The water within the lock boiled angrily as the muskie reached the front of the cement-walled containment area. With nowhere to go, it snapped violently around and rocketed into the chain link netting at the back of the lock. The heavy mesh held fast, at least for the moment, and the fish backed off, spinning around and causing a huge spray of water to soak the men standing around the lock.

"Get that gate shut!!" Brad yelled. *"Get it shut!!"*

The back of the lock was slowly swinging closed. The fish again assaulted the netting, spearing into it with its massive snout. It hit with the force of a train, yanking one of the huge cleats completely out of the cement.

The chain netting gave in and began to slide to the bottom. Brad grabbed it and heaved, as did three more men. Two more men rushed to help, while the five men on the other side stood at the ready in case the cleat on their side gave way.

"Watch it! Watch it! Here he comes! He's coming back!" the

lock operator yelled. The door was almost closed.

The fish slammed into the netting with such power that Brad fell forward onto the pavement. He landed near the edge of the lock, still gripping the chain with all of his might. The tumble had knocked the wind from him, but he pulled himself away from the edge and hadn't fallen into the lock.

The man behind him wasn't so lucky.

The jolt had thrown him off balance and he fell forward, trying to recover. He threw his leg out in front of him to try and stop his fall, but he was already too close to the edge. His foot slipped and he toppled, plunging headlong between the long iron bars and into the lock.

For a moment his whole body slipped beneath the surface, but then he arose, sputtering and clambering, trying to climb the smooth cement wall of the lock. It was chaos. He was too far away for anyone to extend a hand to help pull him out. Someone ran to find a rope while the man in the lock swam frantically to the chain netting and began to pull himself up. The other men held the heavy mesh tightly while Brad reached for the man.

"Come on!" he yelled. *"Just a little more!"*

The water exploded furiously as the fish attacked. The man screamed and suddenly he was gone, pulled beneath the surface.

"Lights!!" Brad screamed. *"We need more lights!!"*

The lock operator flipped a switch and six halogen lamps lit up the lock like daylight. The huge muskie could be seen thrashing wildly about beneath the surface, carrying its victim and snapping him from side to side. The man was screaming, screaming soundlessly from beneath the water as the fish tossed him about like a plaything. Brad turned.

"Kill the fish! Shoot him! Anything!"

A conservation officer removed the pistol from his belt and fired at the fish as it rose near the surface. The blast sent water spraying thirty feet into the air. The bullet met its mark and the fish responded immediately, releasing the man and twisting sideways in the water. Another conservation officer removed his pistol as well, and he, too, fired a shot at the fish. The man in the lock struggled to the surface and once again began to swim toward the fence. Shots continued to ring out.

Finally, one of the bullets struck the fish directly in the head, straight between the eyes, just below the large black diamond-shape marking. It quivered and shook in spasms in the water, twitching and shaking. The shooting stopped.

The man reached the chain link netting, but was too tired to pull himself up. Blood poured from dozens of cuts on his body. He looked as if he'd been in a fight with a straightedge razor . . . and the razor had won.

Brad held the chain link fence and reached down as far as he could. He grabbed the man's extended hand and pulled with all of his strength, bringing the man closer up the fence. Another officer was able to help, and he was finally pulled to safety. Blood poured from open wounds, splattering over the cement and running back into the lock. The man passed out just as two paramedics reached him.

Within the lock, the fish snapped violently sideways and thrust upwards, rolling at the surface, shaking uncontrollably. It gave one final snap-like heave, smashing into the cement wall. It stopped and rolled sideways, completely still except for the occasional extraction and contraction of its gills. The fish shook, went rigid and stiff, and sank to the bottom of the lock.

The muskie was dead.

TWELVE

Once again Brad found himself awakened by the gentle knocking on the screen door. Amy tapped a couple of times before letting herself in, carefully carrying two glasses of iced tea. Brad was still in bed, and he squinted in the bright, early afternoon sun that streamed through the window. It had been another sleepless night, as Amy and he hadn't left the backwaters until eight that morning amid a huge crowd of spectators. Television crews still lined the shore and cars jammed the park, the streets, and adjacent side streets. The story, quite obviously, was a major sensation, drawing attention from around the country. Brad himself had given dozens of TV, radio and newspaper interviews and even did a live spot on CNN. The lock was finally drained and the dead fish was hoisted into a large nylon net and placed on ice in a waiting truck. It was sent immediately to the University of Michigan for testing and research.

"It's a little too hot out for coffee," Amy said, placing two glasses of tea on the table.

"Thanks," Brad responded, as he slowly stumbled out of the bedroom and into the small kitchen, taking Amy in his arms for a brief hug.

"You've gotten quite a bit of publicity," she said, smiling. "You're lucky that not many people know where you're staying or they'd be breaking down your door to talk to you. I've already had a few calls from people looking for you, but I told them that you haven't been here for two days."

Brad picked up his iced tea and drew a long sip.

"I don't think I'm going to be much more help to anyone," he replied. "But thanks for the cover." He again sipped his tea and gazed out the window.

"How do you think the fish got that big?" Amy asked.

Brad shook his head.

"I don't know. My best guess is that it probably has been living in the Great Lakes. It could stay deep and hide, while feeding on big salmon or trout and the likes. Muskies eat anything. The theory, according to Frank, is that the longer this strain of muskie went without breeding, the larger they grew. Obviously if that's the case, this muskie hasn't mated for a long time."

"But what about that marking? You said that's not from a typical muskellunge."

"No, it's not. Frank is pretty excited about the whole thing. I mean . . . obviously he's not happy about people getting killed. But this fish gives us the opportunity to take a look back in time. He's heading to the University of Michigan today to see the fish for himself. He's pretty geeked up about the whole thing."

There was a long pause while Amy sipped her tea. She

stared out the window over the perfect, blue waters of Mullett Lake. Finally, she set her glass back on the table and looked at Brad.

"Do you think there are more?"

"What . . . *fish?* More muskies like *that one?* No. I don't. I mean . . . what we've seen is one chance in a *billion,* so yeah, it *could* happen. But I think that one was the last of the last. See . . . muskies spawn in April and May . . . right around the time you said that river was high because of all the snow run-off. I'm sure that's how it got into Mullett Lake. It probably came up that river from Lake Huron since there was obviously no lock to keep it out. When the fish wanted to go back, it found that the stream was gone because the water table had lowered, as it always does in the spring. It was trapped in the chain of lakes, and probably didn't like it one bit."

"What do you mean, 'spawn'? You mean lay eggs?" There was a look of horror on Amy's face as she spoke. Brad quelled her fears instantly.

"Not a chance. This fish was a male. To spawn, a female swims along releasing eggs while the male fertilizes the eggs. A male muskie becomes intensely aggressive if it can't find a female. It literally goes *crazy.* I think that's what happened here. There was no female around, so the fish just kind of lost it. It's almost like a steroid rage. The fish becomes so unbelievably temperamental that it just snaps. It does crazy things . . . like attacking boats. I've seen smaller muskies—only two or three feet long—do that. Plus there's the fact that it couldn't find its way back to the lake. I imagine that it had been in the Cheboygan River a number of times but just couldn't make it out through the lock." Brad paused a moment, then continued. "But again . . . no. We've seen the last of any giant muskies."

CHRISTOPHER KNIGHT

"I hope you're right."

"I'm not sure about *much*, but I am certain about *that*. We'll never see a fish like that again in *these* lakes, thank God."

✳ ✳ ✳ ✳

Amy's head popped up from beneath the surface and she wiped the water out of her face with her hands. It was evening, still very hot, and the water was delightfully soothing. She looked around. It had been nearly a week since the muskie had been killed. Brad had stayed at the cabin for an extra few days, and a team of scientists had arrived. He went along with them as they scoured Mullett, Burt, and Crooked Lakes with high-tech sonar equipment, searching for any signs of any more of the huge muskies. Besides a few very large sturgeons, they found nothing out of the ordinary. The three lakes were declared safe, people began returning to the water, and the lake was finally getting back to normal. A few boats had ventured out, and children were once again swimming near the shore. But there were still some people that would be afraid to go back in the water for a long time, and some that probably never would again.

Amy began to crawl arm over arm back to the dock when suddenly her head snapped under the surface, pulled beneath the waves with a fervent intensity. Beneath the surface, her arms spun madly and water churned. Terrified, she popped back up again in an instant . . . and so did Brad, who had quietly slipped underwater and snuck up underneath her, grabbing her ankle and yanking her downward. He emerged laughing and sputtering. Amy swam to him and pushed his head below the surface, not really appreciating the prank, but laughing just the same.

"That's *not* funny," she said, as he reappeared on the surface. Beneath the surface he slipped his arm around her waist.

"I *owed* you that one," Brad laughed.

They swam to the dock and climbed up the new wood ladder that Amy's uncle had replaced the day before. Brad picked up his towel and handed Amy hers.

"I'm gonna call it a night," he said. "I've got to go back to Ohio in the morning."

Amy was quiet for a moment, her disappointment showing, and Brad continued.

"But I was wondering, if . . . well, I guess I was thinking about maybe coming back up next weekend. You know. Get here Friday night . . . leave Sunday afternoon. That is . . . if you'd be around. And might want to do something."

"Well, you know I'd like to, but . . . ." Amy replied, not looking up as she dried herself off with a towel. Brad finished the sentence for her.

"But it's against company policy to date any of the guests, right?"

Amy laughed and looked up. It would have been impossible to miss the sparkle in her eyes and the sweet, inviting smile on her face.

"Well, maybe I can make an exception for just one weekend . . . ."

EPILOGUE

UNIVERSITY OF MICHIGAN
BIOLOGICAL CENTER
ANN ARBOR, MICHIGAN

Calvin Parker leaned over the huge fish, split open and dissected on the lab table. He stared intently, Not sure of what he'd just found. Parker spoke without removing his eyes from the enormous carcass.

"Phil . . . come check this out."

Footsteps clicked on tile. They were tired, sluggish steps, unenthusiastic steps. Both men had worked well beyond evening, long after everyone else had left the lab. It was now near midnight, and Phil was about to call it a day. If Calvin wanted to stay longer, that was fine . . . but *he* was going home.

"What's up?" He even sounded tired.

Parker remained motionless, hunched forward, his gaze fixated on the dead fish split open before him on the table.

"That," he said quietly, squinting his eyes as he reached a

latex-gloved hand toward the dead fish's abdomen. "Ever seen that before?"

Phil didn't show much interest. He'd gone over the fish earlier in the day when it first arrived at the lab. An amazing specimen, yes. But it had been a long day and he was tired. It was time to go home.

He leaned forward to see what Parker was poking at. Suddenly he crept closer to the table.

"I'll be a sonofabitch," he whispered. The carcass held his complete attention now. He leaned even closer and spoke again. *"The damned thing's an hermaphrodite."*

Calvin turned and stared at Phil. He said nothing, then turned his head back to the dead fish. He touched the egg sack with his gloved hands, rolling the wet tissue through his fingers. His eyes roamed across the fish's innards that were sprawled out over the table.

Hermaphrodite. Parker had always thought it was a silly word, far too long and clumsy. But he was well aware of what it meant. The term actually came from ancient Greek mythology. *Hermaphroditos* was the son of Hermes and Aphrodite, united in a single body with a nymph, therefore possessing both male and female sex organs. There were many plants, animals and insects that exhibited this characteristic. On more than one occasion, Parker had dissected a fish that was an hermaphrodite, not by its own nature but by some genetic flaw or defect. It was a rarity among fish, but it happened nonetheless.

"And the egg sack is empty," he said finally, shaking his head.

"Son of a bitch," Phil replied in amazement, still glaring at the squishy tissue rolling through Parker's hands. *"The damn thing spawned. It spawned and fertilized its own eggs."*

✳ ✳ ✳ ✳

TWO MONTHS LATER

"Be careful with him!" the old man exclaimed. "Don't horse'im in!" He held the net in one hand, waiting for the fish to near the boat. His eight-year-old grandson, a pudgy, fidgety towhead, sat rigidly on a cushion in the front seat of the small craft, clinging steadfast to a fishing pole. The rod was bent almost in half, and the fish splashed the surface as it grew tired of the fight. It was all the boy could do to hold the rod upright.

"Is he a big one Grandpa?!?!? Can I keep him!?!" the boy exclaimed, his eyes watching the fish splashing at the surface.

"Well, we'll see . . . we'll see. Just be careful . . . bring him on over . . . that's it . . . a little farther . . . *there we go!*" The old man scooped up the fish in the net and brought it into the small aluminum boat.

"Wow! Is *this* one big enough to keep?" the boy asked hopefully, his eyes wide in eager anticipation. The long, slender fish fought viciously within the net, chewing at the nylon and trying to leap away from its captors.

"I'll be dog-gonned," the boy's grandpa said, his brow furrowing as he stared in wonder at the fish. "It's another one of *them.*"

"What kind is he? Is he big enough to keep?"

"Well, it's another muskie all right. But . . . ."

The old man pulled out a tape measure and laid it along side the fish, pressing the muskie firmly to the bottom of the boat with his foot to keep it from flailing about. "Twenty-nine inches long," he continued solemnly. He glanced at his grandson. "Not quite legal size, I'm afraid. But a good fish. You sure did good." His gaze returned to the fish pinned on the bottom of the boat. *"Strange, though. I've been fishing Mullett Lake for fifty years, and I've never seen one with that funny black thing on his head like that. And we've caught four just like this one in one day."*

The boy, disappointed once again, said nothing as the old man took a breath and raised his foot.

"Whelp. Throw 'im back in. We might catch him again on another day. You just never know how big he may grow up to be."

THE END